Ethne Cullen was born in South Africa, but left at the age of twenty-one to travel and explore the world.

She enjoyed a career in education in both schools and universities.

Now retired, she enjoys golf, bridge and painting landscapes in oils and acrylics. She lives with her husband in Victoria, British Columbia.

This is her debut novel.

The Tenth Commandment

Best wishes,

Ethan

Ethne Cullen

The Tenth Commandment

Vanguard Press

VANGUARD PAPERBACK

© Copyright 2018
Ethne Cullen

The right of Ethne Cullen to be identified as author of this work has been asserted by her in accordance with the Copyright, Designs and Patents Act 1988.

All Rights Reserved

No reproduction, copy or transmission of this publication may be made without written permission.
No paragraph of this publication may be reproduced, copied or transmitted save with the written permission of the publisher, or in accordance with the provisions of the Copyright Act 1956 (as amended).

Any person who commits any unauthorised act in relation to this publication may be liable to criminal prosecution and civil claims for damages.

A CIP catalogue record for this title is available from the British Library.

ISBN 978 1 784653 39 2

Vanguard Press is an imprint of
Pegasus Elliot MacKenzie Publishers Ltd.
www.pegasuspublishers.com

First Published in 2018

Vanguard Press
Sheraton House Castle Park
Cambridge England

Dedication

To my husband, for his support and patience.

Sorrow

When you are sorrowful look again in your heart, and you shall see that in truth you are weeping for that which has been your delight.
Kahlil Gibran, *The Prophet.*

It rained the day they buried him. Dark clouds hung low over the city, hiding what sliver of sun attempted to penetrate the gloom. Covering the sky in a blanket of grey, the clouds gave the sky a flat, bleak look as the storm gathered in wads of grey cumulous until, at noon, they finally opened up and shed the accumulation of rain in their moisture-laden depths. The streets ran wet as water gushed into the gullys and poured down the sewers. All colour that had been in the buildings was washed out, leaving only tones of grey and black – the colours of mourning.

At the cemetery two men stood with raincoats tightly fastened and hats pulled down on their heads in an attempt to keep the dampness from seeping into their clothing and running down their necks.

"Merde, this is dreadful bloody weather. As if death were not foul enough to bear, the gods have to punish more," muttered one of them, a short man with a stout build, who was moving about, trying to find a dry place to set his feet. "Why the hell do we even need to be here? Are we really going to get any answers by getting ourselves drowned in this downpour and catching our death of colds. Death of colds, good joke in this location, non?"

Getting no response from the other man, he gave him a nudge and continued, "Awe come on, mon ami, you don't want to be here any more than I do, so please laugh at my jokes."

His only reply was a scowl and a grunt from under a large black rain hat that dripped from all sides. Water ran down under the edge of his turned up collar, and soaked his shirt. He was just as uncomfortable and damp as his companion, but was staying stoic about this assignment they had been given.

They stood together looking out over the grey landscape of headstones and granite memorials to Montreal's dead, and waited for the funeral procession to arrive.

"Yea, but why a coffin and a burial? Most unusual these days," he finally commented.

"Mais, ils sont Catholic. C'est traditionnele. The wife is from France, remember."

"And his lover?"

At his question they both looked over to the slope where a young woman stood alone; the third observer of this burial.

The woman they saw was enveloped in rain gear as they were. She was staring directly at the prepared grave nearby. They recognized her, and knew why she had come.

They could not know that she was focused on the dark space into which the centre of her life would disappear. This was not how it was all supposed to end for her; with sorrow and grief, she thought. All she had wanted was a new life; one filled with joy. She had believed that she had turned evil away, but that had not been so. Her obsession had consumed all that it touched, and had left nothing but a trail of tears.

Do they think that by covering the hole it will make it any easier for us to bear? To not imagine him disappearing forever into that cold hole in the earth? The woman shuddered and turned away from the upsetting site. That was when she saw them – the two other observers.

What the hell are they doing here? she thought. And her anger rose like a gorge in her throat. Can't they leave us alone to mourn and weep without being here to spy on us? The sound of car engines drew her attention away from the men to a black hearse approaching, followed by a long procession of cars.

By the time the funeral cortège entered Mount Royal Cemetery, the sky had lightened and the rain had eased to a slow, steady drizzle. The three watched as the cars parked, and mourners followed the cortège; a coffin, a priest, the grieving wife, and two children. As the coffin was placed into position they heard the priest intone a final blessing: "'I am the resurrection and the life,' saith the Lord; 'he that believeth in me, shall never die.' Go in peace and may the love of God be with you in your time of sorrow."

The mourners moved away from the site to their cars, until only the wife and children were alone with the priest. He escorted them slowly to the waiting black limousine. As they reached the vehicle, the grieving woman stopped, lifted her head, and looked towards the lone woman standing on the slope. She raised a hand in greeting, and an arm was raised in response. She bent, seated herself in the car, and the limousine drove slowly from the cemetery with its sorrowing passengers.

"So, they know each other," observed the taller of the men, seeing the exchange between the women. "Very interesting."

"I'm not surprised. She's been that woman's husband's lover for years. How could they not?" his companion responded as they watched the young woman walk down to the grave.

Kneeling down, she whispered quietly, "Goodbye my dearest love. Please forgive me for the hurt I have caused. I will try to make it right."

Her face was wet, tears mingling with the rain as she walked back up the slope, ignoring the mud clinging to the hem of her coat. She looked over towards the two men with fury in her eyes and left the scene of the funeral to go home and weep alone.

Turning to his companion the tall man shrugged. "Nothing more for us to do here today. But our work starts tomorrow. Let's see if we can find out what really happened to the dead guy in the coffin."

Two Years Earlier
Temptation

The only way to get rid of temptation is to yield to it.
Oscar Wild.

Adam was bored. The sound of voices buzzed around him like so many hornets after something to suck on. He closed his eyes in an effort to blot out the image of the dozen dark suited men hovering around the room. They all seemed to be talking at the same time, trying to outdo the person alongside them. With a loud sigh he rose from his comfortable seat and stood. He had to escape before he found himself saying something he would regret.

"You're leaving, Adam?" someone asked at his elbow.

"Have to get some fresh air. I'll see you all later," he responded quickly before he said anything more.

He had borne the company of these men, yes, all men, he thought, for as long as he could bear. If I did not have to be here I could be at home with my girls, enjoying their antics and laughter.

"Maybe I'll come with you, I need to get away from the noise as well," said Peter Cox, a man who had been standing close to Adam. "And I could do with a coffee. What about you?" Together they walked out of the room.

"What did you think of some of the ideas they were discussing in there?" Adam's companion asked.

The last thing Adam needed was to rehash what they had just spent hours discussing.

"To tell you the truth, I'm not sure how often some of the scenarios he was painting actually happen. I found them interesting, and I was curious, but I don't think any of the brokers at Stark, Nesbitt and Bouchard would ever participate in some of those underhand schemes and by-plays he described." And if they did, I would never tell you or anyone from outside the firm, he thought to himself.

"Maybe we should all be a little more alert to the possibility though," Peter went on.

Why is he pushing the point? Adam mused. Does he know something I don't, or is he fishing for gossip?

"Yep, I agree," he responded non-committedly.

I suppose I am naïve if I think that all the staff are pure and lily-white, he thought. Maybe this is an alert for me to pay better attention to some of the transactions that go through at the brokerage.

The conference in Toronto had been in progress for four days and Adam had done all the schmoozing he hoped he would have to do for the next year. Lawyers from other investment houses from around the country as well as a few from abroad, had discussed, argued and pontificated over minutia for all that time, and he was tired of it all. Not very professional, he thought, but I have to get out of here for a while.

The floors of the hallways in the Sheraton Hotel in Toronto were covered with soft patterned carpet that deadened the sound of his steps. Embossed paper covered the walls between the triple light sconces that threw soft lighting down the passages. All was elegance and muted sophistication. Every effort had been made to ensure that the conference attendees were comfortable and well cared for, and Adam had appreciated the luxury. If he had to suffer through boredom, it may as well be first class boredom.

Stretching his legs felt good. Maybe he needed a jog to clear his head and then think about how he could escape a business dinner for the fourth night in a row. If he went to his room and changed into jogging gear he could do a few miles before he had to think about a plan for the evening. With that thought in mind, he went with Peter to find a coffee. He would take it to his room as he changed. A run to stretch his legs that had been sitting idle for too long would provide a boost of energy.

But fate intervened, and he never did go for the run.

Walking past the doorway to the main ballroom the two men noticed that a large plenary session was underway. He glanced in and saw an attractive blonde woman standing at the podium.

"Quite a looker," Peter commented, giving Adam a nudge. "What do you think? Shall we go and watch her do her stuff?"

Adam just stood and stared at the woman on the stage. She appeared to be holding the audience in rapt attention. A ripple of laughter went through the rows and Adam wondered what she had said that was so amusing.

"What's she talking about?" he asked.

His companion glanced at the notice on the board at the door identifying the session.

"It says here that it's *The Pros and Cons of Strip Bond Investing for your Clients – A Possible Safety Net.* How on earth can she make that topic amusing?"

Keeping his eyes on the stage, Adam walked over to the coffee service area, poured a mug and settled into a back row.

"I'm going for a walk, Adam. Enjoy drooling at the blonde." And Peter gave Adam a wink as he walked away.

Adam looked around the ballroom. It was set up for a large session. Two huge screens flanked the walls on each side of the stage. A podium and microphone were centre stage. Rows of chairs filled the hall, seating a few hundred, he estimated, and the seats were almost all taken. Maybe it was the speaker that was the draw and not the topic, he guessed. She certainly was easy to look at, but in a no-nonsense business sense. He sat mesmerized as he watched her.

The woman standing at the podium appeared to be in her mid-thirties. She was tall; Adam guessed about five foot ten at least. That seemed to give her more of a presence at the podium. Blonde hair fell to her shoulders in soft waves. On the large screens, he could see her features clearly. Her complexion was flawless; mouth wide and full, and large blue eyes looked out at the audience. She wore a skirted suit in deep purple with a white blouse. The contrast was startling, but effective.

Adam sat back and admired what he saw. She projected an easy yet confident manner from where she stood, speaking clearly, but softly. This forced her audience to focus on her words as she gave emphasis by using her hands and arms, never moving her body from its position behind the podium.

Adam listened with little attention. The topic held no interest for him, he was not a broker and did not need the information she was sharing. He was more tuned onto the woman's body language; her poise, her voice, her hands. What he saw intrigued him. She was captivating. He thought that she looked vaguely familiar but he could not think where, if ever, he might have met or seen her before.

A solid round of applause brought his attention back to what was taking place on the stage. He realized that she had stopped speaking. He had been so wrapped up in his detailed examination of her physical appearance, that he had not paid much attention to what she was saying. Obviously the audience had, and they appeared to be appreciative by the applause they were giving.

A few questions were posed, and she relaxed and moved away from the podium, walking to the side where the questioner sat and spoke directly to the participant. This gave Adam a clear look at her body; her long, slim legs showing from the knee length skirt, and her high-heeled dark shoes. This is a very poised woman, he thought. Eventually, she ended the question period by raising her hands and thanking the audience for their attention.

Leaving the stage, she came down and mingled with the crowd, chatting leisurely with many of them as they asked questions and congratulated her on the quality of the presentation. A tall grey-haired man in his late fifties pushed through the throng and took her by the elbow, gently moving her away. She stopped him, pointed to the refreshment stand, and they made their way together to the coffee and tea urns. There they stopped and had a long discussion. The man, who was elegantly dressed in a dark pin-striped suit, looked to Adam, like a very successful business executive, if somewhat dandyish.

I wonder what their connection is, he thought with a jealous pang. The man obviously felt that he could push her around and was speaking to her in a very strong tone. But the woman was not backing down; looking back with a firm gaze as she listened. Then she spoke, and Adam heard her voice say very loudly.

"Avery, this conversation is over. The presentation was exactly what I wanted to cover, and it was well received, so please back off. We can talk about this again when we get back to the office. Now, I am going to get a cup of coffee and congratulate myself on a job well done."

With that comment, she turned away from her companion towards the refreshments. The older man stepped back in surprise, muttered something under his breath, and stormed out of the room.

As Adam watched intently, the woman poured a cup of coffee and then reached into her pocket for something. Pulling out her iPhone she started reading a text on the screen. She turned, picked up the mug of coffee and, while still reading, moved towards the exit doors.

Adam moved quickly towards the exit doors when he realized that she was leaving. He was desperate to meet her. He had to stop her somehow, and talk to her.

At an angle, he walked directly into her path. Continuing to read her text messages, she did not notice him as she moved to leave the room. She collided straight into him. The cup of hot coffee caught him full in the chest; spilling dark liquid down his shirt front, his tie and his suit jacket.

"Oh no, what a clumsy thing to do. I wasn't looking where I was going. Are you all right? Are you burned? Oh, look at your clothes. I must pay for the laundry – and the cleaning. I am so sorry…"

She turned towards the table and put down her now empty coffee cup. Picking up a wad of paper napkins from the refreshment table she started dabbing at Adam's chest where coffee was dripping off his shirt. Looking flustered, all her poise was now gone.

Adam put out his hand and took hold of hers. He removed the wet napkins from her hand and continued to dab at his soaked shirt himself. The woman blushed and put her hand to her mouth. For the first time she looked at him directly, and not at his soiled clothing. The open smile in his dark blue eyes relaxed her.

"No apologies needed," interrupted Adam. "I should have been looking at where I was going. I too was distracted. I was still thinking about how well your presentation had been received by the audience, and I was in a reverie. You really did wow them in here."

"Thank you, I was pleased with the response. But, do let's deal with your condition. Where are you staying? Can I send someone to pick up the clothing for cleaning? It's the least I can offer to do for my ineptness. Please," she begged, looking back at him for forgiveness.

"No, it would be less embarrassing for me if I dealt with it all by myself. However, if you're feeling really guilty why don't you agree to join me for dinner tonight?"

The woman looked at him with her mouth open, and then burst out laughing.

"Well, that's the best pick-up line I've had for a long time!"

"Apologies on my part. I just thought that dinner with an attractive woman, who obviously is bright enough to wow a crowd of hackneyed money people, would make for an interesting dinner companion. But if you're not free tonight, maybe just a drink after I clean up would be recompense enough."

"I'm not doing anything tonight. I never make plans for dinner at these conferences; I prefer to be alone after the crowed days."

"Oh, is that a rain check, or a straight no?"

"It's neither. I would love to have dinner with you and see what you look like without dripping coffee decorating your front. The choice of venue is yours but it's my treat, or rather a very sorry payment."

"Hmm, now, that *is* an offer! I will have to think of somewhere very expensive – the cost of dry cleaning has really gone up recently. Especially for coffee stains, I hear."

She burst out laughing again and said, "Well then, why don't we try the Scaramouche on Avenue Road. It's reputed to be where all the rich and famous hang out. I can meet you there at about seven-thirty."

"It's a date," he responded. "But you don't know who you'll be dining with. I'm Adam Lambert. I'm a lawyer with Stark, Nesbitt and Bouchard," and he held out his hand. "And I know who you are from the session board outside. It's Claire Hardick isn't it?"

"Pleased to meet you Adam Lambert from Stark, Nesbitt and Bouchard; and yes, I'm Claire."

"Can I meet you at your hotel, or would you prefer to meet at the restaurant?"

"The restaurant at seven-thirty will be fine, thank you. Now I must get another cup of coffee as I have someone waiting to meet with me. See you later, Adam, and successful cleaning up!"

She smiled, turned and walked out of the conference room, looking down at her iPhone, reading the messages that he had interrupted.

Adam watched her walk away and smiled. What had he just done? he wondered. He had gone out of his way to get her to walk into him. He had been so determined to meet her, but he had to make it look accidental. And his ruse had worked. He was not usually so devious; it had been a spur of the moment action. Feeling light-headed at the thought of sharing dinner with her he left the room and walked towards the elevators to go to his room. He needed to change out of the clothes, that he suspected, were probably permanently ruined. But the price was cheap if she turned out to be as delightful a companion as he expected she would be.

Whistling his way down the hallway, he entered his room and slowly took off the coffee stained clothing. Turning on the shower he stood under the hot water savouring the warmth, together with a feeling of excited anticipation for the evening to come. Drying off, he pulled on the hotel terry cloth dressing gown.

In the mini bar he found a bottle of scotch and poured the golden liquid into a glass. There was no ice in his room, so he splashed a little water onto the drink and walked over to the bed where he sat down with a sigh.

Suffering a sense of guilt at the pleasure he was taking over his encounter with Claire Hardick he reached for the telephone, punched in his home telephone number and heard the ringing on the other end. After six rings a child's voice told him that his family was not at home.

He left a message for his wife, Luce, and the children; told them that his days were thoroughly boring without seeing them, and that he loved them all. He blew a loud kiss into the receiver and replaced it in its cradle.

Sipping his drink, he leaned back on the pillows and stretched out onto the bed. He wondered why he was feeling such anticipation over the dinner to come. He was, after all, a married man with two children. He loved his children. They were a delightful pair. Even with a father's pride he knew that they were great kids. He and Luce had raised them well, balancing love with control and both the girls had responded well. He felt some regret that he and his wife had very little to share these days, and had not had for years. They still respected each other and maintained a good relationship for the sake of the children, but the marriage was – well, he was not sure what it was any more.

He remembered how they had first met. It had to be fifteen years ago and he had only been twenty-eight at the time. He had been a junior associate in a large law firm in Montreal and was enjoying the work. One day the senior partner suggested that he accompany one of the partners to Paris; to look, listen and learn from negotiations that the firm was doing on behalf of a client who was selling their company to a French one. Adam had been working on the research for the transaction, and the partner felt that he would be a valuable asset; that it would be a good learning opportunity for him.

Adam was delighted. When they landed in Paris he was given the first day on his own to relax before the meetings started the next morning. So Adam was free to amuse himself.

He walked for hours the next morning; down the Champs-Elysées, past the Arc de Triomphe, across Trocadéro Park, past the Eiffel Tower, and along the banks of the Seine until his feet and his stomach told him that it was time for lunch. He found a little restaurant with a sidewalk café that looked inviting. As he approached the entrance a young woman walked past him, up to the waitress, and asked for a table. He hesitated, thinking how pushy that had been; to overtake him so as to get a better table. The waitress indicated that there was only one table left and suggested that maybe, if they would not mind, they could share the table. He looked over at the young woman who looked up at him with liquid brown eyes framed by a headful of shiny, dark curls. He nodded in agreement and followed those gorgeous eyes to a table.

That had been the beginning of a wonderful ten days. Luce, the owner of the liquid eyes, lived in Paris. She was an artist, and was all alone in the world. Her parents had been killed in a fire that had burned down their home in the countryside just south of Paris. From that shared lunch, the two spent every free moment that Adam could escape from meetings, together. She showed him all the tourist sights first.

She made him take a ride on the bateau mouches down the Seine. She made him kneel and pray in Notre-Dame Cathedral. She ignored the Eiffel Tower as too uninteresting and obvious. She showed him the views across Paris from Sacré-Coeur at the top of Montmartre, as well as the panoramic view across the rooftops of Paris from the top floor of the Pompidou Centre. They wandered the halls of the Louvre, trying to give him a peek at the Mona Lisa over the heads of the dozens of tourists who stood in front of the painting. Then, and only then, did she take him to her favourite art gallery, the Musée d'Orsay.

After they had exhausted what she termed *touriste Paris* she showed him the Parisian Paris. They explored the little back streets of the Marais, Montmartre and the Latin Quarter. They sat at outdoor tables in restaurants to eat croque monsieur or madame for lunch; they cut slices of salad off a large cabbage and drank wine from crockery jugs in Nos Ancétres les Gaulois on the Isle de la Cité.

They shared nights of passionate sex in her studio apartment off the Rue Francois Miron, and woke early so that Adam could return to the hotel, shower, and be on time for his daily meetings. He found that he was being pulled in two directions, work and pleasure, both of which he was enjoying immensely. Luce's energy and enthusiasm had him besotted. She had infused new life into him in this wonderful city.

As well, he was engrossed in what was occurring in the meetings he was attending. He found that the research he had done in Montreal provided useful background information. He would jot notes onto the legal pad between himself and the partner. Then he would tap the pad, and the partner would glance at the notes, nod, and continue the discussions and negotiations, now including the information Adam had provided. He was pleased that he was making a meaningful contribution. As well, he was fascinated by the negotiating process, and felt proud of his role when they finally had a completed contract to take back to their client in Montreal.

On the last day of business, he requested a stay-over from the partner who smiled and commented, "You want to stay and enjoy more time with the young Parisian who has obviously been keeping you up all night. Oh, I can tell by the shadows under your eyes as well as the glow in them. Of course you can stay. You made a valuable contribution here for your first negotiating experience. Take a few days. Just call the office and they will make the necessary changes to your ticket. The hotel, however, I can give to you for one more night, then your fun is on your own dime!"

He wished Adam well and departed alone, leaving him with a last few days to spend with Luce.

The next day he asked Luce to marry him, and she agreed with a laugh and a kiss. He purchased a plane ticket for her for the next month, giving her time to pack up her life in Paris and join him in Montreal. He had never done anything so rash in his life before, but he was totally enraptured by this young woman, and did not want to lose her.

He met her at the airport three weeks later, and she settled into the apartment with him. The following months were as exciting as Paris had been for them. It was now Adam's turn to show Luce the sights and sounds of Montreal.

Lying on the hotel bed in Toronto he smiled to himself as he sipped at the mellow scotch in his hand. He remembered their first times together in Montreal.

They explored the city like tourists, Adam showing her the sights first. They took a taxi up to the observatory on the top of Mont-Royal for an expansive view of the city. They walked through the park, hand in hand. They stopped in Schwartz's for a smoked meat sandwich that was four inches thick. Luce curled up her nose at the amount of meat packed between the layers of rye bread and remarked that the French did not eat like this.

"How can Montrealers call themselves French if they eat so much?" she had wanted to know.

Adam walked with her down St. Catherine Street, the main thoroughfare of the city, and then up Avenue Montagne to Sherbrooke Street where they explored the small boutiques and galleries. They went on to the Musée des Beaux-Arts where Luce said she should erect a tent so that she could explore Canadian art every day.

They walked down to Vieux-Montreal, the old city, and along the cobbled stone streets of Rue Saint-Paul with its old buildings now housing an enticing mix of art and craft galleries, boutiques and restaurants. They visited the beautiful Notre-Dame Basilica with its twin towers, and sat quietly in a pew and admired the interior with its Romanesque and Rococo influences.

Adam drove her around the residential areas to get a feel of how and where the citizens of the city lived. They drove along the Lachine Canal with its quiet, meandering waterway. They drove through Westmount with its elegant homes and Luce remarked that one day, when they were very rich, they were going to live in a house just like the ones they were looking at, right in Westmount. Adam had laughed, and told her to keep dreaming.

They dined at night in some of the city's funkiest restaurants, as well as some of its finest. Adam wanted to show her the sophistication of the city, and the excellent French cooking Montreal chefs were proud to serve.

One weekend they drove to Toronto to meet his parents who had been very surprised at the sudden news of the impending marriage. In the double winged Toronto City Hall they were married in a civil wedding service. This was a compromise, as Luce was

Catholic and Adam had been raised Anglican. Adam's parents were cool, but polite towards Luce.

They confided in him their concerns regarding different cultures, languages, countries and religions. He brushed off their worries, saying that their love would overcome all those challenges.

But they had been right. Love had not conquered all. The first year was bliss, with Luce getting pregnant almost immediately with Andre. The two girls, Juliette and Michelle had followed soon after and they suddenly found themselves with frantic lives; very little time for each other, and both trying to get their own careers started.

Luce had tried to keep her art projects going. She was very talented and sought out galleries that would show her work, occasionally selling a piece. Adam was working twelve-hour workdays, often bringing work home at night. They quickly found that the small apartment would not accommodate space for her art work, a crib for a baby and then for two, so they moved to a larger apartment, and finally, when Adam was established, into a house in Point Claire. Later, Luce got her wish fulfilled when they moved into the large house in Westmount where they now lived.

Luce had found that she was losing her French identity in a foreign country, a new city, and not enough time to cultivate her own interests. Over the years she had slowly drifted into her own silent world and buried herself in her art. She felt that she had given up an essential part of who she was to make the marriage viable and so had drifted back to her art to recover some of herself.

However, with three children she was busy enough with her home and children. They hired a housekeeper to assist on the home front while she spent more of her time in her studio. Adam did not mind, as he felt guilty that their planned utopia had not materialized. At least they had each found something fulfilling in their work.

They had agreed to make the marriage work. They both adored their children and so never fought, always agreed on discipline for the kids, and tried to appear as a couple on formal occasions. When he made love to her it was with a dutiful passion. Their bodies going through the attitudes of surrender and possession. The death of their oldest child had drawn a final curtain down between them.

As he lay on the bed in the hotel in Toronto, remembering the history of his marriage, there was a knock at the hotel door.

"Room service," said a voice from outside.

Adam was surprised as he had not ordered anything, knowing that he was going out to dinner in a short while. When he opened the door, a hotel staff member carried in a tray and set it down on the table.

"Thank you, sir," he said, "it has all been taken care of." And he left the room quietly.

Adam moved to the table and saw on the tray, a bottle of Lagavulin single malt scotch, a bucket of ice and a single glass. Tied to the bottle was a small envelope. He reached over, untied it, and pulled out the note inside.

The message read:

My apologies. I have been called to an emergency meeting this evening so will not be able to join you for dinner. Please accept this as a double apology for ruining your clothes and your dinner arrangements. I hope my guess that you're a Scotch man is correct.
Regards,
Claire Hardick.

Adam felt an acute sense of disappointment. He had found the woman to be extremely attractive. She had roused his senses more than any one he had met in a long while. For a few moments that afternoon he had felt young and alive again. Maybe it was just as well that they could not meet for dinner. Not being close to her for an evening would be a relief. He could now go home without a sense of guilt hanging over him.

With a sigh, he decided that an early night would suit him well. He picked up the telephone and ordered room service.

The next morning Adam arrived at the airport to catch the flight back to Montreal. The airport was crowded with early morning travellers. He could tell the business commuters from the tourists by their dress and luggage. He noticed a group of traders from Stark, Nesbitt, and Bouchard, joined them, and was amused by the stories they regaled each other with about the secret side of the proceeding; the pairings they had noticed, the goofs that speakers had made and the quiet negotiations for trades behind closed doors.

The flight was called, and the passengers moved to board the aircraft. As he handed his ticket to the flight attendant checking him in, he noticed another passenger walking down the ramp to the plane and thought her back looked familiar. His heart skipped a beat when he realized that it was the woman he had missed dining with the night before.

Boarding the aircraft, he looked around for her. She was seated not far from the entrance. He glanced down at his seat number and slowly moved down the aisle, checking numbers as he went. He held his breath as he moved closer to the row in which she was sitting, and stopped. His seat was across the aisle from her. How kind the fates were, he mused. Placing his small bag in the overhead bin he sat down. She had not looked up from the computer that she had on her lap. As the last of the passengers found their seats and the doors closed, she looked up at the flight attendant who was doing the safety checks.

"Hello again," said Adam. "They have not started serving coffee yet, so I assume that I am quite safe for a while."

She looked across at him in surprise and then recognition dawned on her face.

"Oh, hello. Yes, I think I can assure you that I am not going to ruin another suit of clothing just yet," was her laughing response.

"Thank you so much for the gift of that very smooth Scotch, I will enjoy it; and yes, I am a whisky drinker."

"It was the least I could do to make up for my clumsiness."

The passenger next to Claire leaned over and asked if they would like to sit together so they could chat, and said that she would be happy to change seats with Adam.

He glanced at Claire before answering. She just smiled back at him, so he agreed.

Sitting so close to her made Adam's body heat rise, and he felt his heart start to beat faster. This was not supposed to happen. He had been relieved when they had not had dinner together, and now luck, or whatever controlled these happenings, had thrown them together again.

"I think fate has had a hand in this. We were meant to have another meeting. If not over dinner, then in an airplane a few thousand feet about the ground," he remarked.

"It appears that is the case. Are you going home? Do you live in Montreal?" asked Claire.

"Yes, I do. Are you going home as well?"

"Yes," she replied. "I was just in Toronto for the conference. I apologize again for standing you up last night, but I have a boss who likes to have all the i's dotted and the t's crossed, so we had to meet last night. He was staying in Toronto to complete some projects we'd been working on and he needed some confirmations from me."

As the plane flew towards Montreal, they continued to talk about the conference, the work they did for their respective firms, the highs and lows of working in the world of investment. They talked about what they enjoyed doing when they were not working. Both laughed and agreed that there was not much time for that.

"But when I can escape, my winter passion is to ski," admitted Claire.

"I ski as well, mostly with my older daughter who is getting to be very good. She wants to snowboard and I am resisting for now."

He saw Claire react at the mention of his daughter. "Where do you and your daughter ski?" she asked.

"We go to Mont Tremblant a lot. We like the village atmosphere, enjoy the crowds, and the ski runs are well groomed."

Adam discovered that Claire went up to Mont Tremblant almost every weekend, but that she liked to go alone. It was her escape from being with people all week. Then she asked him about his family. She looked directly at him. She wanted to see what his eyes would tell her about his response. She wanted to know if he was going to lie to her, and cover up the fact that he was married.

Looking back at her, he saw the acute interest she had in his answer. He knew that he wanted to see more of this woman; but he also knew that if he lied he would never see her again. He told her that he was married, that he had two adorable children, and that his older daughter enjoyed skiing, and the younger only occasionally. He told her that his wife never skied, but that she sometimes went up the hill for a break. He told her about Luce, her artistic talents, and her success at selling her work.

"That is a very unusual name, your wife has," remarked Claire.

"Yes, it's really a nickname. She would not tell me what her real name was, so I had to peek at her passport to find out. Her mother, I gather, had read an English novel with a heroine called Lucinda, and called her daughter after the book's name. Luce was always teased as a child, and hated the name so much, that she started calling herself Luce."

"I can't blame her for that. Luce is short – a no-nonsense name. Does it suit your wife? I'm sorry, that is a very personal question."

"No, I don't mind, and yes, I think that it does suit her."

During the long discussion of his family, Claire watched Adam intently and knew that he was telling the truth. That he loved his family, and possibly even his wife. She knew that, however disappointed she was, that was where he belonged and where she was going to keep him. As much as she felt an acute attraction to this man that she had just met, he was not going to be hers.

They discovered that they were both planning to be on the ski hill the next weekend and laughingly suggested that they would probably ski into each other somewhere on the slopes.

"Sounds like you will be too good to ski with me, and I don't want to be caught lying upside down in the snow when I go headfirst over a mogul," Adam commented.

He wanted this woman to suggest that they meet at a certain time. He did not want to know that she was on the hill, and not able to find her. However, she did not make the suggestion, so he believed her when she had said that she preferred to ski alone.

As they disembarked, he held out his hand to say good-bye. Holding her hand in his, he felt as if he wanted it to stay there always.

"Au revoir, Claire, I will definitely see you again," he said quietly as they turned and disembarked in Montreal.

The Triangle

The measure of a man's real character is what he would do if he knew he never would be found out.
Thomas Babington Macaulay.

The city of Montreal is nestled between the banks of the Saint Lawrence River and the slopes of Mont Royal. The heart of the island city is a wonderful mixture of old and new; from the cobbled streets, historic squares and fine buildings of Vieux-Montreal, where the early French settlers left their mark, to the busy modern streets of downtown with its many skyscrapers and dazzling underground malls and walkways.

Montreal owes much of its charm to its French heritage, and is the largest French-speaking city in the west after Paris. The French influence has resulted in many fine restaurants serving superb French cooking.

Besides the French influence, there is a dynamic influence from the English residents and the thriving immigrant population. Overall, there is a wonderful atmosphere of joie de vivre in this cosmopolitan city.

Just north of Montreal, in the Laurentian Mountains, is a ski resort that draws skiers from across Canada and North America. The breathtaking views from the four slopes of the resort provide skiers with over ninety runs of varying challenge. Chairlifts and gondolas move people from the base of the slopes up thousands of vertical feet to dismount and challenge the runs.

The heavy snowfalls provide for a long ski season and the chalets and hotels are always full throughout the winter season. This is Mont Tremblant, the pride of Quebec and a place of retreat, fun, and hours of skiing for both the avid skier as well as the ski bunnies who prefer to sit in the restaurants, admire the views, and be admired themselves.

Three residents of Montreal frequent Mont Tremblant on a regular basis: two are avid skiers, and enjoy the snow and the challenging runs to the fullest. The third comes up to draw, and to seek inspiration for future art projects.

Adam sat on the chairlift as it moved slowly up the snow-covered mountain. He looked across the expanse of the snow with its undulating moguls and ski-carved ruts. The winter sun created long shadows, emphasizing the whiteness of the terrain. Snow hanging off the branches of the tall evergreens sparkled as if embedded with a million small diamonds. Heavy with snow, the trees bent under its weight, creating shapes and patterns that were fascinating and entrancing. He loved this wonderful white world.

What a beautiful mountain this is, he thought. It is a world of such contrasts of nature, and each season brings something fresh and new. I wonder how many of the hundreds of skiers rushing down the hill at great speeds ever stop and admire the beauty of their environment. Not many I think.

He watched as a group of teenagers, yelling and whooping to each other, flashed down on snowboards below the chair. I wish I could warn them of the dangers of that activity. He thought of Andre, his son, and a wave of fresh grief overwhelmed him. He felt close to his son here on the hill, but he had to remember the wonderful times they had enjoyed together on this and other ski hills. There were no more runs to be taken with him. Andre was gone, and he needed to be strong for his family.

This was why he came up to ski at Mont Tremblant as often as he could. It gave him a chance to get away from the stress of the city and spend some time in solitude and quiet. The hill, with its endless trails, provided the variety and the challenges he needed. He could get onto the hill's Nanson Trail and forget about the world for a while.

One of his chair lift companions broke into his reverie with a whoop.

"Mon Dieu, did you see her, the lady in red? She is such a good skier; and she takes, how do you say, the risks. I see her all the time here on the hill. Always in rouge et blanc. Nobody can miss her, or ski into her. But she is worth watching, non?"

Adam smiled at the French accent. He appreciated the man trying to speak to him in English; he must have heard him speaking before they got onto the chairlift. Living in Montreal meant the French language constantly surrounded one. Adam was bilingual, but the courtesy of his lift companion was pleasant.

"Yes," he replied, "I have noticed her before. I agree that she is a very accomplished skier. Do you know who she is?"

"I hear that she lives in Montreal and comes up to Tremblant many times. She must have the big job because she always stays in the Fairmont Hotel. But, always she is on her own. People have tried to ski with her, and she makes the excuse and skis away. I, myself tried once and that is what I got, the excuse. Oh well, there are lots of pretty girls up here, don't you think?" the francophone skier laughed.

"Oh, I agree that there are many very attractive woman skiers; but I'm married, so I can only look."

"Sorry that you cannot have the fun with the girls, but some married men do you know. Your wife, does she ski?"

"No, she does not ski. My two daughters do ski and they come up with me sometimes, but not today."

The chairlift slowed as the cable took them to the turnaround, and the three skiers pushed themselves off their seats and skied away as the chair turned and started downhill again.

"Enjoy the day," said Adam to his chair companion as he pushed himself off to ski down the Glades run.

Adam's job as legal counsel with Stark, Nesbitt and Bouchard was busy and stressful, but he found it to be extremely rewarding. He had never taken to court work, so his expertise drifted towards a specialty in the investments sector.

He found the money managers and brokers with whom he worked were an interesting mix of personalities. As well, he assisted in negotiations with takeover bids by large companies, especially on an international scale.

Born in Toronto to parents who were both lawyers, they had always assumed that their older child would follow in their footsteps. His sister, two years younger, never felt the same pressure, even from their ambitious mother. She had chosen a life in the arts and owned a very successful art gallery in Yorkville. This, together with her own talent as a water colourist, seemed to satisfy their parents' ambitions for their talented offspring.

As children, Adam and his sister often joked about the parental ambition they had to face. They would play games at being basketball stars, and then say, "Oh no, not a sportsman," in their father's voice and roll on the bed with laughter.

So, Adam found himself at Osgoode Hall in Toronto studying law. He found that he actually enjoyed the studies, as well as the competition with his peers to be near the top of the class. His parents were delighted and encouraged his every success.

Because he was living at home during those student days, he found his social life to be relatively staid, despite the encouragement to party more from his fellow students. The lack of late pub night distractions helped with his studies and made his success easier.

When he graduated, his parents wanted him to join one of their own legal firms, but Adam was insistent. He had spent enough time at home, following in his parents' footsteps. So he applied to law firms in Montreal and soon received numerous offers from which he could choose.

He thoroughly enjoyed the international flavor of Montreal with its French influence, as well as its bilingual and multi-racial citizens. He found that, unlike Toronto, Montreal came to life at nine at night, and the restaurants and bars on Rue Montagne and Crescent Street were alive with revellers until the small hours of the morning, even on weekdays.

He settled into a rental apartment on Hill Park Crescent so that he could walk to work. His new home he furnished with a truckload of furniture sent from his parents' house in Toronto, and he quickly settled into a routine in a new city. He felt alive, energetic, and excited about starting a life of his own making.

His first years were exhausting. He worked at becoming established at the firm, and quickly gained a reputation for being bright, and thorough. As well, the clients enjoyed his good looks and easy manner, despite his lack of experience. At night he lived another life. After his staid years in Toronto, he decided to taste the good life. He frequented the bars, often rolling home inebriated, falling into bed for a few restless hours before starting work the next day. He also found that there were plenty of attractive, bright young women in the bars. The temptation was too much for him, and he often woke up in a stranger's bed.

One morning he woke up, looked at the body lying in the bed next to him, and could not remember who she was, or how he had got there. Driving back to his own apartment he decided that he had sown enough wild oats, and that it was time to become more adult. He needed a regular girlfriend, and a more sophisticated life style. He was nearly thirty and he wanted a change.

A new larger apartment was the beginning of the change for him. He started hosting small, catered dinner parties at his home. He invited the lawyers with whom he worked and they came with their wives; the single men often bringing dates.

This tactic changed his social life. He was now on the dinner party circuit and he found that he became a popular guest at many homes. His peers quickly decided that he was ready to get married and started inviting single women for him to meet. He smiled at their efforts, but appreciated them; dating a number of these women with pleasure. However, he was in no hurry to marry.

All these good intentions were thrown aside when he found himself in Paris on business and met Luce, his wife.

His life had changed. He found himself with little time for himself, and when he did, he escaped to the ski hill where he swept the city and its obligations away in a rush of powder snow and speed.

He loved his wife and his family dearly, but the monotony of corporate life, interspersed with family obligations, tended to drive him to look for distractions. The ski hill was a wonderful outlet for release from the pressures of life.

The suite in the Fairmont Tremblant was large and luxurious; the living room furnished with soft floral furnishings that warmed the room. A small dining table of dark mahogany stood in one corner. In another was a gas fireplace that added a glowing atmosphere on cold, snowy days. The bedroom contained a king size bed covered with a down comforter, and thick white spread; numerous pillows were banked against the headboard. The dark mahogany chests lent a contrast to the stark white of the large bed. An en-suite led off the bedroom. It was large and sumptuous with a jacuzzi bathtub, glass-enclosed shower, and a marble top on the vanity that held a variety of toiletries.

Claire Hardick used this hotel suite on a regular basis. She was too busy with her work life in Montreal to allow for the maintenance of her own chalet, so she had sold the one that she had inherited when her parents died. Now, she chose to live in the hotel when she was skiing on Mont Tremblant. She was aware that the cost of this luxury was extravagant, but it was one that she allowed herself. She was a wealthy woman, having received a large inheritance from her parents; but she was still very aware of how much this indulgence was costing her, and she revelled in the privilege.

Standing at a window in the living room of the suite, she looked out at the spectacular view of the mountain. It rose from the white snow base to pale blue peaks that appeared to reach the heavens. No matter how many times she stood there and admired the view, it never failed to take her breath away. She felt carried away by the awe of the scene; the grandeur that nature was capable of presenting.

She loved this mountain with its glorious majesty, its variety of ski opportunities, as well as the amenities it offered to those who made the effort to drive up from the city. For her it was the ultimate escape. It was a way to unwind after a week of long days and the stress of keeping clients content. This was her meditation, and she came to the hill as often as her agenda allowed.

She had been coming here for years; first with her parents until they died. More recently alone. It had become a habit to take the comfortable way, and so she rented a suite at the hotel. It provided her with housekeeping as well as meals that she did not have to prepare herself.

A quiet knock on the door was followed by a voice saying, "Your breakfast order, Miss Hardick."

Smiling to herself at the service she was enjoying, she opened the door for the room service waitress, and stepped aside to allow her space to wheel the breakfast trolley into the room. Claire thanked her as she left the room, and sat down to enjoy her start to the day.

Room service was how she ate when at the hotel. She did not relish the idea of facing dozens of curious faces in the dining room before starting the day. This quiet time alone was very precious to her. Once she got to the mountain slopes she would be in the middle of ski line-ups, crowded gondolas and numerous skiers on the hill. This was her time to be alone and enjoy the breakfast she had ordered. The Fairmont Hotel now knew that her order was always the same; grapefruit juice, two scrambled eggs, three rashes of crispy bacon, two slices of whole grain toast and a large pot of coffee with milk, not cream. She never ate breakfasts like this at home, so she indulged when someone else was preparing the meal; and she rationalized that she would be burning off the calories in the hours of skiing to follow.

Pushing away from the table that held the remains of her breakfast she walked to the closet and pulled out her ski suit. She looked at it pensively. The redness was certainly eye-catching. She smiled, remembering the comments she often heard as she skied down the hill. *Lady in Red, come dance with me* was the most common. But then, I suppose I ask for it by wearing this bold colour against the white snow. I can't help but be noticed. Maybe it's time for lady in black, she mused, just to fool them all. However, this is what I have with me today; so this is what I will be wearing.

She pulled on a white turtle-neck sweater to go under the suit for warmth. With the red suit, the white neck showed up starkly. Grabbing her white ski cap and white ski gloves she looked at her reflection and smiled. I look like the Canadian ski team she thought. All I need is a maple leaf pasted on my back.

She giggled to herself and made for the door. She was more than ready for an exciting day on the slopes.

Luce Lambert sat over her sketch pad, putting the final strokes on the landscape that she was drawing. A wide angle view of the slope of the mountain was what she wanted, so she had sat herself close to a window. She was interested in capturing the shapes of the snow-laden trees. When the white snow lay heavily on the branches, they bent under the weight and formed grotesque shapes against the sky. She was sketching when she noticed a group of teenagers stumble into the lodge, laughing and pushing at each other. The noise caught everyone's attention as they watched the energetic young people.

Sitting quietly in her seat by the window she watched them come in from the chill of the snow-packed hill into the warmth of the lodge. They were laughing, pulling off toques, goggles and gloves, and plopping down onto the benches at the tables close to her.

She watched as one of the youths pulled off his toque, exposing a mop of red hair. His face was flushed from the cold, and snow clung to his chin. Glancing up he saw her watching him, and broke out into a broad grin, showing perfect white teeth.

"Gee, it was so cool out there today. The snow is just super. You don't ski, lady?"

"No, I'm afraid that I don't any more. I come up here for the scenery, both outside and inside. I like to draw what I see, and this is a wonderful place for that."

"Well, whatever turns you on. I'd rather be on the snow *in* the trees than drawing them!"

"I'm sure you would," she laughed, looking at him carefully. He would make a wonderful study with his colouring; his hair, eyes, cheeks, bright ski clothes.

"Would you mind sitting there for a moment while I do a sketch of you? I think you would make a very good subject for a painting. But if it's too much to ask I'll understand."

"Hey, that's cool. But I need a coke and a burger first. Can I eat while you draw?"

"Certainly. I'll wait right here for you."

Twenty minutes later Luce had a detailed sketch of the youth, complete with notes on colouring and tints. She was excited about what she had captured on her sketch pad. The energy in the youth would show through in a painting. This was the subject she needed to help her forget about her loss, to ease the pain of missing her son. He would have been about the same age. This project would be a therapeutic healing for her.

She gave the boy her name and phone number, and took his. Fortunately they both lived in Montreal, so could stay in contact with each other.

"I'll let you know when I have finished the portrait, or if I need you for one more sitting. Could you do that for me?" she asked.

"It would be fab if my folks will let me."

"Tell them what we did here today, and ask them to call me if they have any questions," she responded.

"Thanks," he said as he pulled his toque over his red hair. Goggles and gloves were grabbed as he ran off to join his friends and attack the slopes again. At the door he paused, looked back, and blew a kiss to her.

What a delightful young man, Luce thought, and she felt a tear form in her eye and roll down her cheek. Is this the substitute for my lost son who is gone forever?

She looked again at the sketch, and thought that this was one of the best things she had done on the hill for a long while. She often came up to Mont Tremblant with Adam when he wanted to ski. She used the time to sketch the mountain scenes, the unusual shapes of the snow-covered trees, and sometimes the people. It was a time when she could share something with Adam, even if he wanted to be alone on the hill. She understood his need to be alone after the pressures of work. But they did not share much these days. Over the past few years she had felt them moving apart, finding different interests and, after the death of their son, Andre, different distractions in an effort to forget.

She had been quite young when she had met Adam in Paris and fallen in love. Their whirlwind romance had resulted in a quick marriage when she moved from France to be with him in Montreal. Coming to a French-speaking city had made the transition easier, even if she sometimes wanted to put her hands over her ears at the Quebecois French that she heard. Still, it was French, and the familiar language helped to make her feel more at home.

Slowly, she and her husband had drifted into busy routines; children and home for her, with some painting at an easel when she could find the time; a busy career with long hours for Adam. It was the death of their son on the ski hill that had finally opened the rift that was difficult to close. Instead of clinging to each other in their sorrow, they had found different avenues for healing. Adam worked harder, and skied more frequently than before. To give his wife an outlet for her sorrow he had built for her a large well-lit studio attached to the rear of their house in Westmount. Luce turned to her painting, and spent more and more time alone in the studio, creating works of art to compensate for her loss.

The few times that she came up the hill to Mont Tremblant were a change for both of them, and these times seemed to bring them closer for a while. That was why she had made the effort today. She was glad that she had, as she now had this wonderful study of the young lad to take home to work on.

Advice

It is well to give when asked, but it is better to give, unasked, through understanding.
Kahil Gibran. *The Prophet.*

The telephone rang loudly on her desk for the second time. Claire glanced down at the call display and ignored the ringing. She could hear the phones ringing throughout the outer office.

This was a very busy time for the company; in fact, the word chaos tended to come to mind when trying to describe her work day, but she was learning to handle the pressure. Years of working around phones, the partners' demands, her clients' wishes, and keeping everything on an even keel had taught her to decipher which demands were urgent, and which ones she could leave on the back burner, to be dealt with later.

She ran her hand through her hair, twisting it into a knot at the top of her head. This was a habit she had when she was problem solving. It played havoc with her hairstyle, but it had the effect of slowing her pulse rate and steadying her breathing. Her long, blonde hair was one of her best features. It was thick and luxurious, and fell just below her shoulders in soft waves. It softened her face that tended to look businesslike and determined. The waves of her hair softened the mouth that could stretch into a firm line when she was crossed or pushed; it softened her eyes which could look right through you when you questioned her decisions. Yes, she knew her hair was her saviour, and she made the most of keeping it looking luxuriant.

She looked down at the folder on her desk knowing that what it contained was good work. She was very pleased with how successful her presentation at the conference had been. She had been prepared, she had been ready, she had been polished, she had been credible. She had not worked this hard for so long not to make the most of the opportunity that had been offered to her. Now that she was back, it was time to catch up on work that had been pushed to the back burner as she had prepared for the conference.

The phone rang again and this time she answered the call, "Claire Hardick here."

"Oh, Miss Hardick, I'm so glad I found you in. Do you have a moment? I have a concern that my shares in Pontifish are not doing as well as I think they should be doing, and I wondered what I should do about it. You see, my friend's husband has some of the same shares, and he thinks we should all be selling them as the company..."

"Excuse me," interrupted Claire, "to whom am I speaking?"

"Oh, oh, I am sorry. This is Mrs. Potter. Do you need my account number?"

"No, Mrs. Potter, not until we talk about your question. Did my assistant tell you to speak to me about this?"

"No, I did not speak with her; the call came straight through to you."

"Thank you. Now, about the Pontifish Gold shares. I can assure you that there is absolutely no reason to panic about selling that particular holding. The company is very sound, and anything you may hear to the contrary is just gossip. However, if you are feeling uncomfortable about holding them I can get my assistant to call you and she will be happy to process the sale."

"Oh, so they are safe. I did not want to sell them as my husband bought them before he died and he was very good at investing. No, I won't sell them just now. Thank you, thank you so much, I do feel better now," and the line went dead.

Her phone rang again. She sighed and looked at the caller ID.

"I'll be right up, Avery," she said into the speaker.

"Good, I want to go over a few things to make sure we make the most of this opportunity. There is a lot of money in this for us all, and I don't want anything to misstep," replied the voice on the other end of the line.

"I agree," responded Claire sharply.

Oh yes, thought Claire, there's a lot of money in this for us all – you mean you! I'm doing all the work and taking all the risks. You'll make sure that you grab most of the headlines for the company; as well as the money.

Avery Heap was the senior partner who worked in a sumptuous office on the upper floor of the building. The office, with its antique furniture, Persian carpets, and original oils on the walls suited the man. He was polished, suave, and confident. He liked to know what was going on in every nook and cranny of the business.

Claire picked up a file from her desk and headed out the door. In the outer office her assistant was just returning to her desk.

"Oh, Miss Hardick, I'm sorry I was not here; I had to go to the ladies' room."

"Did you put the phone on messages when you left, Nathalie?" Claire asked.

"I always do Miss Hardick."

"Well, please check. A call came directly through to my phone while you were away from your desk, and I did not need the interruption when I was in planning mode."

"Yes, I will, I – oh, ooops. No, I did not put it on messages," said Nathalie. "I am so, so sorry. It will not happen again."

"Fine," said Claire curtly, and started for the door to meet with Avery Heap.

As she walked down the hall she reflected that it was most unlike Nathalie to make such a simple mistake. The young woman was extremely efficient and ambitious. Claire stopped, took a deep breath and pulled herself into the here and now.

My mind has been so focused on the conference and now catch-up, that I have not been aware of my surroundings and other people, she thought. Have I really looked at Nathalie in the past few days? Maybe I have. And what, if anything have I seen? On reflection, she's been very quiet and subdued which is unlike her. Maybe I thought she was just being considerate of my workload and stress.

Claire stopped, turned around and headed back to her office. As she entered she noticed that Nathalie had her head down on the desk. She looked up when Claire came in and opened her mouth to speak, but Claire spoke first.

"Nathalie," she started, as she noticed tears glistening on the young woman's lashes. "I don't have to go up right now, why don't we go and get a coffee and bring them back to my office for some girl talk."

Nathalie's mouth opened and closed, and opened again. "Oh, I'll get the coffee, Miss Hardick. And would you really give me a chance to talk to you? I must ask somebody to help me and I don't know how or who to ask."

"Oh no, Nathalie, I don't need you to get my coffee, we'll go together." As Claire walked back into her office she realized that she would now not have time to meet with Avery and she still was not ready for her next meeting.

"On second thoughts, Nathalie, can I take you up on that offer to fetch the coffee? I'll phone and tell Mr. Heap that I'll be late for the meeting."

Avery will be anything but happy, thought Claire, but she spent more time working with Nathalie than with Avery, and she wanted to make sure that she was happy and comfortable in the job. She only hoped that, whatever the problem, she could solve it; and that it did not have to go all the way up to the human resources department.

"Avery, Claire here. I have a problem that has just come up that I have to deal with before I leave. It can't wait I'm afraid, so I won't have time to come up and meet with you. I'll see you later this afternoon if you have time. I will clear my agenda if you let me know what time will work for you."

She was just about to put the phone down when she heard Avery yelling over the line.

"Now wait a moment. This will not do. I have to speak to you this morning."

With a sigh, Claire answered. "Avery, this issue could be very problematic. I don't want it to escalate, so I'm going to deal with it now. I will see you later. Goodbye." She switched off the phone.

Waiting for Nathalie to return, Claire started packing files into her briefcase. She was pushed for time, but she felt that whatever was bothering the young woman should be dealt with before she left Nathalie to simmer. She tried to guess what it might be. Could she have been involved in a sexual harassment incident? Was she unhappy with the workload? Were the other staff members treating her poorly? She hoped that it was something that she could deal with.

Nathalie returned with two cups of coffee and put one down in front of Claire. "I took two cookies out of the staff cookie tin as well for you. I know you like them. I don't think anyone saw me."

Claire laughed and thanked her. "Now, you look like you're feeling a little better. Please sit down and tell me what is making you so unhappy. Is someone harassing you in the office?"

"Oh no," shrilled the young woman. "Oh no, no. I am *so* happy working here. It has nothing to do with work. I am so sorry if you thought that was my problem. You see, it is trouble at home, especially with my mother."

Claire leaned back and relaxed. Oh well, she thought, I'm here now, I may as well hear what she has to say; but Avery is going to be rather upset when I tell him my delay was not work related. Sometimes people have to come before money.

"So," questioned Claire, "what's the problem with your mother?"

"Well, actually, it's my mother and the man she wants me to marry. You see, we are Jewish, as you know, and my mother is determined that I will marry as she puts it 'a nice Jewish boy'. There is this boy, I mean man, that has taken me out a few times and he's nice, but…"

"So, what's the problem?" Claire prodded.

"Well, he's a dentist with his own practice, so he earns a good salary and he takes me to very nice restaurants, and buys nice presents, and he's quite good looking, but um…"

"He sounds ideal to me," laughed Claire.

"Yes well. The problem is that he is very, very boring to be with. He talks about work and sport all the time. He never wants to go dancing. He watches football on the television constantly, and I just sit and watch him watching. And now, my mother thinks that he is going to propose. But I don't want to spend my life with him. What am I going to do? All my Jewish girl friends are married and they think I should snap this guy up before someone else does."

"Well, I think you need to think about the big picture of your life before you decide what to do. Where do you see yourself in ten years' time, or even five years? Would you like to be married with a comfortable house with lots of children? Do you see yourself as a career woman? You need to see beyond this month, or even next year."

"Oh yes, I do want to marry. It's just that I'm waiting for the man of my dreams to appear. I want to be swept off my feet. This does not always happen in the Jewish community. We are expected to marry someone from within the Jewish faith, and I have not met anyone who has set my heart pounding even faintly yet. I want passion!"

She looked across at Claire who was watching her with an amused smile on her face.

"I didn't mean to say so much. I am feeling so much pressure from home that I don't know which way to turn. Have you met the man of your dreams, Miss Hardick, if I can be so personal? You have never married have you?"

"No, I have never been married. I suppose, like you I have dated a few men, but have never been swept off my feet either. I really am much too busy with my work right now to even think about a big romance. I don't know how I will react when the big passion arrives – whether I will give up my career for home and family. I will just have to wait and see I suppose. Right now my work comes first in my life."

Nathalie looked puzzled as she replied, "I am sure you will give up everything if you get bowled over by the right guy – we all seem to do that."

"In the meantime," laughed Claire, "why don't you go on a few more dates with the dentist and see how things turn out? Why don't you suggest doing a few more exciting things together? He may be more interesting than you think, and you will make your parents very happy. And now, I have a meeting to go to."

She picked up her briefcase as she left the office.

"Thank you, Miss Hardick, you are always so kind and supportive."

Claire made a grimace with her face. "We do what the job demands. You can reach me on my mobile phone if there's an emergency."

With that comment, she walked out of the office.

Family Life

Come live with me, and be my Love
And we will all the pleasure prove.
Christopher Marlowe.

Breakfast was always a rather hectic, rushed meal in the house. Adam sat and looked at his family sitting around the kitchen table. His two daughters usually grumbled about the family requirement to eat a good breakfast before they left for school, but Luce, his wife, never compromised. She insisted quietly that they had to eat, and made a point of providing them with a variety of tempting options. She was not enamoured of the North American habit of eating dried, cold cereals at the start of the day. Instead, she made delicious French pastries for them. This morning they had warm chocolate croissants with butter and a choice of jams or honey. The girls squealed in delight when they saw the croissants, as this was their favourite breakfast. No complaining today, Adam thought as he watched them fill their mouths with hot chocolate.

The two Lambert girls were generally well behaved, but like all children, they often tried to get more than their parents were willing to give. Adam and Luce tried not to overcompensate for the loss of their son by indulging the girls, so they tended to be more strict than usual. They both missed their son very much. He would have been fifteen if he had survived the ski accident and his absence was felt by the entire family. It was now four years since the accident, and the girls were beginning to make lives for themselves without their older brother who had been their champion, their hero.

"Are you going away again, Papa?" asked the older girl, Juliette.

"Yes, I am off to Quebec City for a few days. I will miss you all, but I'll phone every evening to find out what nonsense you've been up to that day, so don't disappoint me."

"Oh, Papa, we don't do nonsense. We are very serious people. Even our teachers say that we are serious, don't they, Michelle?"

"Yes, they do. But Papa knows that we can be foolish at times too. We will try not to disappoint you, Papa," replied Michelle.

"How long will you be gone this time?" asked his wife in an exasperated tone.

Adam caught the inflection in her voice so answered carefully.

"I am booked into the Chateau Frontenac for two nights, but if there's nothing of interest for my role in the firm, I may come home earlier. I will let you know what happens. I'll phone home every night to check in, and you know where to get hold of me if you need anything, or if there's an emergency. I am not looking forward to these meetings, as I suspect they will be rather boring for me, but I can't afford not to go. I am not making any major contribution to the discussions, I am only there in an advisory capacity. That can be rather tiresome if there is nothing of particular concern for the firm. There will be a lot of group lunches and dinners. They call them power lunches, so let's hope some of them produce some power," he explained with a smile on his face.

Luce smiled in response, but she sometimes wished that he did not have to be away so often. With their son gone, she felt that a male influence was needed around the house.

"What's an advice capability?" questioned his younger daughter.

"It's called an advisory capacity. That means I am there to advise. As a lawyer, the firm wants me to watch for anything that could be illegal, or give the company a problem in the future. We have to make sure that everything we do is always on the right side of the law. Do you understand that?"

"I think so. So you're like a mistakes policeman?"

With a laugh Adam tousled the hair of the child sitting next to him, and bent to give her a kiss on the cheek.

"Sort of, but I don't have a badge, or carry a weapon to do my job."

"Wow, that would be cool if you did," interjected his older daughter.

"No, it would not," interrupted Luce firmly. "No weapons allowed in *this* house. We don't want anything that is going to hurt other people around us. Do we?"

"Non, Mama," came a duet of response.

"So kiss your Papa au revoir as he will be away for a few days."

Looking longingly at his family, Adam knew that he would miss them. All through the breakfast meal he had been watching them and wishing that he did not have to travel out of town again. But duty called, and he would again be apart from them, if only for a short while.

Temptation

Is this her fault or mine?
The tempter or the tempted, who sins most?
William Shakespeare

The week after the conference was a blur of activity for Claire. Her presentation had been well received, and she had received a number of enquiries about the possibility of visiting other brokerage houses to work with their staff on a more intimate basis. Some of the calls had come from European brokerage houses that had attended the conference and were keen to have her visit their firms for further discussions.

She was very flattered by the attention, but she knew that there was no future in rushing around the world talking with other investment houses when her own clients required her attention. Avery, however, had other ideas. He was extremely excited about the attention that Claire had garnered for the company and he wanted to capitalize on it.

Avery was owner of a boutique investment house that had established itself as a credible firm with which to invest. He had hand-picked reliable, hard-working money managers and brokers from around the country. This handful of talented people had earned for the firm, a reputation for honesty, integrity and a Midas touch for making money for their clients. Claire, in particular, was one whom Avery had nurtured carefully. She had a second sense for thinking outside of the traditional investment box and had often put the group ahead of the investment curve.

For Claire, the company had provided an introduction to the field of her choice after she had completed her MBA at Queen's University. Her father had been her mentor and guide through all her teen years and had helped her to understand how the world of money and investment worked. She had been fascinated since she was a little girl, when he had opened her first bank account into which she had carefully stowed away much of her pocket and chore-earned money. Then her father had encouraged her to open an investment account and to read the market reports. She had started selecting stocks, checking her choices with him, and then watching the results – as they either increased her wealth or lost her money. Those formative years, when it had all been a fun learning experience, had provided a grounding in how the world of big money worked, and developed in her a sixth sense for sorting the wheat from the chaff when it came to picking investment stocks.

She respected Avery, the man who had hired her and who showed every confidence in her ability. As she sat and listened to him, she told herself that she had to be patient with this man who had provided her with many exciting opportunities during the past years; but she was not going to be pushed around by his curt manner.

"This is a wonderful opportunity to put our firm on the international map," he stated firmly to Claire when they sat down together to talk about the response to her presentation. "We need to strike while the iron is hot. This attention will fade very quickly if we wait."

He was eager for Claire to go back to Toronto as soon as possible, and also to answer a call from Calgary that presented a lucrative consulting opportunity.

I know what you want, thought Claire. You just want me on the money trail, so you can get richer. I had better make sure that this works for me as well, both to benefit my career, and to benefit the firm financially.

"What's in it for me, Avery?" she asked brazenly.

Avery was taken aback. He looked at her quizzically. She had never been so forthright before.

"You get to keep your job of course," he retorted with a smirk on his face.

"I know that I get to keep my job. If I go on these jaunts for the firm, I have to get more out of them than jet lag. Or I will leave the firm and go out on my own and service these clients in my own way. Don't play games with me, Avery. I think we both know that you need me as much as I need the profile of the firm. So let's talk sense here."

After that exchange, the conversation became more reasonable and they worked out a response to the potential clients. Claire would travel to some of these places, but not ignore her commitments in Montreal.

She left his office thinking that, done right; she would enjoy some of these mini-breaks away from the office, as well as using it to do some sightseeing and shopping in Europe – all at client expense. Smilingly congratulating herself for playing hardball with Avery, she returned to her office and the workload waiting for her there.

When the week ended, she was more than ready to climb into her car and escape back up the mountain to the luxury suite, the delicious breakfasts, and the new snowfall on the slopes. She had watched the weather during the week and conditions looked to be particularly good that weekend. So she left the office early on Friday afternoon and headed up to Mont Tremblant and her favourite hotel suite.

The mountain seemed to her to be at its glorious best. Sunlight appeared to glint off every snowflake on every tree, making the world around her look like a giant crystal ball in which the skiers moved.

Saturday morning found her waiting in line at the gondola to ascend the hill when a voice said, "Now I know that the fates are on our side. Hello again."

Startled at the voice so close by, she looked over her shoulder to see Adam Lambert standing two lines behind her, also waiting to board the lift.

She smiled at him. "Good morning to you as well. I think it's going to be a wonderful morning. The snow looks good today."

"Next group get on," called the attendant at the gondola loading station. He signalled to her to hurry up, as she was the last person he could fit into the gondola waiting to be filled. She hesitated for a moment; should she get on and miss having time with this new acquaintance? They would probably never meet up for the rest of the day among the crowd of skiers. Or should she wait and go up the hill in his company?

"Let's go, lady," the attendant called again.

"You take the space," Claire turned and said to the woman standing behind her who appeared to be a single.

The woman thanked her, stepped into the gondola, and it swung away on its cable to ascend the hill.

"Okay. Move forward everyone," the attendant signalled and Claire moved forward with the next group, that included Adam Lambert.

"Thank you for doing that," he said. "Now I have a chance to get to know you better. I was hoping that we might meet, so this *is* a good morning."

He had no intention of telling Claire that he had been waiting at the gondola since the lifts had started operating that morning, hoping to find her there. Her bright red outfit had caught his attention as soon as she got into the line-up and he had cursed softly to himself when he realized that she was going to be squeezed into the gondola in front of him - and that he would still miss a chance of skiing with her. That's when he had taken a chance and spoken up, leaving the decision up to her whether to join him, or to ride up without his company.

A wide grin spread across his face, and Claire could not help but return the smile. They climbed into the next gondola together and headed up the slope. Adam looked Claire up and down as they rode. She felt self-conscious, as his eyes ran up and down her figure; she had the sensation of being appraised.

"I think I've seen you skiing on the hill, your red and white outfit is very distinctive. You stand out under the lifts as your bright suit goes flashing by. I've noticed how well you handle the moguls."

Claire blushed. She knew that her suit was distinctive but had not expected it to be *that* noticeable. In the midst of the babble from the other passengers, their conversation was brief and polite.

When they exited the gondola they agreed to take a few runs together to see if their pace matched. Much to their delight, they enjoyed the rhythm of skiing together, matching their skis as they carved to each other's curves and descended the slope. Finding such mutual rhythm in their ski patterns, they enjoyed a few more long runs in tandem. Later, they stopped at the ski chalet for a hot chocolate as Adam had arranged to meet one of his daughters there.

He introduced Claire to Juliette who was full of excited news about her morning ski lesson and the young group with whom she had been skiing. She hardly noticed that her father was giving more attention to the lady in the red ski suit than to her excited stories.

Claire then wished them well, and left to ski by herself for the rest of the day. She had explained to Adam how important these times alone were to her.

"I don't want to appear rude, but this is my meditation for the week. I could sit at home on the floor with my legs crossed and hum for an hour, but I prefer to ski. To be out in the air, moving fast; it blows away the cobwebs in my head.

That night, back in the hotel suite, she ordered a room service meal of beef bourguignon and a bottle of Argentinian dark red Malbec. As she sat in the hotel suite dining on her delicious meal, she recalled the conversation and skiing that she had enjoyed with Adam. He was a very interesting man. They had talked about their work briefly; they had rehashed the highs and lows of the conference they had attended in Toronto. They also found that they both had a keen interest in music, attending symphony concerts, and shared a deep admiration for Kent Nagano, the new Montreal Symphony maestro as well as Charles du Toit who had conducted the musicians for many years. They had discussed their enjoyment of opera performances and critiqued the last production of *La Bohème* performed at the Place des Arts. Adam felt that the soprano who had sung the role of Mimi had been too shrill; Claire thought that she had been too fat to be credible as a romantic heroine.

"When Rodolfo took Mimi's hand in his, and started singing, *Che gelida manina* – 'Your tiny hand is frozen' – and he was holding a very plump lump of a hand in his, I had difficulty controlling my laughter. I know opera is all about the music, the melody and the voice, but to me, it still has to be visually credible." They both laughed and agreed on that point.

For someone who prefers to ski alone, I certainly enjoyed having company riding up on the lifts as well as skiing down the slopes; how unusual, she thought.

The next few weeks found her meeting with Adam on Mont Tremblant on a regular basis. They got into the habit of arranging a time and a place to meet. They would ski together, meet up with his daughters for hot chocolate, and then spend the rest of the day skiing separately; Claire alone, Adam with his children.

As the weeks passed, a special friendship developed between the two. They did not ask more from each other than a few hours of interesting conversation and skiing a few runs together. However, when their eyes met, there was more communicated in those looks than any words could express.

Adam felt that he was not in a position to tell this woman how desirable she was, and how he wanted more from her. The more time he spent with her, the more enamoured he became. The times that he was with her, out in the open, Adam could make himself believe that he was n o t harming anyone.

For Claire, the friendship was rather confusing. She knew that Adam was married and devoted to his children. But she could not control her body's reaction when he was close to her. She told herself that she was extremely attracted to this man, that he was a man with whom sparks could fly for her, as Nathalie had wanted; but she also knew that he could never be hers. So she kept her emotions well in check when they were together.

One day, quite out of the blue, Adam stopped Claire before she could ski off on her own. He took her by the arm and gently guided her to ski away from the crowds with him and find a quiet place on the side of a run.

Looking at her very intently he began, "Claire, I don't know how to say this, but I think I want to ask you this. Where is our friendship going? You are my secret lady in red – like the words of the song. I don't mean secret as in sneaking away together, because we're in the middle of a crowded hill, but we may be starting a gossip mill with our constant skiing together. Does this bother you?"

Returning his look, she stayed quiet for a long while.

"Are you suggesting that we should stop meeting this way?" she finally asked. "If it is, I will understand that you have family commitments, but I will truly miss these times together. They have become very special to me."

"To me as well," responded Adam hoarsely. "I do want them to continue, and nothing will compromise my family. The girls did not come up with me today, you will have noticed."

"Yes, I did wonder where they were. I thought they were skiing with pals. If you are alone, and not in a hurry, would you like to have a drink together after the lifts close?"

"That would be very pleasant," responded Adam quickly, "but I think it should be earlier, as I have to be home by seven. My wife and I have a commitment for the evening."

"Well, why don't we plan to make it next time you are up here alone."

Looking disappointed, he nodded, and Claire skied away to the chairlift. She was aching with feelings of regret.

When Claire met up with Adam on the slopes during the following Sunday, he made a point of mentioning that he was alone, as the girls had a birthday party back in the city.

Claire looked at him intently and said, "So you want to take advantage of the raincheck I gave you last week for drinks after skiing?"

"Caught out. Can't hide my blatant gaffe can I?"

Laughing, they agreed to meet at Claire's suite at four. She left the hill earlier to get back to the hotel to order a cheese tray and a bottle of Lagavulin scotch from room service. She had learned from him that he had enjoyed the gift bottle that she had given to him in

Toronto, and that this bottle had started him on a habit of drinking it as his Scotch of choice.

"See what an expensive drinker you have made of me," he had remarked jokingly.

By the time Adam arrived at the hotel, Claire had changed into a casual chiffon two-piece in shades of cerise and burgundy. She had brushed her blonde hair out so that the waves hung loosely to her shoulders.

When he knocked at the door of the hotel suite she opened it with a broad welcoming smile.

"Come into my parlour," she sang.

"Said the spider to the fly?" questioned Adam.

"Oh my, did I sound like the wicked witch luring in the unsuspecting?"

Adam stopped and looked at the beautiful woman in front of him, her blonde hair a shining halo around her face. The softness of her clothes fell loosely over her lithe body, emphasizing the roundness of her breasts, and the length of her legs.

"You are certainly no witch, unless they come in alluring disguises these days," he said softly.

Embarrassed, Claire quickly responded, "Enough of this; let's have a drink. I hope you're ready to eat as well. The hotel staff did wonders with the cheese tray I ordered. I think they expected I was entertaining the entire Canadian ski team, not just you and me. Would you please do the honours with the Scotch."

Adam poured a generous amount of amber liquid into each glass, added two ice cubes to hers, and handed the glass to Claire. He sat on the couch and turned to look at her.

I cannot give this woman up, he thought. She has become such a part of my life by now. I find myself anticipating the weekends when I know that I will be with her. How can I welcome her into my life without hurting anyone in the process? He wanted to be with her, but he did not want to encourage a difficult entanglement.

Claire smiled back at Adam thinking, I am falling in love with this man. How could it happen? Now that I finally find someone who has totally engrossed my attention and desires, he turns out to belong with someone else. My timing and my luck are not working.

Sipping at their scotch and eating generously of the crackers and cheese selections, they continued the conversation they had started that afternoon on the slopes. They had disagreed on the penalties imposed on brokers who had been caught in insider trading deals. Adam saw the issue from a legal perspective, Claire from the brokers' angle, although she could still not approve of the practice.

They agreed to some difference of opinion on the issue and changed the topic to the more pleasant one of the promise of an early spring in the city. They had mixed feelings about the arrival of the warm sunshine. The warmer weather was always welcomed in a city often blanketed in snow for many months of the year; but the warm weather also meant the close of the ski season that they both enjoyed so much.

"How will we get to continue these conversations once the ski hill is closed?" prodded Adam, hoping she would suggest meeting with him in the city.

"There's always next winter," joked Claire in reply.

When Adam stood at the door to leave, they stopped and looked at each other. They were both heady from the alcohol and being so close to each other in private. He bent his head and kissed her softly on the lips.

"Thank you for a most enjoyable time. I will certainly see much of you before next winter."

"Adam," Claire replied. "I like being with you too much; I do not want to lose a friend."

"We will make sure that does not happen," he said.

The moment was frozen as they looked at each other. Adam felt himself stir and bent to kiss her again, not so gently this time. He opened her lips with his and prodded with his tongue into her warm open mouth. He felt her relax into him and could not contain his desire.

In one swift motion he picked her up in his arms as he closed the door shut with his foot and headed for the bedroom. Placing her gently onto the bed he ran his hand up under her soft skirts and along her warm thighs. Claire lay back on the bed and opened her legs to his exploring hands as she pulled his mouth down to hers again.

Adam sat back and looked at her, spread out on the bed, and pushed her clothing up to reveal her naked thighs.

"Oh, I want you so much," he whispered as he lifted her garments over her head. She lay naked in front of him.

He quickly disrobed and together they fell onto the bed in a passion of arms, legs, and hungry mouths. Searching each other for as much intimacy as they could find, they rolled together, until Adam pushed his erectness into her welcoming warmth and thrust out all the pent up desire that had been accumulating over the past weeks. When they had released their passion they lay side by side and looked deeply into each other's eyes.

"Should I apologize and say that I am sorry if I did something that I should have been able to control? But I am not sorry, so I hope that you are not. I have been in lust with you from the moment I saw you on the stage in Toronto, talking to a room full of interested listeners. My willpower could only last so long."

"Oh, Adam, Adam; have you not been able to see how much I have wanted to do this as well, but felt unable to say so? I have been mentally urging you to do this for a long time."

Her words were so honest, and so exciting that Adam felt a wave of desire that hardened his erection, and he rolled over onto her again. This time he caressed her gently; her breasts, her thighs, and explored her secret crevices with his hands. He felt her thrust up towards him and he lowered himself onto her again, entering her slowly, feeling himself sink into her. She felt his thrusts and moved in rhythm with his movements, finding satisfaction in their coming together.

When they had finally dressed and Adam stood at the door again ready to leave to return to the city, they both hesitated, knowing there was an unspoken issue to be resolved. Neither wanted to talk about the future; about where this relationship was headed. They both knew that they wanted more time together. When and how that would happen, neither of them was prepared to discuss.

Their ski meetings continued for the next few weekends, enjoying time and conversation together as they rode the chair or the gondola, and pacing their skiing rhythm to match each other. However, there was a new intimacy in their togetherness that they both felt intensely. There was no opportunity for time to be alone with family commitments pulling at Adam, but they savoured their times together.

Time to be alone again came one dull, snowy Sunday. As the snow fell heavily and the runs became covered with soft white blowing swirls they stopped skiing. It was now difficult to see the runs, despite the ski goggles they wore.

Adam suggested that they stop skiing and share an early dinner. They made their way to the restaurant, Des Petits Ventres, in the village.

As they sat and enjoyed their meal, a weather report was issued by the management. "All patrons heading back to Montreal today should leave immediately as the roads are becoming dangerous with deep blowing snow covering the highways. The report is that the roads will be closed within the hour if this heavy snowfall continues."

Adam rose without looking at Claire. "Wait here for me, I will be right back," he said as he left the table.

When he returned he sat down and looked up at Claire who was watching him questioningly.

"I hope this meets with your approval," he started. "I phoned home and told the family that I could not drive home tonight as the roads were closed. I told Luce that I will be staying at the Fairmont Hotel."

He waited with bated breath for a response from the woman he wanted to be with tonight, hoping she would respond with the invitation he desired.

Claire searched his face for a long moment and then quietly said, "Let's go to the hotel now, I want to hold you very close to me."

The breath that Adam had been holding slowly escaped from his lips, and he reached across the table to take her hand. He searched in his wallet for enough bills to cover the cost of the meal, and led her outside. They pulled on their ski hoods and goggles and together, hand in hand, fought the wind and the snow as they walked up the road to the Fairmont Hotel.

Laughing, they stumbled into the hotel lobby, shaking snow off their clothing. When they entered the elevator they pressed the floor button and turned to each other, brushing snow from their faces. Adam leaned in and took a lump of snow off Claire's chin, then moved closer and kissed her gently.

"So cold," he said softly. "You need warming up I think."

"Please do," responded Claire as she leaned into him.

They moved into each other's arms, Adam licking snowflakes from Claire's eyes and mouth. They stood clutched together in an embrace that they wanted to never end.

Neither noticed that the elevator arrived at their floor, the door opened, and then closed. The elevator descended to the ground level again where the door opened.

A loud cough caught their attention and they slowly pulled apart, still with arms wrapped around each other. In a daze, they looked out at half-a-dozen faces smiling back at them.

"Well, love-birds, do you mind if we share your elevator? We won't watch if you wish to continue."

The group of watchers all burst out laughing as Claire and Adam blushed and stepped to the back of the elevator.

"You two have found the best substitute when the hill is not skiable. Enjoy. We are all jealous," commented one elderly woman.

When they finally left the elevator at their floor they stumbled to the door of the suite, opened it, and entered with a burst of laughter that brought them back into each other's arms.

"Oh, how embarrassing," stuttered Claire. "So much for trying to stay discreet about our relationship. I hope that none of those people in the elevator recognized us. We will have to be more careful with our passion in public."

"I don't regret one second of what I was feeling," stated Adam firmly as he began to strip off his ski gear, tossing the wet clothing onto the bathroom floor.

"Come here, you glorious woman, I want to warm you up all through." He turned to Claire and helped her peel off layers of ski clothing.

Together they stood under the shower, turning up the temperature until they both felt warm and relaxed and then wrapped themselves into the warm towelling gowns provided by the hotel.

"Would you like a drink to warm up inside?" Adam questioned. "The Scotch worked wonders for us last time we sat here drinking together."

Claire was still feeling a little shy around this man. They had spent so much time together on the slopes; but as lovers, they were only just discovering each other. She needed a drink to warm her, but also to give her courage to enjoy this man whom she felt guilty being with, but could not control her desire for.

So she agreed, and Adam poured two generous glasses of Scotch and carried them through to the bedroom where Claire was drying her hair and rubbing herself down.

"Cheers," said Adam, clinking his glass against hers. "Here's to a whole night of pleasure with the woman I desire with my entire body."

They both drank, and, never taking their eyes from each other, slowly sat down on the bed together.

The power of the emotion between them was electric as they felt the strength of their mutual longing. Adam leaned forward and put his mouth on her warm eager lips. Perhaps it was the excitement of the thought of an entire night together, but he felt a heightened awareness of every sensation.

Unfastening the ties of her gown he reached underneath the fabric to cup her breast. Her body ached with the desire and expectation of his touch. He squeezed a hard nipple, and bent to suck it, running his hand down her thigh to feel its warmth. He wished he could have all of her at once. Pushing her down onto the bed he opened the gown fully, exposing her naked body to his desire. Claire felt his need – the bulge in his groin, and melted into him.

Hearing her moan with pleasure, Adam moved his hands down to her hips, her stomach and the insides of her thighs. She opened to his touch.

Much later they collapsed back onto the bed, wrapped in each other, and lay together without speaking for a long moment.

When Adam rose, he picked up his Scotch and took a long drink. He turned and looked at the beautiful woman lying there, arms stretched out, legs apart, and felt that he had never felt this way about any woman before. He was lost in her; he could not think clearly when he was with her. And when he had her under him, when he was inside her, he was transported to a place he had never known. This, he knew, was a feeling he would not want to let go. The erotic sensations were like an addiction that he had to feed. He decided that he would do anything to have these feelings continue.

"Do you realize what you are doing to me?" he asked hoarsely. "I need you desperately. When I am not with you, I am thinking about you all the time."

Lying back and enjoying the look of lust in this gorgeous man's eyes, Claire smiled. She had wanted him. She had desired his attention; she had lustily wished for what they had just enjoyed. Now she knew that she could enjoy him at her leisure. They would find ways to be together. They would continue to see each other and be intimate during the summer. They would not wait until the next season of skiing to be together.

She motioned him down to her and kissed him gently on the mouth, placing his hand on her naked breast.

"You are a lusty man, Adam. I will be there when your desire is as ripe as it was this evening. You would have noticed that I was not objecting."

He smiled back at her, running his fingers over her nipples and watched as they hardened under his touch.

"Thank you for being so wonderfully warm and receptive. I will continue to adore you with my eyes, my mouth, my hands, and my constant erectness."

They both laughed as he handed her the glass of untouched scotch. Sitting up and fastening her gown closed they sipped the single malt scotch in satisfied silence.

Claire woke at first light to find herself twined together with Adam; their bodies warm and luxuriant beneath the covers. The storm had abated and the world was still. She rolled over and noticed that Adam was still asleep. Lying very still, she watched the man for whom she had such deep feelings breathe beside her. She examined every inch of his face. The lock of dark hair lying across his forehead, the long eyelashes resting on his cheeks, the rough stubble of growth on his chin, the softness of his mouth now closed in sleep. She adored every plane and hollow of that face. As she watched, she tried to imagine what their future together would look like. How would they meet? What could they share during the summer months? They had so much of each other still to explore, to enjoy, to share.

Adam left early in the morning, planning to be home as soon as the roads were passable. The forecast for road conditions was not positive, but he decided not to linger. Claire felt cheated by his leaving so soon. This, she knew, was the reality of wanting to be with a man who already had another life and other commitments.

They kissed goodbye, and promised to contact each other, both acknowledging that this relationship was going to move forward during the months to come.

Marriage

In practice it is seldom very hard to do one's duty when one knows what it is, but it is sometimes exceedingly difficult to find this out.
Samuel Butler

With the warming of the weather in Montreal the ski season came to an end. Mont Tremblant continued to attract visitors, but they were there for the other pleasures that it offered. The gondolas continued to operate, taking hikers up the mountain for challenges other than skiing. As the summer approached, the activities in the village increased and crowds arrived hoping to enjoy the warm weather fun that the mountain offered. They came to golf, to fish, to swim, to cycle, to ride horses. There was even a dune buggy track. And, for the really adventurous, a zip line which whisked them across the valley to the peak beyond.

The first few weeks after the skiing closed down Adam and Claire had managed to talk with each other only once. They had arranged to meet for a drink at the Queen Elizabeth Hotel in downtown Montreal, and had sat in a quiet corner of the bar, talking, sharing stories of their workdays, and looking at each other longingly. They were both feeling the loss of time together, but accepted that this was the new reality of their relationship.

Coming home from work later that evening Adam noticed that the lights were all on in the house. He pulled into the drive, pressed the remote to open the garage doors and pulled into the space alongside Luce's Hyundai Santa Fe. He smiled as he glanced into the back of her wagon and saw that it was piled high with easels, and boxes.

She must be going to a paint-in tomorrow again, he surmised. She was a talented artist and he was very proud of the work she did. He was also relieved that she had an activity that kept her so absorbed. Somehow, it made him feel better, more at ease with his life. The space that had developed in their relationship was not closing, but widening. Not knowing how to deal with it, he compensated by working harder and spending more time with their children.

Walking into the house and into the den, he saw that the two girls were playing a game of cribbage, both leaning over the board with concentration. He watched as Michelle moved pegs down the line. The two young heads were close together, one dark like their mother, the other sandy, like his.

"Well, who's winning?" he asked.

"I have to watch all the pegs she moves, as she doesn't count very well. I think she's trying to cheat and win," his thirteen-year-old daughter, Juliette, replied.

"I do not," the younger girl responded, "and this is a game to make my math better, so I *can* count. At least I can count up to fifteen all the time."

All three of them laughed at her clever response.

Adam went over and gave each of them a hug and a kiss on the cheek. His children were a joy to him. The teenager, Juliette was bright, full of energy and good at sport. His younger daughter, Michelle, was a typical nine-year-old girl. She was into the latest fashions, loved shoes, and often appeared with her hair in some new, wild hairdo. "I am going to be a fashion model," she often stated as she pranced around the room, showing off a new outfit or hairdo.

Adam often took Juliette up to the ski hill with him, and they enjoyed long runs together. She was an accomplished skier, and was constantly nagging him to get a slalom board to try hot-dogging like the older teenagers. But Adam felt that the boards were too dangerous for a thirteen-year-old, and kept resisting.

"Where's your mother?" he asked the children.

"In the bedroom I think, but we haven't seen her this afternoon."

Adam walked into the living room, stopping at the bar cabinet to pour a Scotch. He returned to the den where he took off his jacket and tie, threw them over the couch, and relaxed into one of the large, comfortable wing-backed chairs. This was his favourite room in the house. The atmosphere was warm and inviting. It was the one room in the house where Luce turned a blind eye to tidiness, with the result that it was often strewn with evidence of the girls' activities.

The room had been furnished with large, comfortable seating. Two large wingback chairs sat on either side of a long four-seater couch that was covered in a floral fabric. Bright cushions in deep green and burgundy sat along the backrest, but quite often were on the floor where the girls liked to lie and watch television.

A large-screen television dominated one wall, and a state-of-the-art stereo system was enclosed in a cabinet beneath the screen. This technology was an indulgence that the family enjoyed together. Evenings curled up together watching a family movie was a favourite, and they all appreciated a variety of musical genre.

Adam stretched his legs out and put his feet up on an ottoman. He took a long drink of his Lagavulin and watched the children at their game for a while. He thought about what family life could be like if only his wife was warmer, and became part of the group more often. His thoughts were interrupted when Luce came into the room and smiled at him.

"Tiens! I did not hear you come in," she commented as she watched the children. Her voice was soft and melodic, still retaining a strong Parisian French lilt to her English.

"Would you like a drink?" Adam asked.

She nodded in assent, and Adam went through to the bar and came back with a glass of dark, French red wine – her drink of choice.

"Oh, Papa, I saw you and your ski lady go into the Queen Elizabeth Hotel today," Juliette remarked casually.

Luce looked up quizzically. "Who is the ski lady?" she questioned.

"She's the lady that Papa skis with a lot on Mont Tremblant. I forget her name, but she's very nice. She's a real hot-dog skier. You should see her, Mama. Papa struggles to keep up with her," explained Juliette. "And you can't miss seeing her because she always wears red with a white hat."

Luce turned to look at Adam. "Have I met this woman?"

"I don't think so, but I did mention her. I met her at the conference in Toronto and we discovered that we both skied at Tremblant. We bump into each other occasionally up there and ski a few runs together. She is very good, as Juliette says. She often has a snack with us in the chalet. That is where Juliette has met her."

"Well maybe if everybody knows her, we should invite her for drinks here so that I could meet her as well. Where were you going to this afternoon in the hotel, Adam?"

Adam thought quickly. *How much can I really explain without causing complications? The girls have already told her about Claire, so she knows we are* friends. Maybe some of the truth is by far the best way to handle the situation.

"When we were on the hill a few weeks ago she asked if I knew anything about stereo equipment. She was going to purchase a new set, complete with good speakers, and she didn't have time to do all the research. I mentioned that we had replaced our system last year and told her what we'd purchased. I offered to take her to the store that supplied ours. So, we met this afternoon in the hotel, and then I took her to the store and introduced her to the manager. He gave her good advice, and I think she'll buy a good system from him." Adam tried to explain without meeting his wife's eyes.

"That was kind of you," Luce remarked curtly.

Adam looked up at his wife slowly. He saw a beautifully groomed woman; slim and dark haired, who had kept her figure in good shape. She had aged very well, with hardly a line showing on her face. She was a serene woman who was always calm and in control of her emotions. When had they become so apart he wondered? When last had they had a real conversation about anything meaningful? Most of what they talked about these days were issues related to the children. When did she ever tell him how she felt about anything? When did he ever feel the desire to confide his innermost thoughts to her?

Then his mind shifted to Claire who was so different. She was so open, so warm. She questioned and prodded and laughed until everything inside her, all her emotion, came pouring out. He found himself opening up to her sympathetic ear as well, sharing his innermost thoughts and desires with her.

He loved Luce, his wife, of that he was sure. They had a history together. They'd created a family together; they'd created a life together. But they never really communicated anymore.

"She appreciated the assistance I gave her," Adam said finally.

Luce looked back at him for a long time, and then got up and went to the kitchen to prepare dinner for the family.

Adam watched her leave. How was he going to find a balance in this new life he had created for himself?

Surrounded by his family, as he was at the moment, he felt the urge to stop the double life he was starting to live; he knew that he should give up the infatuation he had with Claire before it got out of hand. He did not want to hurt Luce. Was he just being selfish, grabbing for himself something that he knew he should not have – like the forbidden fruit? Maybe he was just being a proverbial weak male; the clichéd kind that women's magazines criticized so often.

Despite these disturbing thoughts, he felt the pull back to the pleasure he had found with Claire. He would not, could not, give up the woman he had just met, and was feeling so drawn to. He believed that he could find a way of fitting this new-found pleasure into his life, without hurting the family he loved.

Adultery

Sexual pleasure, wisely used and not abused, may prove the stimulus and liberator of our finest and most exalted activities.
Havelock Ellis

When the snow melts in Montreal, the city sheds its winter clothing and pulls itself out into the summer sun. The dirty, wet sludge of snow and street dirt wash away down the street sewers, leaving the paving shining, and the sidewalks clean. Even the buildings, that have stood like dark spires in a clouded sky for months, appear bathed in a new veneer, washed clean by the rays of sun penetrating through the last of the winter clouds. Bodies that have been wrapped from head to toe in down-filled jackets and head toques against the winter chill, now appear in shorts and tee shirts, exposing white, sun-starved limbs.

Summers in Montreal are hot and humid, so the window air conditioners in older buildings start pumping cooling air into stuffy rooms, as residents wipe heat- induced sweat from their brows. Deck-chairs appear on balconies overlooking the streets, and everyone lounges outside at the end of the day with cool drinks, enjoying the summer evenings.

For Claire and Adam, the end of the ski season brought challenges of a different nature. They now had to find moments, stolen from their summer routines, in order to share time together. With the children home from school, Adam felt obliged to spend more time with them after work and on weekends. With these pressures pulling on their time, they both arranged to lengthen their lunch breaks from work, by starting work earlier in the mornings. With time in the middle of the day, Adam could join Claire at out-of-the-way restaurants for lunch, and occasionally to meet at her home.

For Adam, the deepening of the relationship with Claire engulfed him in a new sensation. He had never before felt this close to another human being. A feeling of fulfillment wrapped around him when he was with her. He realized that it was not just the sexual pleasure that she provided, but also a deep emotional comfort that he had not been aware had been missing from his life. When they were together, he felt a self-righteous sense of loyalty to himself, and pushed aside any thoughts of conflicting needs.

To Claire, it seemed that this new passion in her life was most inconvenient. The last thing she needed was an uncontrollable romance, especially with a married man. She took time to inspect her feelings for her lover from every angle; to imagine, and to wish for these feelings to lessen in intensity. However, her intellect and her emotions both answered that she wanted them to remain. She understood that the life of her mind and the life of her senses were separate.

Both lovers were in agreement that their adulterous relationship was intoxicating, and they fed on the stimulation and eroticism that accompanied it.

Activities available in Montreal in the summer months provided numerous opportunities for the two of them to enjoy more than sexual encounters together. The International Festival Jazz de Montreal found them on the downtown streets listening to the free concerts offered to the walk-by audience. The Montreal festival is the largest jazz festival in the world, and offered to the two of them, music from about two thousand artists from roughly thirty countries – truly an international occasion. And together they soaked up much of it. The ten free outdoor venues allows anyone willing to join the crowds, for the ten days that the streets in a major portion of the downtown core is closed to traffic, to enjoy the stirring sounds of jazz out of doors. And they joined in whenever they could.

One night they went separately to hear Melody Gardot's honey-coated voice perform songs from her album *Worriesome Heat*. Adam and Luce were both attending the concert, and Claire watched as they entered the Salle Wilfrid-Pelletier in Place des Arts and take their seats. She was seated some rows behind and took as much pleasure in watching Adam's enjoyment of the music, as the music itself. It seemed strange to be enjoying the experience with him, but not *being* with him. Watching him with Luce at his side stirred up conflicting emotions. Later, when they were together they analyzed the performance and shared their mutual enjoyment of the songstress's wonderful voice.

A day stolen from work found them together in the Parc de Rapides near Lasalle where they spent the day hiking through the hills and valleys.

"This reminds me of the times we enjoyed together on Mont Tremblant during the snow months. I really do miss those days. We were out in the open, but could still be together – without feeling as if we had to hide, or feel guilty," observed Claire as they sat on a rock and looked down on the river and the gushing rapids.

"I agree, my darling," sighed Adam, "but our circumstances won't allow for any more than I can give."

He was fearful that she was feeling frustrated by the on-going secretive nature of their relationship and did not want to lose her. He could not give more time to be with her, as much as he wished he could.

Leaning into him, Claire placed her head on his shoulder and took his hand. "I never feel that our being together is anything but a joy. How can something that brings us both so much pleasure be wrong? How can it be considered unlawful? You are giving your family your love and attention; and you are giving me a little bonus time."

Looking down at her, Adam smiled. Was she trying to justify his adultery in her own mind? He did not feel guilty about his time with her, even if he knew, logically, that what he was doing was considered sinful. He knew that he would never leave Luce and the girls for this woman. He could not conceive of causing any pain for his family. So how could this relationship be wrong? Maybe, he too, was trying to justify his adultery.

Leaning down he kissed her deeply and enjoyed the sensual, responsive opening of her mouth.

"Do you realize that this may be the first time that we have been alone and not made love to each other? Should we start taking bets to see if we can last out without fucking each other?"

"Now, that's a bet I know I would lose. In fact, I don't see anyone around right now, unless of course, there are some Peeping-Tom hikers' binoculars trained on us from across the valley. We surely are not going to let our quota get lost are you?"

Walking off into a quiet, secluded wooded area, they stopped beside a large spruce. Pulling down her trousers to expose her loins, Adam ran his hand up Claire's thighs as she unzipped his fly, encouraging him to enter her.

Replete, they sat down on the pine needles under the tree and relaxed against each other.

"Just how many women have you done that with?" Claire teased.

Adam sat very still, not answering. Then he turned, and looking straight at her told her the secret that he had always kept to himself.

"I want to tell you something that I have never shared with another soul. I don't want you to think less of me, but I want to be honest in this relationship. Can I tell you?"

"I don't know whether it's something I want to hear, or not," prodded Claire tentatively. "Will the knowledge make me hate you? Or hurt me? If so, then I don't want to hear it."

"No, but it is something I have done in my past that I would like you to know about."

"Then tell me," Claire answered quietly.

"There have been other women in my marriage. Other women that I have had affairs with, before I met you."

He watched Claire for a reaction, but she just looked right back at him, waiting for him to continue.

"They were very fleeting liaisons that meant nothing to me other than a titillating diversion from – I suppose boredom and stress. That's an excuse I know, but I think it's also the truth. Luce never knew about them; and if I can help it, never will. I would not hurt her for the world. She has always trusted me completely and I do not want to betray that trust."

Claire looked away as he continued to talk about his relationship with his wife.

"I was always extremely discreet, as were the women involved, so there was never any gossip. One of those relationships was with a young woman who worked in an art gallery where Luce showed her work. And the other, I'm ashamed to admit, was someone who lived close to us. Luce knew her, and she later helped her when the woman was ill with breast cancer. Sad to say, she died very quickly from the disease."

He turned and looked at Claire, but she was not reacting to his confessions at all. She was sitting very still and listening. She did not want her relationship to end the same way as that of these other women.

"I was thankful for their discreetness when the relationships ended," Adam continued. "I had promised myself that I would never again indulge in another adulterous relationship. And then, my dearest, I walked into a cup of hot coffee."

Claire turned back to look at him and saw the tenderness in his gaze. She smiled back at him, and relaxed.

"And look where that cup of coffee got you!"

"Yes, in a place that I never want to leave. I will find a way to make us safe from gossip and pain." He leaned forward and kissed her very gently on the forehead.

Standing up, he helped her to her feet, and they slowly hiked their way down to the start of the trail and back to the car park.

Poisoned Pen

The end justifies the means.
Machiavelli

Claire was beginning to realize that the times she was spending with Adam were becoming more than just pleasurable sexual encounters. She looked forward to his phone calls with breathless anticipation. Each time they met, she felt like a teenager again, waiting for her first date. She had always been able to control her emotions with the men she had dated. There had been a few lovers that she had become very fond of, but she had never felt an overwhelming passion for any of them. She'd become accustomed to the thought that she was never going to be one of those women who became obsessed by one man. All the passion that romance novels espoused had passed her by, until now.

How had this happened so suddenly to her? Why did it have to be that, when she finally felt this elusive emotion, it was for a man who was already entangled with another woman and a family?

She felt an overwhelming desire to be that woman – to be the one whom he spent all his time with. To be someone who did not have to share him and his time. She did not want to have to hide when she was with him.

She wanted to be able to flaunt their relationship; to let the world know that they were a couple and that they shared intimate times together.

Her common sense told her that this was never going to be possible. When Adam spoke of his family it was with such endearment that she realized he would never leave them willingly. If he would not leave them, she wondered if there was any way to make his wife leave *him*. What would make her want to walk away from him, and possibly take the children? What would make her feel such disgust or anger towards her husband that she would leave him?

Why did most women divorce their husbands? What was the impetus that forced them to make that final decision to leave? This thought motivated her to explore the statistics about separations. She discovered that many separations were caused by violence inflicted on the woman or on their children. Adam, she knew, would never do that to his family.

The other major reason for divorce was infidelity, especially on the part of the husband. Would Luce leave Adam if she knew that he had been unfaithful to her with numerous women? She was not sure.

Claire liked Adam's children; she would miss them if they were not in their lives. The children knew that she and their father were friends. They had skied together; they had lunched together on the ski hill. But she had never met Luce, his wife. She suspected that Luce knew about the friendship because the children would have said something. However, she was sure that Luce did not know that her husband was her lover. They had been very discreet about their meetings, and were only seen together in very public places like the ski hill, or occasionally enjoying lunch together in town in very public restaurants. If they were public about those times together, they both thought, no one would suspect them of being lovers.

One evening she sat relaxing in the den after dinner. She had loaded her new audio system with a number of CDs to shuffle through a range of soft classical choices. An after-dinner liqueur of grappa sat on the table alongside her chair, which she sipped at occasionally. She was enjoying reading a pulp fiction romance novel, one of her favourite ways to switch her brain into neutral after a busy day at the office. She picked up the book, looking at the cover showing a picture of a beautiful woman with long tresses leaning back, as a well-muscled man with a handlebar mustache kissed her deeply on the lips. She smiled at the image and opened the book. Taking a sip of grappa, she continued to immerse herself in the plot between the pages.

Suddenly she stopped reading, looked up from the book, stared into space as if lost in thought, and then bent back to the pages in front of her. She re-read the paragraph that had so suddenly caught her attention. She read the words on the page again.

She stood with the letter in her hands as tears rolled down her cheeks. She had never suspected that her husband would ever be unfaithful to her. She had trusted him so implicitly for all these years. Now she was reading these dreadful words, telling her that their marriage had been a farce from the beginning, that he had been Geraldine's lover for many years. The letter was so damning. It told her in graphic detail exactly what he had been doing with this other woman.

How can I ever stay with him? she thought. How can I ever look at him with love in my eyes again? Every time he looks at me I will see the other woman. This is the end of my marriage...

Claire stopped reading. Then she read the section again. Putting the book down, she lay back on the couch and closed her eyes.

What would happen if she wrote such a letter to Adam's wife? What was the worst thing that could happen? Would his wife react as the woman in the novel had? It was fiction of course, and that did not guarantee that the same reaction would occur in real life.

However, if his wife received a poison pen letter accusing Adam of adultery, would she show the letter to Adam? If she did, how would he react? It might make him apologize and end their affair. It might make his wife so angry that she would demand a divorce.

Could she take a chance and risk the possibility that it might end their marriage? That was what she wished. Then Adam would come to be with her alone.

She lay for a long time with her eyes closed, running every possibility through her mind. Then she slowly rose from the couch, went to the desk and pulled out some paper. Sitting at the desk, she picked up a ball point pen and started to make notes on what could be included in such a letter. She scribbled, *Mrs. Lambert, your husband is cheating on you...*

The words looked so bland written down that she took the sheet of paper, crumpled it up, and tossed it into the waste basket. She pushed the chair back and spoke aloud to herself, trying to better sense the tone of what she was trying to write.

"I have to pretend that I'm supporting her by telling her this information. I have to sound like I'm on her side, and not her husband's. I have to make her angry. I have to make her feel that her husband has embarrassed her. I will have to plan the wording out very carefully. And most important, whatever I say, must never be traced back to *me*."

Part of the challenge was that she did not want to do anything that would hurt Adam in the process. She had to ensure that the letter was specific enough to create anger, but not accuse her husband of anything specific. She knew from her conversation with Adam that she was not the first extra-marital affair that he had indulged in. She also knew that these relationships had been short-lived encounters; that t h e y did not mean anything other than a need for warmth and someone to talk with. She had teased him about his roving eye, and wondered if his wife knew about them and was tolerant, or whether she knew nothing about them at all. She suspected the latter, as Adam was particularly discreet, and she herself had never heard any rumours about his straying behaviour.

Walking back to the desk in the study she sat down and tried to compose this difficult missive. She had to describe, for the wife, the affairs that her husband had enjoyed with other women. She had to tell how he had been seen around town with them, how her friends were laughing behind her back, and so on.

Claire sat with her head in hands and looked at the blank sheet of paper in front of her. She would have to grit her teeth against her better nature, and try to be as painful as possible with the words she wrote. That was the only way that such a note would work to achieve the results she wanted.

She sat and wrote sentence after sentence, erasing some, scrunching up page after page until she felt that she would never be able to get the letter written. Eventually she gave up and decided to sleep on the decision before taking any further steps.

Her night was restless. She kept imagining Adam with his arms around his wife, comforting her as she held a burning sheet of paper in her hands. Then she saw Adam telling her that his wife was going to divorce him because of his affairs with other women.

When dawn finally broke, she was still tossing about trying to decide what to do. As the first rays of light penetrated the window shades she fell into a deep, dreamless sleep and did not wake until nearly midday. The sound of the telephone ringing at her bedside startled her awake. Reaching over she lifted the handset to her ear and muttered, "Yes."

"That's a very abrupt greeting. Did you wake up on the wrong side of the bed on this lovely morning?"

The sound of Adam's voice brought a sigh to her lips and she smiled at his greeting.

"You won't believe it, but you have just woken me. I can't believe that I was still asleep. What time is it?"

"It's nearly noon and I thought we had a lunch date. I was just calling to say that I am going to be a little late, but I'll still meet you at the restaurant, if you are up to it."

"Yes, I'd love that. And thank goodness you're late as I'm still in bed."

They agreed on a meeting time and Claire smiled as she quickly went about making herself ready to meet her lover for lunch.

It was mid-afternoon before she returned to the house. She and Adam had enjoyed a relaxing meal together. They had sat outdoors at a table under an umbrella to shade them from the sun that coloured everything with bright hues and warmed their bodies. She was feeling very mellow as she walked into the den and bent to tidy the desk.

Then she saw the crumpled pages and the lines that she had left scrawled on the single sheet lying on the top of the desk. Picking it up she read again the words she had written. She held her breath and thought about the moments she had just shared with Adam. She thought about how many more of those times she could enjoy if he did not have a wife to go home to. Am I prepared to act on the old Machiavellian saying of *The end justifies the means*? Yes, I believe that the end that I want justifies *any* means. If this is the means, then I will have to do it.

Sitting down at the desk she moved the handwritten pages aside and opened the computer. She started to type and kept typing until she had a letter written. A letter without a signature. A hurtful letter. A letter that she hoped would drive a wedge between Adam and his wife.

Before she printed the page she stopped. Caution ran through her mind. I cannot touch the paper on which this is written. I cannot leave my fingerprints on any part of this page. Everything has to be wiped clean, or kept clean before I print.

Walking through to the bedroom, she took out a pair of gloves and put them on. They made her hands feel bulky; the only time she wore gloves was in winter. But they would have to do. They would keep her fingerprints off the paper and envelope.

Back at the computer, she read the note she had written. She reread it, and made some changes. She tried to imagine herself receiving such a note, and felt ashamed of what she read on the page.

Taking a deep breath, she printed it out, put the sheet of paper into a plain white envelope and wiped it clean. She addressed the envelope in bold black print to Mrs. L. Lambert, at her home address in Westmount, and attached a stamp to the envelope.

The addressed and sealed envelope lay on the desk as she stared at it. She was very cold and felt shaken by the exercise of writing something so hateful. Her gloved hands hovered over the damning article, and she pushed it away, pulling off the gloves. Now that it was written, she was not sure that she could bring herself to mail it.

She picked up every sheet of paper on which she had been scribbling the drafts, and pushed them through the paper shredder. Glancing around the room she made sure that the only evidence of what she had done was the white, addressed envelope lying on the desk. Her last action was to erase the words from the computer.

Still feeling very cold, she pulled on a sweater and went outside to walk around the garden in an effort to warm up. There she sat for a long time in thought, staring out at the dark trees at the bottom of the garden, watching as the gloom of night rolled in.

Her mind recalled all the times that she and Adam had sat out on this back patio; how many times they had succumbed to deeply intimate moments outside. She grew hot thinking about Adam's hands on her body; how their sexual encounters drove her to heights of passion that she had never experienced before. As these visions passed through her mind, Claire knew why she had written the note in the den.

She would never give up her relationship with Adam. In fact, she was finding that she was not content with the brief times they shared. She wanted all of him.

She needed to be with him, to be able to turn over at night and find him curled up alongside her in the bed. There was so much that she wanted to share with him, but could not because of his loyalty to his family. If he would never leave them, she reasoned, she had to find a way to make *them* leave. The note would do that. She hoped that it would.

The white envelope sat on her desk in the den for three days as Claire went about her daily routines. At night, she would gingerly pull the envelope out and look at it, holding it carefully in a tissue to avoid leaving fingerprints. She would look at the name on the front, and wonder how much hurt she would be inflicting on this woman who had never done any harm to her. Guiltily, she would replace the envelope and walk away.

It was Adam who made the decision for her.

One evening, as he sat at her table enjoying a casual pasta dish and a bottle of French Pinot Noir, he looked across the table at her and said longingly, "Don't you sometimes wish that we could do this every night? That we could just be together without my having to rush off somewhere else? I always feel so cheated when I need to leave; when really, all I want to do is to stay right here. I know it's all a dream, but I can't avoid the thoughts that crowd in on me at moments like this."

He got up and walked around the table, took her face in his hands and kissed her deeply on the mouth.

Claire's mind absorbed his words, and she relaxed into his tenderness. He wants this as much as I do, she thought. I know that I am doing the right thing.

It did not need anything more to spur her into action. The next evening she left the house with the envelope wrapped in a scarf. She took a long walk to a postal station some distance from her home. There she dropped the envelope into the red mail box.

The walk had a therapeutic effect on her. The cool evening, the tree-lined streets, and children playing in a local park relaxed her fears. This was how life in the city should be. The mellowness of the surroundings calmed the agitation she had been feeling about the action she was taking. She reasoned that this move could provide the answer to getting what both she and Adam wanted; to be together all the time, with no family pulling him away from her.

Luce, Adam's wife, was sitting in her studio at home working on a study of a small child playing on a beach. The sky in the painting was a clear cerulean blue, and she had painted the water in the ocean a softer shade, phthalo blue with a hint of light green to balance the bright hue of the sky. She was putting some touches to the pale yellow dress the child was wearing when she heard the sound of the mail dropping through the slot in the front door onto the floor. She leaned back and studied the painting. The sand on the beach would have to be toned down with more sepia to balance the effect of the blue of the sky she thought. Stretching, she decided that it was time for a break and a café au lait.

Walking through to the kitchen, she picked up the mail in the hallway and placed it on the kitchen counter as she prepared the coffee. She poured a cup and stood at the counter, sipping, as she sorted through the bundle of envelopes.

She glanced at a large brown envelope that obviously contained papers for Adam. Some window envelopes she just flipped through, sighing as she thought of the bills they contained. Then she noticed the white envelope addressed to her. Frowning, she turned it over. Seeing no return address, she wondered who had sent it. Tearing the envelope open, she extracted one sheet of typewritten paper. Sipping on her coffee, she read the message on the paper.

Mrs. Luce Lambert,

I write this as a friend, because I feel that you are being treated very badly by your philandering husband. Somebody needs to tell you the truth so that you don't go around being embarrassed any longer. Your husband has been fooling around with other women for many years. Either you haven't a clue what's going on, or you are too much of a coward to deal with the problem.

First, there was the woman who lived two doors down from you, the one who died of breast cancer. Then there was the woman, or more like a girl she was so young, who worked in a downtown art gallery. That one did not last very long.

And now, he's screwing around with a financial broker. She's a blonde that everyone sees him with all over town.

How can you stay with a bum like that? Be a strong woman and throw him out. The rest of womanhood will thank you for it.

Your Friend.

All colour drained from Luce's face as she read the note. She felt herself sway and put a hand out to hold onto the kitchen counter to stop herself from falling. She gulped at the air that she felt was choking in her throat.

Reading the note again, she turned slowly and collapsed onto one of the kitchen stools. Feeling dizzy, she put her head down on the counter. Her mind was swimming. Her world had suddenly turned on its axis and she was about to fall off the edge. She felt battered by the hatred she felt in the words on the sheet of paper – the note that was now lying on the floor where it had fallen from her hands. She could not understand what she had done to hurt the writer; that would cause them to be so full of venom directed towards her and Adam.

Slowly, her breathing modulated and she began to control her shaking. She lifted her head from the table and looked at the paper on the floor. Bending down, she picked it up and read the words once again, more calmly this time. As she did, tears formed in her eyes and rolled, unchecked, down her cheeks. She could not believe the accusations that were being levelled at her husband.

She had sometimes wondered if there had been other women in Adam's life. But if there had been, she had felt that he was being extremely discreet and considerate so that she would never find out, or be hurt by any scandals. Now she had to examine what could be clear, cold evidence of specific liaisons with particular women, all of whom she had met and known.

Feeling shattered by facts that she now had to deal with, she rose from the stool, opened the fridge and removed a bottle of white wine. She opened the bottle and poured a full glass. Standing at the counter she drank in large gulps as she stared at the note; this one page of paper that had brought her world crumbling at her feet. She realized that part of what was upsetting her, was that the affairs appeared to be public knowledge. How many of their friends and acquaintances knew of them? If the note writer knew, then she had to assume that there were many others whom were privy to the information.

She picked up the bottle and poured another glass of wine. Taking the note, she walked out to the back patio and sat on one of the deckchairs. As she sat sipping at the wine, feeling it slide down her throat, her thoughts began to calm. She needed time to absorb this information, to figure out what it really meant to her and to her marriage.

It was an hour later before she stirred from her reverie. She realized that she had been daydreaming of all the possible eventualities that could accrue from her knowing that Adam had enjoyed intimate times with other women while being married to her. She wondered if she could ever trust him again. The realization struck her that the last woman mentioned in the note had to be Claire, the woman Adam called his *ski buddy*, but who was probably his latest lover.

She made up her mind that she was not going to say anything to anyone about the note; she was going to deal with the situation in her own way. That thought gave her the spur to go back to the kitchen, and refill her glass.

"What the damn," she said aloud, "I may as well solve this problem with a good tizz on, as sober – ça ne fait rien!"

Maybe it was the alcohol, but sipping at the third glass of wine gave her courage, and then the courage turned to anger. She suddenly found that she was furious. She was furious with the mean-spirited, so-called friend who would write with such venom. She was angry with her friends for never hinting at a problem. She was angry with Adam for his adulterous behaviour. And most of all she was angry with herself for being so naïve that she did not suspect that something like this could happen.

All she could think of was revenge; but who to take it out on she was not sure. All she wanted to do was to run away and hide and be on her own to lick her wounds and try to find herself again. She walked through to the bedroom and hid the note in her underwear drawer where she knew no family member or the housekeeper would ever go.

Somewhere in her depths she wondered if she was the one to blame. Had she become undesirable to her husband? If he still wanted her, would he stray? Walking over to the full-length cheval mirror in the room, she looked at herself. She was well groomed. Her hair was always done attractively. Her clothes were in style, if perhaps, sometimes a little on the artsy side. She studied her reflection in the mirror carefully.

Unfastening her skirt, she let it slip to the floor and stepped out of it. Her legs were firm and slim. The long-sleeved top came off next, and was tossed onto the floor with the skirt. Standing in her brassiere and panties she looked at her body. Was she desirable? She turned and examined her buttocks. With her back to the mirror, she stepped out of her pants and turned. She still had a pronounced bush of dark hair between her legs. Was that a turn off? she wondered. Standing up straight, she released her breasts from the confining brassiere and let their weight fall to her chest. Slowly, she turned around studying every curve of her now naked body. She was surprised by the physical reaction she was experiencing seeing herself so exposed and reflected. She felt her nipples harden and she lifted her hands to cup each breast and push them upwards as she watched her body in the mirror. She did not recognize the sultry woman who looked back at her, standing brazenly open-legged with a breast in each hand. Was this the woman Adam wanted; the one that she had not given to him? Now it was too late. He had found other interests. Dropping her hands from her breasts, she turned in disgust and moved to the bed where she crawled under the covers and sobbed.

She woke with a start and realized that the shock, the alcohol and her tears had been too much for her to cope with. Sleep had overwhelmed her, but it had also soothed and calmed her. Lying in the bed, she knew that she had to find a way out of this predicament. Could she confront Adam? Could she continue to live as if the note had never arrived?

What, she wondered, were her options? She wanted to be alone; but how was that possible with a husband and family? Adam had not considered that he had a wife and family when he had enjoyed his adulterous liaisons. Maybe, she thought, it was time for her to think only of herself for a change, and take the option that she felt was calling to her. She had to be alone; alone to think, alone to heal, and maybe over time, to forgive.

Where could she escape to, to be alone? Her first thought was back to where she had always been happiest; and that was Paris. Without stopping to think further, she got off the bed, dressed and walked to the den where she sat at the desk. She phoned a travel agent that they had never used before, and booked a flight. Then she pulled out an old diary, opened it to a list of phone numbers and dialled long distance.

When Adam came home from work, Luce was busy in the kitchen putting the finishing touches to the family's supper. The children had arrived home from school in a flurry of noise and news of their day. She had sent them off to change out of their school uniforms and to pass the time in the den so that they did not notice her slight intoxication, or her dark mood.

As she tossed a salad to go with the chicken dish that was baking in the oven, she told Adam that she had been feeling a little restless recently and had decided that she needed a change of scenery.

"Oh, good idea," said Adam. "Where shall we go? Do you want to take the kids with us?"

"No," replied Luce without looking at him, "I don't want to take anybody with me. I want to go away alone." She raised her head and looked straight at him for a long time without blinking. "I have booked a flight to Paris, and I leave tomorrow at eight in the morning, and I'm going alone," she told him.

"I have a friend in Paris who needs me to be there," she lied, "and as well, I want to explore some of the work that the art community is doing. I have seen some of it reviewed and want to connect with that group again. I have missed them a lot. And I cannot do all this if I have you and the children with me."

"But we can come with you for a week, and I can be with the children while you tend to your friend, and then we'll leave you for a while with your artist friends."

"I do not want you with me," affirmed Luce. "I am going alone and that is my decision to make this time."

Adam looked at his wife in surprise. He had never seen her be this adamant about anything before. He wondered what had happened during the day. She must have received an upsetting phone call that he did not know about.

"Did I meet the friend that you're going to see?"

"No, you did not."

"How long do you think it will take to assist the friend and explore the art work? How long will you be away from us?" he prodded.

"I don't know. You will just have to trust me on this. I will return when I am ready to be here again."

Adam thought that was a strange way to phrase her stay, but he noticed that she was quite upset about something, and he did not want to make matters worse. He was very confused and did not know how to handle the situation. He'd never been left alone with the children for any length of time before, and knew that this new arrangement was going to present challenges.

"Don't worry about the children," Luce added, "I've arranged for Susan to be here every day at seven in the morning. She will pick the children up from school in my car, and get a supper prepared. She will do this on weekdays only. You will have to deal with the weekends. You may want to ask your mother to come and stay for a while as well; she will enjoy being with the children and feeling useful."

Adam just stared back at his wife. Not knowing about the note, he could not understand why this had all happened so suddenly – in one day. Why had she not discussed her plans with him? Why was she just ready to get up and leave?

"Do the children know that you're going away alone?"

"No, I have not told them yet. I thought we could do that at supper time when we are all together."

Luce had no intention of accusing Adam; of presenting him with the hurtful note. She did not want to give him the opportunity to deny, or worse, to confirm what it said. She just needed to get away and assess where their marriage was. She needed to find out how she felt about staying in Montreal, away from her beloved Paris, with a man who did not care for her.

When she told the children that she was going to be away for some time they were both upset, until Adam reassured them that they would now both be mothers, and would have to be very grown up and take care of him as well as themselves.

"You see, I am the papa, and I don't know how to do some of these house things like mamas usually can. I am sure that you will both make your mama very proud of you with all you can do around the house, and take care of yourself as well. And Susan will be here to keep us all in order."

With that, they laughed and said that they would make a list of all the things that they knew how to do on their own.

The children clung to Luce as she left the house in the waiting taxi the next morning. She had refused Adam's offer to drive her to Trudeau Airport, telling him that he needed to comfort the children who were upset about her leaving. She had hugged them both and kissed them on the cheek. She did not hug or kiss Adam but looked straight at him and said that she would tell him when she was coming home. And she left.

Indulgence

*There is no such thing as pure pleasure;
some anxiety always goes with it.*
Ovid

Claire tried to continue her life with as much routine as possible. She moved through the days holding her breath, waiting for some response or reaction to the note she had sent to Luce. Nothing happened. There was no communication from Adam for three days. Suspicion began to creep into her mind that the words she had written had upset his wife, and that he was staying to comfort her. The despicable action that she had taken had to remain secret from Adam, so she was reluctant to make contact with him. So she did nothing, and waited.

Lying in bed at night her mind would not be still. Feelings of guilt at her action stayed with her constantly. Her mind would rationalize that she had taken that course of action because of her need to be with the man who now engulfed her life. She began to fear the results of her deed when there was silence from Adam. He did not come to the house, he did not phone, he did not try to explain his absence – there was only silence.

On the third day she could wait no longer so she phoned his office. The staff at Stark, Nesbitt and Bouchard informed her that Mr. Lambert had taken time off to deal with family matters. Hearing this, her fears increased. Her desperate act had resulted in losing the man she craved - her obsession. Her desperate act had backfired. Instead of chasing his wife away, she had chased Adam away – right into the arms of his family who now needed him more than ever.

She could not sit still; she could not relax. Like a caged animal she paced around the house. She talked aloud to herself, telling her head to relax and wait to hear from him. The only answer her head responded with was one of regret for what she had done, and that it had cost her dearly.

The Lambert household was in chaos. Adam and the children clung to each other when Luce disappeared. Juliette and Michelle were heartbroken that their mother could leave them without telling them why she was going.

"What did we do to make her go away?" asked Juliette perplexed.

"Doesn't she love us anymore?" sobbed Michelle.

"I think it was because I went into her studio and borrowed some brushes for my project at school."

"No, it was because you didn't ask her. She told you that," was Michelle's rationale.

"Who is going to look after us, Papa?" they both wailed.

Holding the girls close to him, Adam tried to reassure them both that their mother had left to go to Paris to help a friend who was in need. He did not know if this was the truth, but that was all he had managed to glean from the scrap of information Luce had given him before she had left. He knew that he had to reassure the children that it was not their fault that their mother had left. They should not feel any guilt, he reassured them.

If there was any guilt, he knew it should be his. He wondered if Luce had found out about his relationship with Claire, and that she had decided to leave him for that reason. He felt sure that, if she had known, he would have sensed some reaction from her; or that she would have tackled him up front about the relationship.

No, he felt sure that there had to be another legitimate reason for her to go running to help an old friend in Paris. He knew that she still missed her home city, even after all the years that she had lived in Montreal. He would often find her sitting and staring into space; and when offered a penny for her thoughts, she would smile and say, "Oh, it's more costly than that to fly to Paris; très cher."

The children stayed home from school for the first day in order to give them an opportunity to see that their lives would be fine without their mother. Adam rose early to make sure that everything was ready for their breakfast. Instead of their mother's delicious pastries it was cereal and toast that was served. When Susan, the housekeeper, arrived she assured the children and Adam that she could keep the routines going until his wife and their mother returned. She had promised Luce that she would be available as much as they needed her. She was happy to help, and she was pleased to have the additional income.

On the second day of Luce's absence, Adam insisted that the children go back to school, and participate in their regular activities of piano and ballet lessons. He knew that the more they were in contact with their friends, and participated in these activities, the less abandoned they would feel. However, he stayed away from the office to organize a routine with Susan, and to ensure that the house was stocked with the provisions they would need.

It was not until the fourth day that he felt ready to contact Claire and to share this new information with her. How the absence of his wife was going to affect their relationship, he was not sure. This new freedom would allow more time to be together without explanations and excuses, but he was not sure that his loyalty to his wife would permit him to over-indulge in the affair. He was still feeling very uncomfortable about the state of affairs when he finally called Claire one evening and asked if he could see her.

Asking Susan to stay with the children after their evening meal, he drove to Claire's house.

It was with trepidation that Claire answered his ring at the door. She did not know what to expect from this visit. In order to prompt some information from him, she watched his reaction carefully as she asked, "Adam, how good to see you again; how are the children?"

"Claire, let's sit down, I have to tell you what's just happened."

"Come into the den and I'll get drinks for us. Scotch as usual?"

"Thanks, I could use a stiff one."

Sitting together on the couch in the den, Adam turned to her and quietly stated, "Luce has gone to Paris suddenly. I don't know how long she'll be away, but the children and I are going to have to cope alone – with the help of the housekeeper."

Claire stared back at him as she felt her face suffuse with heat. Her heart started to beat rapidly and she had difficulty breathing. *She* knew what had probably happened. Luce had read the note and had decided to leave her husband. She continued to look at Adam, this man whom she now knew was hers. Her actions had achieved the hoped-for result. What Adam had just told her was overwhelming. She was having difficulty containing the emotions that welled up inside her.

Trying to cover up her feelings, she rose from the couch and went into the kitchen. She had to get away from Adam for a moment to gather her thoughts, and to get her breathing under control. At the fridge, she pulled out the ice tray and added ice to her Scotch. She took deep breaths in an effort to control the shaking of her body. She felt light-headed, euphoric.

"Claire, are you all right?" Adam called from the den.

"I'm just getting some, some more ice," she managed to stammer in response.

Holding onto the kitchen counter, she bent her head low to gather herself together. She had to be surprised and supportive when she returned. Nothing she said or did must allow Adam to suspect that she had manipulated his wife's departure.

Slowly she turned, and went back to the den.

She asked, "I am stunned to hear this news, Adam. I did not know that she was planning a trip to Paris."

"We did not know either, the girls and I. She just informed us one evening, and was gone the next day. She said something about a friend needing her. She seemed to be quite upset, so I think it must be a close friend. She must have been very worried about her."

Claire could not look at him. She turned away so that he could not see her face. She was filled with joy and longing for this man. Her feelings of guilt must not stop her from enjoying being with him. Now that her plan had worked, she was free to reap the benefits.

She turned back and looked at him with such longing in her eyes, that Adam could not resist the urge to lean forward and kiss her gently on the mouth. He felt a surge of longing and lust that he knew was more than just being with this tempting woman. He knew, as his lips met hers and she opened her mouth under his in response, that he would enjoy her to the fullest while his wife was away.

The lovers established a new routine. Adam often came to Claire's house straight from work and they enjoyed time together. They sat outside enjoying the summer weather, relaxing on the comfortable loungers on the back deck, bantering back and forth about all the troubles of the stock market, the political climate, or the world of music.

Their times together usually ended with passionate coupling. They stripped off all clothing while lying on the chaise chairs outside, they lay entwined together on the couch in the den, they relaxed together on her king-size bed in the bedroom, and once, in a sudden burst of passion, Adam lifted her onto the kitchen counter, unzipped and entered her. They jokingly took bets to see if they could enjoy a time together that did not end in sex; but the bets were always lost as their lust and physical need for each other overwhelmed them both.

The guilt they had suffered when Luce had left soon faded as they settled into this routine. The children appeared to be comfortable with the support of Susan, and their father was now home more evenings than he had been before their mother had left.

One evening Claire asked whether the children would like to come to her home for supper. Adam was reluctant. "I don't think that would be a good idea. They should not become too intimate with our life together.

You know what children are like, they tell the truth, and may say something to Luce when she comes home."

Claire flinched at his reference to Luce's return. She realized that Adam expected his wife to come back to Montreal. This was not *her* wish. She had been hoping that his two girls would come to regard her as a very close friend of their father, and get used to having her with them.

"Maybe what we could do is to take them out to dinner with us. Go somewhere public, so that it doesn't appear to be too intimate. What do you think of that idea?" suggested Adam tentatively.

Claire nodded in agreement. "Would they enjoy that?" she asked.

"Oh, they always like being taken out for a treat. Why don't we try something on Friday or Saturday evening when there's no school the next day."

"That could work," acknowledged Claire. "But I do insist on going somewhere better than McDonalds. I know that kids like it, but I don't think I could manage that."

"You don't know my girls," Adam smiled. "They have been raised by a French mother who likes good food. They never get to go to fast food outlets."

"Do they like Italian?"

"They love Italian, but Luce does not; so this is a chance to give them a treat we normally would not do as a family."

"Do you know that lovely little restaurant on Boulevard Saint-Joseph, right across from the Lachine Canal? If we go early, in the light, they will see the water. Maybe we can walk along the canal afterwards."

"I think you have a date with three people, lady," concluded Adam, taking her in both his arms, giving her a loving hug, and a loud kiss on the neck.

The dinner together was a huge success. The girls used this as an excuse to root through their entire wardrobes to find just the right outfit to wear, and were determined to be on their best behaviour for Papa's friend.

"We will be at a grown-up place to eat, and we'll be with your special friend, so we want to look special too," offered Michelle.

Il Fornetto is a little Italian restaurant in a residential neighbourhood, facing the Lachine Canal. The twenty odd tables are crammed into the small space, but nobody seems to mind as the noise level is always low, allowing the patrons to converse without being overheard. The serving staff are attentive and knowledgeable so could answer all the questions the girls had about items on the menu. They wanted to order pizzas, but Adam suggested they try something different for a change as they had frequently been ordering in pizza while their mother was away. They both then selected a pasta dish with lots of tomato-based sauce.

Adam and Claire sat together, enjoying the delicious Italian dishes, a good bottle of Italian red wine, and watched the girls messily enjoying their penne and linguine meals. Looking across the table at each other they both knew what the other was thinking, but neither was prepared to voice the wish in their eyes.

After they had eaten, the four left the restaurant, crossed the street, and wandered along the bank of the canal. The girls ran on ahead, enjoying the freedom to stretch and run along the water's edge.

"They can only play at being grown up for so long," laughed Adam as he watched them scampering off together.

"This was most enjoyable. Your idea of eating out was a good one. Let's do this again. I think we all had a good time."

Adam looked at her thoughtfully, glanced up to see where his children were, and then pulled Claire to him and kissed her gently.

Regular phone calls from Paris came for the girls. Their mother always asked what they were doing. How school was going? What they were eating? She never asked about Adam, and so the children never thought to tell her about the meal with Claire. They talked a lot about school, how kind Susan was being, and how they were being very grown up to get their own breakfasts every morning.

Her absence still confused the children. They wondered why she did not want to speak with their father when she called. If he answered the phone, she would ask to speak with the children. Once or twice Adam suspected that she just put the phone down when she heard his voice, as there was no reply on the line when he answered. He knew that they never had much to say to each other when they lived together, and concluded that this was why she did not wish to speak with him now.

Her behaviour did perplex him, but he knew that Luce was more concerned about the children and their needs than of his. She would obviously want to speak with them on a regular basis. With each phone call, they asked when she was coming home. She was evasive and did not give them a set date. Her only answer was that she was not ready to return to Montreal yet.

When the schools closed for a mid-term break, Adam suggested to the children that they go to Toronto to spend time with their grandparents. They were overjoyed, as they loved his parents who spoiled them outrageously. This also meant that they would get to ride on an airplane. Adam's father had offered to drive to Montreal to fetch them, but Adam decided to give them the additional treat of an airplane ride, which he knew they would love. He drove them to Trudeau Airport, and ensured that they got onto the correct flight. He told them that their grandparents would be waiting at Pearson Airport in Toronto for them when they disembarked. He was not worried about their safety, as both girls appeared to be more excited than nervous about the upcoming stay with their doting grandparents. He turned his car out of the airport lanes and drove straight to Claire's home.

"Come on, you sexy wench, I am taking you on a very dirty week's holiday!" he announced as he walked into the house.

Smiling, Claire met him, carrying a small suitcase, and gave him a loud, lascivious kiss.

"How is that for an appetizer, you sex-crazed man?" she responded.

Laughing nervously in each other's arms, they thought about the time they had arranged to share together. Adam had suggested getting away from Montreal so that they could enjoy being together without constantly looking over their shoulders. Claire had agreed that it was a wonderful idea. They made a reservation at an exclusive resort in the Eastern Townships, close to North Hatley.

The drive from Montreal to North Hatley took them just under two hours, heading almost directly east into the heart of what had been best known as the Eastern Townships, or was referred to as the Cantons de l'Est by the Francophones. A warm sun slanted out of the autumn sky, transforming every tree into a kaleidoscope of colours. The golds and yellows, oranges and reds of the fall leaves shone in the sunlight. They admired the scenery of rolling hills and small villages along the route. There were many small ski hills in the region and they picked them out visually, discussing their skiing facilities pros and cons. Nigel Kennedy's performance of *The Four Seasons* on the CD player kept them company as they relaxed together; frequently holding hands as they drove.

When they arrived at the resort they parked and walked up to the reception desk. The elegance of the rural buildings was impressive. The sign on the front wall stated that the establishment had a five star rating, and that the dining room had a Relais and Château designation. They looked at each other as they read this information and nodded in approval. They anticipated a wonderfully luxurious stay.

That night they dressed in elegant casual clothing and enjoyed the sumptuous meal the chef had provided in the restaurant. The service was attentive and the wine list extensive. When they had finished dining they retired to the small, cozy bar to enjoy a glass of Armagnac, a brandy that they both enjoyed, but was not always available in restaurants in Montreal.

Falling into bed together that night, they took pleasure in the fact that they could hold each other until the sun rose, and then still lie together. Their love making that night was slow and gentle, both savouring the pleasure of the freedom that this time on their own would afford them.

Light filtered in through the blinds at the window. Two bodies lay intertwined in the king bed. Watching Adam sleep, Claire thought that he looked boy-like when he was tousled; his hair mussed and the stubble on his chin beginning to sprout. She touched his face gently, then leaned over and kissed him on the tip of one ear, on his cheek, on the side of his neck. She ran her tongue down his throat and chest, stopping at a nipple to run her tongue around it.

Adam opened his eyes and looked at Claire for a long moment. This woman had him entranced. He felt lost in her depth when they were together. Leaning forward, he pulled her face down to his, kissing her gently on the mouth, feeling her respond with her tongue, exploring his.

Running his hand under her nightgown he pulled it up and over her face so that she could not watch his exploration of her body. She lay very still and closed her eyes under the shield of the soft cloth. His hands stroked down the length of her body, tracing the shape of her shoulders, her breasts, her abdomen. Every one of her nerves tingled in anticipation.

"So beautiful," Adam murmured, as bent his mouth to her breast. He felt the nipple harden under his lips, and became more aroused.

She arched her body up into his, as he ran his tongue down her body and nuzzled her navel.

Adam moved up and pushed into her wetness, enclosing himself with pleasure. Slowly he moved with her until they both moaned in fulfillment; relaxing together intertwined on the bed. Adam rolled over and slid the fabric from Claire's face.

"How did you enjoy a sightless exploration?" he breathed into her now exposed ear.

"Oh, Adam, I never realized how cutting off one sense could enhance the acuteness of all the others. Every nerve in my body was on high alert to your touch."

They lay together as the morning light grew brighter and flooded through the window. Adam looked at the woman lying in his arms and wondered when he had last enjoyed a sexual experience more than with her. He had enjoyed the company of several women, but none of them had aroused or satisfied him like Claire did. She opened her eyes and looked at him questioningly.

"You look as if you have something immensely profound to say, Mr. Lambert."

"Yes, in fact I do have. You have worked up an enormous appetite in me. I am ravenous, and need more than just your body to feed on. You have heard that man cannot live on love alone – although at times I feel it's all I crave. Let's go and find out what this five star restaurant can produce for breakfast."

Claire laughed. They enjoyed a quick mutual shower, and dressed quickly. Together they walked down the path to the dining room, appreciating the view of Lake Magog and the clear, fresh air. As they got close to the entrance a voice called out, "Adam, I thought that was you. Fancy seeing you here! Are you alone? Sorry, I did not see your companion."

Adam and Claire stopped in their tracks, glancing at each other quickly.

Claire recovered first and said, "I will catch up with you later, Adam. It was nice running into you.

Maybe we can have lunch or dinner together while you're here." She turned and walked away briskly.

"Oh, I'm sorry I chased your friend away," said the stranger.

Thinking quickly Adam responded, "No Peter, I just bumped into her on the way to breakfast. I think she's staying here for a few days, so I'll meet up with her later. What are you doing here?"

Peter Cox was a broker at Stark, Nesbitt and Bouchard, and not one that Adam thought of as a friend. If he was staying at the Manoir as well, Adam and Claire would need to be very careful of their activities, he realized.

He walked into the dining room talking with Peter about uneventful topics. The waiter came over to them and asked, "Are you alone this morning, sir?"

"Yes, I am alone. I thought I would just get four croissants and some jams and take them to the suite so that I can continue working there."

Taking the pastries, Adam returned to the suite. Claire was not there, so he brewed a pot of coffee and set the croissants on the table, waiting for her to return.

An hour later she came spilling into the room, laughing as she did so. "I thought I was going to burst when that guy spoke to you. How did you pull it off? I assume you made up some interesting excuse about why you're here alone. Who is he anyhow?"

Adam sat and watched her with a broad grin on his face. "He's with the firm, and is here for a break I gather. But, you were wonderful! How did you manage to think up your get-away so quickly? Are you sure you've not had an illicit affair before, my dear Miss Hardick? And, you are late for breakfast. I ordered some croissants from the dining room and can perc a fresh pot of coffee. Where did you get to?"

"I came back for the car keys and drove into North Hatley. I too, picked up some breakfast and brought it back. So we can both eat our fill!"

Congratulating themselves on their ingenuity, they tucked into the pastries and coffee.

"If he's going to be hanging around here, why don't we take the car and go somewhere today and give Peter time to leave? I know that there's a wonderful Abbey close by that's worth a visit."

When Claire agreed to the plan for the day he added, "I'll have to pick you up at the end of the road in case Peter sees us, but we can then be together without being noticed. So much for us finding a place where no one else would find us!"

They drove through the rolling hills of the countryside to the Abbey Saint-Benoit-du-Lac. Approaching the abbey down a winding road, they were impressed by the size of the main building. The façade of the structure was impressive from the outside, with large domed clerestory windows spanning the entire length of the building. Overlooking Lake Memphremagog, the abbey was situated in a large open expanse of fields and orchards, making the building appear cloistered from the outside world, surrounded only by nature.

The interior of the abbey was cool, and they gasped as they took in the detailing in the ceiling of the long corridor leading to the interior chapel. The use of multi-coloured bricks arranged in natural geometric forms continued down the entire length of the hallway.

They entered the quiet of the chapel and seated themselves on an aisle where they could observe the front refectory. At ten o'clock a group of fifteen monks entered from a side door and stood quietly in the chancel. At a signal they slowly and quietly began what continued to be a half- hour performance of Gregorian chants. Moving up and down through the limited melodic range of the music, the sound created a quiet monotony that enhanced the peace and serenity of the experience.

The couple were very quiet as they left the chapel. Holding each other's hands in a strong clasp, they made their way back down the beautiful corridor and then descended the stairs to the large gift shop. Their mood did not change until Claire saw the large array of cheeses on display. She let go of Adam's hand and picked up a slab of blue cheese.

"Look at the texture of this cheese, Adam. The notice here states that all these cheeses are produced on site, from milk taken from the Abbey's herd. I think we should take some of these varieties back to Montreal. The girls would love this rich cheddar."

Selecting a number of cheeses she paid for the purchases, and clutched the package as they made their way outside and back to the car.

Two months passed with Luce still away in Paris. She had given no indication of her return to Montreal and her family. Adam was becoming more and more concerned as she continued to be silent about her intentions. He was reluctant to voice these concerns to Claire, as he did not want to embroil her in what he was beginning to suspect was going to be a difficult future with his wife.

His relationship with Claire now felt like a pseudo marriage, leaving him with feelings of schizophrenia as he moved from his home to her house. He felt very comfortable in the warmth of Claire's house; her spaces were smaller than the house in Westmount, but had character and charm in its aged beams and paned windows.

He felt very relaxed one evening as he and Claire sat together in the warmth of the den and read. They were immersed in the content of their books until Claire looked up and asked.

"Did Luce ever ski with you on Mont Tremblant?"

"Yes, she did when we were first married. Why do you ask?"

"I just wondered why she gave up on the sport, when the girls are so keen on skiing."

Adam closed his book, placed it on the side table and turned to look at Claire. He sat still for a long while, until Claire felt uncomfortable and asked, "Is there anything wrong with my asking, Adam? If there is, I'm so sorry. Please ignore the question."

"No, you have every reason for asking. It's a difficult question for me to answer, as I have never really discussed this with anyone. I will try to explain to you, but it won't be easy," he continued. "But first, I think I need a drink to fortify myself. Would you like one?"

"Yes, thank you," a puzzled Claire responded.

Adam brought two glasses of Scotch back to the den and offered one to Claire. He did not sit down, but stood at the window, staring out at the evening sky. His silence disturbed Claire, but she did not want to push him into an answer that he did not want to give.

Finally he spoke, not looking at her. "Luce and I had another child."

Turning, he finally faced her and continued. "A son. He died four years ago in an accident on Mont Tremblant. Luce has not skied since then. She can't bring herself to put on skis and pass the place where our son lost his life. I have not pushed her."

"Oh, my darling. I never guessed that you had this tragedy in your life."

"Yes, it was a tragedy for all of us. He was the joy of our lives, and the big brother hero for the girls. We still miss him dreadfully, but we had to move on with our lives, especially for the sake of the girls."

Claire was dumbfounded. She did not know how to react to this tragic news. She knew that Adam was telling her something that was very painful to remember, and she wanted to share his grief with him.

"Our marriage was not in a good space before the accident," Adam went on. "We had both found ourselves busy with separate lives – and then our son was taken from us. It was as if the gods were punishing us for something we had done; or not done. But we could not find a way to grieve together. We spent all our energy comforting the two girls, who were so young then, that we forgot, or did not want, to think about each other. We did not cling together as maybe we should have."

He took a long drink of scotch and stood up again, pacing around the room before he continued. "You cannot understand what one goes through losing a child. The emotion. First the shock; then just numbness. Denial and disbelief follow. He did not die, you tell yourself. There had to be a mistake."

He paused and looked out of the window for a good while before continuing. "I think these emotions just cushion the loss for a while. But when they wear off you are left with worse; feelings of guilt, of anger, of despair."

He stopped talking and walked backward and forward across the room as he spoke. "Luce and I experienced these emotions differently. She withdrew into herself quietly, with her grief. I ranted and roared. I could not forgive myself for allowing him to use a snowboard, to allow him out on some of those difficult runs. I was on an emotional roller-coaster for months. I could not sleep, I could not concentrate at the office, until I was so exhausted that I became ill and needed time off work."

Claire felt a tear run down her cheek, and wiped it away before Adam could notice. She wanted to be strong for him, to let him know that she was there for him.

"I think that Luce blamed *me* for the accident." Adam said softly. "She never said so, but I could sense her withdrawal. She got medical advice as well as support from a counsellor. They suggested a mild tranquilizer for her. She still takes a low dose every day. She had to deal with clearing out Andre's bedroom. I found that I could not look at all the stuff in that room without his energetic young body in it."

"Eventually, I could not bear the pain that was in the house, and I escaped back to the office and work to try and forget. But I did try to be there for the girls. If I could not comfort my wife, I could support *them*. It was very difficult not to overcompensate for the loss of their brother by cosseting them too much; by being overprotective. Luce and I seemed to have a silent agreement that they should not be ruined by this catastrophe. That we still had two chances to raise wonderful children."

"Oh, and they are wonderful little girls, Adam," Claire interjected.

"I know. We have all learned to live with the loss, but it is still very painful to remember, to talk about."

Claire rose and walked over to her lover. She put her arms out and wrapped him in her embrace, putting her head onto his chest and rocking gently.

"I am so glad that you shared this with me. Now, I know you so much better. I know who you are. Another piece of your life falls into place for me, that I can share with you – not the grief, but the healing."

Kissing her gently on the top of her head, Adam unwrapped her arms and walked to the couch where he sat down, picked up his glass of Scotch, and drank deeply of the golden liquid.

"That is why I will not give Juliette permission to get a board for hot-dog skiing," was his final comment. "I cannot talk about this anymore, but I am glad that I have told you. I knew that I would have to tell you sometime, but I did not know how to start the conversation. Thank you for the prod, you are always so sensitive to my moods, and understand my thoughts. Thank you for just being you at times like this."

Adam's children had settled into a routine that did not include their mother. They appeared, to him, to be settled into a life with just the three of them. However, he never had an answer when the topic of Luce's return was mentioned.

"I wish Mama would come home. I miss her cooking."

"I wonder if she's still painting while she's away?"

"Are you lonely sleeping in the big bed on your own, Papa?"

And very often these comments would end with… "When is she coming home to us?"

He had no answer to give to them.

Revenge

Revenge is a meal best served cold.
Source Unknown

Luce did eventually return to Montreal from Paris. She was feeling refreshed after the long stay in familiar surroundings with old friends, and having been able to focus on her personal emotions without the distractions of family demands. She had half-enjoyed her months away from the family. She missed the children dreadfully, like an ache that would not go away. She had phoned regularly to find out about their lives; had heard that they were keeping well and that they were missing her. But they had also appeared to enjoy some of the freedom afforded them without Mother Hen watching their every move. It also seemed from their conversations that Adam had been a wonderful father in her absence.

She took time to examine her feelings about her husband as she walked the streets of Montmartre. She thought about the years that she and Adam had shared together. She acknowledged that the joy and lust of the early years had faded and that, for many years now, they had lived together with a mutual tolerance, acknowledging that they were together to support the girls. When their son Andre had died, they had experienced a deep grief together, but it was not enough to draw them closer through that very difficult time. She felt that she had lost Adam at the same time as she had lost her son.

The dreadful letter that she had received in the mail had probably contained the truth. She acknowledged that Adam had enjoyed the company of other woman during his marriage to her. Because she had not been aware of them, she assumed that he had been very discreet. However, if, as the note intimated, there were others in the community who knew about these liaisons, then she felt some embarrassment and a certain shame. Why did a woman always feel a responsible guilt when their husbands strayed? It was as if they had not been good enough to keep them happy to stay faithful, she rationalized.

Her sojourn in Paris had made her realize that this was not the life she wanted. She did not want to be alone in the world; without her children and her comfortable home. All the years that she had invested in her marriage had earned her the right to enjoy a happy life with her family. These thoughts led her to decide to return to Montreal with a determination to restore her marriage. She would win Adam's love and desire back. She would hold her head high when out in social circles, and defy anyone who questioned her decision.

Without giving a warning to Adam or the children, she arrived back in Montreal early one morning. The house was empty when she unlocked the front door and walked in. As she wandered from room to room, she felt that she had made the right decision in coming back. She felt at home. She felt comfortable in this house. It was *her* space, and she belonged there.

She unpacked her suitcase, and went through to the kitchen to see what she could prepare for dinner that night when Adam and the children would be home. From chicken that she found in the freezer she prepared a meal and made a salad from ingredients she found in the fridge. Then she sat down to enjoy a cup of tea, and waited for them to arrive home.

At four o'clock the children had not come home from school. She did not worry, as she assumed that they had after-school activities. At seven o'clock they were still not home. She was disappointed when she realized that they were eating out somewhere with their father. Probably some fast food place, she mused. At eight-thirty she was exhausted from the long flight from Europe, and from the waiting.

She was dozing on the couch when she heard the door open and the happy voices of the two girls fill the house. She stood up and waited for them with open arms. They walked into the den and shrieked, "Mama, Mama, you're home – oh you're home."

They hugged her. Michelle started skipping around the house singing, "She's back, she's back, she's back!"

Juliette stayed in a warm clasp, with her arms around her mother, not wanting to let her go. Guilt overwhelmed Luce as she realized just how much the girls had missed her; she knew that she had made the right decision to come home, and to them.

"Why didn't you tell us you were coming home? We went to dinner with Papa's skiing friend, but we would rather have been here," sobbed Juliette, through tears of joy at having her mother home again.

Luce stiffened when she heard where they had been, and she strengthened her resolve to find a way to end the affair that Adam was having with this other woman.

Adam came into the house from the garage and froze when he saw Luce with the children. He opened his mouth to speak, but could not find the words.

He had been confused by her leaving, and was now even more at a loss as to why she had come home without warning him.

"I came home," said Luce.

"I can see that," responded Adam. "Welcome back." He moved over to her and gave her an air kiss on the cheek.

When the children were finally settled into bed, Adam turned to Luce with a puzzled look.

"Were you ill when you left? Did you go there for treatments? Was a friend ill? You never told me why you went, or why you had to stay so long. I thought that you had left us for good. Have you come back for a divorce? I am still in the dark about this behaviour, Luce. You are still my wife, whatever that means to you," he rambled on and on, trying to find an answer.

Luce looked at him quizzically. "You are still my husband, whatever that means to *you*? I am home to stay, Adam. I had an emotional meltdown and had to get away to sort out my life, to examine my feelings and to think about my home, my family, and my marriage. But I have returned, and intend to stay and continue my life – only it is going to be a lot better this time."

Throughout this speech she stood, looking straight at Adam without blanching.

Adam looked back at her steadily. "You are back now. But are you here to stay, or will you disappear again? We cannot go through the past months again. It was very hard on the girls; especially not knowing why you had left. They kept asking if they had made you cross, and chased you away. They need you Luce, so please promise that you are back to stay. I assume that you do not want a divorce. But, if our marriage is too estranged for you, we can think about how we could handle that without upsetting the children even more."

I am sure that you would like a divorce on your terms, mused Luce. Then you can have your ski friend permanently. But, my dear Adam, that is not going to happen, because I am here to take you back. And your relationship with her is going to end. This she silently promised herself.

"Yes," she responded coolly. "I am really back for good, and to stay; in this house, with you and the girls. We have invested a lot of time and effort into staying together, and we can continue to do that. Maybe we could try to find some of the passion we once shared. I have some thoughts on how I would like my life to change; but maybe we can talk about them tomorrow when we are both rested. It's too late now, and I am very tired after the flight. I wish you had not taken the girls out with your ski friend for dinner."

On that note, she walked away to the bedroom where she climbed into bed, and fell asleep immediately.

When Luce awoke the next morning it was with a new resolve. She was determined that she was going to put her marriage back to the way it had been ten years before; before the loss of their son. They had come through that sad period together, and she hoped that they could now find a new passion together, the passion they had once shared.

Walking through to the kitchen she discovered that she had slept through the rush of getting the children off to school. Adam and Susan had dealt with the girls as they had probably done alone for the months that she had been away. She began to regret her quick action in getting away from Montreal, and hoped that she had not damaged her relationship with the girls. She also wondered what had developed with Adam and this woman, the ski friend. They were obviously still seeing each other, together with the children. She needed to find out where she stood; what the challenge was that she faced in getting this interloper out of her marriage.

It took two days of watching her children's joy at having her home again to reinforce for her the need to restore her marriage to where it had been years before.

"First of all, I need to discover the nature of their relationship. Are they really having a sexual affair or could it be what Adam has suggested, a platonic one of business and skiing attachments?" she spoke aloud to herself. "I need to find out how to do that."

She decided to be proactive. The internet provided a listing of private detectives in the Montreal area. Having never needed to use such a service before, she felt at a loss as to how to go about hiring a private eye. From the several names listed, she read through their listings and checked the websites of several; but she was just confused. They all promised the same confidentiality, most were ex-law enforcement, and they quoted reasonable rates. Not sure how one went about choosing a reliable person, she selected the only female name listed. Surely a woman would be understanding and do a sound job for her.

Picking up the phone she called the number listed. It belonged to a Detective Janette la Roux. Maybe she is French speaking, Luce thought. That would be a good sign.

When the phones ring was answered, she discovered that, indeed, Detective Janette la Roux, was French Canadian, and would be pleased to meet with Luce later that afternoon.

They arranged to meet at a café close to the Snowdon Metro Station. Luce did not want to be seen in the detective's office; as well, she did not want the woman to see her in the house.

She liked the female private eye immediately. Janette le Roux was young, well groomed, and greeted Luce with a warm smile.

Luce shook her hand and introduced herself to the woman. The two seated themselves and Luce asked, "Pouvons nous parler en Français?"

She got a warm smile in return and the rest of the conversation was conducted in both their native tongues of French.

"I am Janette la Roux. I was a detective with the Ottawa police force," the detective stated, "but I found the challenges of street work too difficult with a family to care for. So I elected to do a job where I could control my own hours of work, and also one that is safer."

She looked at Luce sitting opposite her at the café table and saw a woman who appeared to be very much in control. Not like the anxious, nervous women who often required her services.

"Now, Mrs. Lambert, how can I be of assistance to you?" she asked.

Luce explained her situation and watched carefully for a reaction from the detective. Janette le Roux sat and looked back at her client without showing any emotion. Luce suspected that her problem was probably something that the woman heard on a regular basis, and that the task was not too complicated for her. Le Roux quoted a fee; they shook hands on the deal, and arranged to meet in the same café two weeks later. They agreed that the detective would report any information she had collected at that time.

Luce sat in the café for a long time after Janette la Roux had left, wondering if she was being ridiculous about the whole situation. She probably could sit down with Adam and ask him directly what he intended to do about having two women in his life. Her fear was that he might tell her that he wanted to be with the other woman. That would force his hand to leave her and the girls. She wanted to give herself an opportunity to pull him back into the marriage completely, and not risk a decisive showdown with her husband.

Two weeks later, when Luce met with the detective again, Janette la Roux pushed a large envelope across the table to her. Luce looked at the innocuous brown package and picked it up slowly. Opening the flap, she extracted a printed report that was attached to a number of photographs. She asked the detective for an oral report, while she glanced at the photographs. She saw Adam and Claire sitting together in what appeared to be a restaurant; she saw pictures of Adam leaving a house. There were photographs of a house, a car, and one of Adam and Claire together in front of the same house.

"I followed your husband every day. Many times he went to the house in the photograph. It is listed to the owner, Claire Hardick. In the past two weeks he went there four times. One evening he went there straight from work and stayed very late. Otherwise he only went to work, and then to the gym, out to lunch, and then home," Janette le Roux started to report to Luce.

"I also followed Claire Hardick, the woman in question. She works at Heap and Associates. The house in the picture is where she lives. The car in the photograph is hers – a seven year old BMW. She spends a lot of time at work, goes to a gym regularly, and often goes for long runs. Otherwise she stays home," she continued.

Then she added, "The photographs show the two parties together a number of times. Once in a restaurant having lunch together, and there are a few pictures of the man leaving the house in question, sometimes with her at the door, appearing to be saying goodbye."

"I don't want to suggest that the relationship is anything but platonic. You can see from the photographs that they are never touching each other. They are spending a lot of time together, but it may not be physical," le Roux offered.

She went on to suggest that she could follow them both for a longer period of time if Luce wanted more details. She stated that she had ways of finding out if the pair was more intimate, but would prefer not to describe what those methods were.

After looking at the photographs again, and reading the details in the written report, Luce felt that she had a good feeling as to the nature of the relationship between the two people that had been monitored. She thanked the detective, paid the fee, picked up the envelope containing the information and left the café.

Back at the house she went into her studio where she pulled the photographs from the envelope, laid them out on her drafting table and stared. She knew that these two people were lovers; that they had probably been lovers for more than a year. She realized that if they were still together after all that time, this was not a quick fling. This was a relationship that could last. The children seemed to like this woman as well, which made her even more dangerous to the well-being of her marriage. She wondered how Adam felt about the dual life he was living; how he could handle the duplicity. She knew that he loved his children and would do nothing to hurt them. How he felt about her, his wife, she was not sure. He had been a good provider; had never physically or verbally abused her; and had certainly been discreet about this and the other relationships he'd indulged in.

Her challenge now was to win him back to the family exclusively. She had to find a way to end the relationship with this other woman in his life. The winning him back had to happen in such a way that she was never seen as the cause of him losing his lover. She had no intention of living with her husband's resentment.

She supposed that she could try to get pregnant. Adam would devote himself to her and any new family member. Was she prepared to start again with diapers, sleepless nights and a large body? And, if the plan did not work, she would be left with an infant to raise on her own. Adam could be angry with her for not being careful, as they had been for ten years or more. She was not prepared to take that risk.

In her wildest imagination she wondered if there was a way to make Claire go away? Could Claire be involved in a fatal ski accident? Could she do something to her skis that would result in a fall? She did not know enough about what that would look like. She walked away from the photographs. What ridiculous thoughts these were. She just had to make sure that home life was more enjoyable, tempting, and emotionally satisfying for Adam than the house in the photographs.

Cutting the report and photographs into small pieces, she threw them into an empty container on the table and threw a lit match on top of the pile. That was the last she wanted to see of the evidence. She knew now what was going on, and she had to deal with this situation in a very competitive manner.

The first act she did the next morning, after she had seen Adam and the girls leave, was to get into her Santa Fe wagon and drive to the address that the detective had provided. Driving slowly up the hill, she found the house that had been shown in the photographs. It was a character Tudor house, set back from the road, with a well-manicured simple garden in front. On the driveway was parked the same blue car that the detective had described; a BMW that looked to be a few years old. The neighbourhood looked to be well established, with mature growth trees and well cared for properties.

Luce drove up to the top of the street and turned around. She was surprised at how steep the street was. It climbed up a hill to a cul-de-sac at the end, and then wound its way back down the steep slope. Luce kept the brakes applied as she drove slowly past the house again.

Her thoughts were jumbled as she looked at the place where her husband had been spending so much time. As she looked at the front door where the photograph of Adam and an attractive blonde had been taken, her heart pounded and rage engulfed her senses.

This woman was going to be a very challenging opponent to deal with, she knew.

Renewal

*A tower of nine storeys begins with a heap of earth.
The journey of a thousand li starts from where one stands.*
Lao Tzu

Luce sat in her studio at the rear of the house and looked at the artwork that was there. It all seemed dull compared with the examples of work she had done while in Paris. She went to the large travelling box that she had brought home with her and opened it.

Taking out the canvases, she stacked them around the walls of the studio. She gave a critical examination of her work as she noticed the variety of the pieces; the different techniques she had explored while away. There were a number of subjects, both human and from nature. The many nude studies that she had done were new for her, and she had surprised herself at how much she had enjoyed exploring the contours and curves of the human form. There were a number of still life studies, done in swift, large brush strokes that left the details blurred, but the shapes recognizable. These were soft, muted works.

She then turned to her studies of the city of Paris. In these, the sharpness of the angles in numerous recognizable buildings and structures stood out starkly.

They included the bell tower of Sacré-Coeur, the solid boldness of the Arc de Triomphe, the repetition of the windows in the Musée de l'Armeé in the Invalides, the pyramid entrance to the Louvre, the exterior air and water ducts of the Pompidou Centre and the skyward point of the Eiffel Tower. These were hard-edged works in thick acrylics, often laced with modelling paste to create three-dimensional textures to the structures.

She could see the progression of her thinking and the techniques she had incorporated while away. The flow of the changes was interesting. The subtle changes in the use of colour, the inclusion of texture, and were all bolder than the work she had done in Montreal. There were more human forms in the new work, and in most of them, the focus of the subject was filtered, rather than starkly clear. They were an interesting mix of boldness in design and colour, but softer in line.

Turning back to the work she had done in Montreal before she had left, she was surprised at how different they were. She had been more controlled in her approach to each subject; more traditional. Her new work was more free, more creative

Feeling very pleased with what she saw on the canvases leaning against the studio walls, she wanted to share these with others. Contacting the galleries she knew would be a start. She hoped that she could find a gallery that would give her a private showing so that she could show her diversity. But being out of touch for months would mean that she would have to do the rounds and renew her contacts.

During the next few weeks she made numerous phone calls, chatting with the gallery owners that she knew, asking about their future plans for showings. However, she was told that there were no openings available in the near future. This disappointed her but it did not stop her from working. She decided to keep the momentum going that she had started in Paris, so spent many hours in her studio painting and creating new pieces.

It was early one evening that Adam came home and found her busy at a large canvas depicting the head of a child looking up at the sky where a flock of white birds whirled around in a multi-coloured sky. Adam stopped and watched his wife for a while, then slowly walked into the studio. He looked around at the work leaning against the walls, encircling the studio. There were canvases stacked on a chair at one side. Canvases marched around the room in no particular order. The room, with light streaming in from the large skylight, was a riot of colour. He stood stunned. His senses were overwhelmed with what he was seeing. He had never seen Luce produce such wonderful work before.

She looked up at him and noticed the look on his face. "What do you think?" she asked tentatively.

"They are stunning," he gasped. "You have really changed your style. Did you do some of these while in Paris?"

"Yes, I did a lot of work with several different groups and they pushed me to explore techniques; to search inside myself for new emotions to guide my work. It was very therapeutic. It kept me from missing you all, and gave a positive focus to my time away."

She said these words looking straight at Adam, wanting to see what his reaction would be. He looked right back at her. He still did not appear to know that she was cognizant of his affair with the Hardick woman.

"You have an amazingly wonderful collection of work here," Adam continued in amazement. "You should be showing these somewhere, you know."

"I had thought the same thing, but I did not have any success when I visited a few galleries last week."

"Hmmm, that's not good. Have you ever thought of opening your own gallery to show your work? I think you have enough here to fill any gallery. You could find a space and make that your own special project," suggested Adam hopefully.

It was a sudden flash of inspiration, but a project like this would keep Luce focused on staying in Montreal, and not be tempted to go back to Paris, where she had obviously loved the art scene and found a welcoming community.

"Wow!" said a surprised Luce. "I never thought about going it alone. I wonder if I could? If I have enough talent? Enough variety in my work to fill a space, and to attract interested art fanciers?"

"Of course you have the talent. Look at the enormous amount of work you have right here. You still have some paintings in other galleries that I'm sure you could recall if they have not been sold. Once you have found a space you could keep part of it as a studio, so that you could continue to work right at the gallery when you don't have customers. You could even hire staff to cover some of the front work while you produce more product."

Adam found himself suddenly very excited by the idea of his talented artist wife showing the world what she could do. He was pleased that she had found something that would give her such an enormous amount of pleasure. From a financial aspect, he knew that he was suggesting a project that could turn out to be very expensive. However, he rationalized, if they never tried, they would never know just how good the work was that his wife was producing.

"Oh Adam, you should never talk about works of art as product, but I know what you mean," said a smiling Luce. "This could be very exciting. Let me think about it for a while."

When they sat at the dinner table that evening, there was a connection between them that had not been there for a long time. They felt that they had found a mutual project, and each had a very personal reason to make sure that it came to fruition. Luce, for self-stimulation and to prove to Adam that she, too, was a capable interesting woman; and for Adam, it was a means of keeping Luce excited about staying in Montreal with the family.

During the next few weeks, Adam spent time exploring the arts areas in Montreal. He walked Sherbrooke Street West and the small side streets leading from it – like de Maisonneuve and Crescent. He checked into the galleries he found, examining their showings. He spent time in some of the more outlying areas, around Rue St. Laurent and Avenue du Parc where there were at least a dozen galleries already. He explored Rue Saint-Paul East and Rue Saint-Jean and visited the galleries there. With all this information, he had a good feel of where the art scene was congregated in the city. He then phoned a real estate agent, and put her to work finding possible available spaces in any of these locations. He did not tell Luce that he was trying to find a gallery space, wanting to surprise her; and he wanted to free her from the drudge of the logistics so that she could produce more 'product'.

It took three weeks before the agent came back to Adam with some possible sites to explore. That night Adam took home a package full of real estate information: locations, square footage of the spaces, as well as some photographs of the sites. When he showed the package to Luce she was surprised, as she was still pondering the venture.

"Oh, thank you, Adam. I didn't know that you had already started on the project . I was still thinking about the possibilities. This is very exciting, but let's see what could be available."

Feeling very pleased with his efforts, Adam raised a word of caution.

"I don't think we should rush into anything. Take your time making a decision as you don't want to find yourself in a space that becomes a white elephant."

"What's a white elephant?" questioned Luce, who had not heard the English expression before.

"Oh, I forgot that it may be new to you. It means something that turns out to be useless. I don't know why white elephants would turn out to be useless – in fact I think if you had one, you'd probably make a fortune with everyone wanting to see something so unusual. Anyhow, let's be careful with the choice of space and location."

They finally selected a large open warehouse-like space that would accommodate a working studio, an open space gallery, as well as smaller rooms for exclusive showings and an office. The space, located on Sherbrooke West, had just been vacated by a designer clothing store that felt there was far too much space for their needs.

Adam hired an interior designer to work with Luce, and within a month the space had been transformed into a modern, airy gallery with richly coloured walls to show off the art. It included an office, a studio, one large gallery and two separate small rooms for intimate showings. Luce was thrilled with the result, and she spent hours in the new space working with a newly hired assistant in hanging her work. She sorted through some of her finest recent work and prepared for an opening show.

Celebration

There is no must *in art because it is free.*
Vasily Kandinsky

As she was nearing the time when she could launch the gallery, Luce decided that she would open with a grand splash. She felt that it was time for her to be seen socially, not only as the owner/artist of the gallery, but also as Adam's wife. They needed to be seen as a couple in more public places. This, she thought, would reinforce for Adam that they were husband and wife, and that the whole city saw them as such. The mean-spirited person who had penned the note to her would also see them together, and she hoped it would put all the rumours to rest.

She and Adam made the decision to host a big opening gala in the new gallery. They had not done any entertaining for some time, and Adam thought it would be good to socialize with his work peers. Luce wanted him to invite his financial contacts, and she would invite some of her best artist colleagues.

They developed the guest list together; Luce listed local artists, and some who worked in the surrounding areas, such as the Eastern Townships. They sat down and brainstormed the community who's-who, particularly those who supported the arts. They also identified the art critics for the *Montreal Gazette*, the *Globe and Mail* and the *National Post*, the French papers, *La Presse* and *Le Devoir* as well as some of the smaller community newspapers. Finally, they hired a caterer to provide a selection of wines and appetizing finger food.

They were both exhausted by the time the party had been planned. It was then that Luce suggested that Adam invite Claire Hardick.

"You know her well, and she has spent time with the children. I have only seen her once at a distance up on the Mont Tremblant ski hill. Maybe she would feel left out if she knew that we were doing some lavish entertaining and she had been forgotten."

Adam was taken aback. He had told Claire about the opening of the art gallery and the party that was being planned. In fact, she had been feeling rather neglected as a result of all the time that he had been spending with Luce, and had told him so. They had both laughed about it, and he had assured her that, once the party was over, she would have his undivided attention again. He knew that Claire would not be expecting an invitation to the event as they had purposely avoided being together in public. Now he was faced with a decision.

"I can ask her when I next see her, but I don't know how interested she is in art."

I am sure that you know very well, thought Luce. She turned to Adam and suggested, "Why don't we just send an invitation to her, like we're doing to all the others and see what she decides to do. At least she will know that we're including her."

Adam agreed, and three weeks before the opening, an invitation was mailed to Claire along with the other hundred invitations.

It was a gloriously sunny fall day as the last of the arrangements for the gallery opening were being completed. Luce made an effort to stay calm and direct the last of the preparations. She was feeling particularly proud as she stood back and admired what she and her staff had accomplished in such a short space of time. The gallery walls were hung with what she and Adam considered the best of her work; and the flow of the hangings emphasized the development and changes she had made in her techniques during the past year.

Her latest works were hung in the front of the gallery; the bright colourful collages representing an array of still life and florals in bright swirls of paint covering large, impressive canvases. These they hung close to the entrance to capture the viewer's attention and to draw them into the exhibition. The show then moved on to her portraits, many of them bordering on the abstract, but still very recognizable as the human form. Lastly, in the smaller rooms at the back of the gallery she had hung her quieter works depicting scenes of Paris and Montreal. In these she had used softer brush stokes, blending the edges to merge the images with each other. Looking at them was like looking at the scenes through a mist, or a light screen. Their effect was calm stillness. Luce felt that this was an appropriate way to view the end of the exhibit.

Lavish vases of flowers stood in the centre of the two main galleries and added to the impact of the art, without being a distraction. The caterers were busy working in her office at the back of the gallery, preparing gourmet bites of food as well as setting out glasses for wine and champagne.

Luce, herself, was a beautiful work of art that night. She had selected her outfit with particular thought to appear as a combination of artist, as well as the wife of a successful man. Her flowing gown in various shades of deep maroon showed off her pale skin and dark hair. The gown, with one bare exposed shoulder, shaped to her body's form and fell to her ankles. The children had clapped and giggled when they saw their mother looking so glamorous, and were nervous to hug her in the beautiful gown. When she had turned to face Adam, the sight of her took his breath away. He had almost forgotten what a beautiful woman she was. This, he thought was the Luce he had met and fallen in love with so many years ago. He was excited for her tonight, and immensely proud of what she had accomplished since first envisioning a gallery of her own. He walked up to her and kissed her gently on the cheek.

"You are going to outshine you own works of art tonight, my dear. I want to congratulate you on your achievement before anyone else does. May tonight be a wonderfully successful opening of your own gallery."

Luce smiled up at him warmly, and took his arm as they made their way to the limousine that was waiting to drive them to the gallery. "I want to enjoy many glasses of celebratory champagne tonight, without worrying about driving home," Adam had remarked as he arranged for the driver and car to escort them. The children and Susan, the housekeeper, waved to them as they drove away.

When they arrived at the gallery the door was open, lights were glowing, and invited guests were streaming into the already full interior. There was a buzz of conversation as viewers moved from one art work to another; discussing, criticizing and commenting in what appeared to Luce and Adam to be an appreciative hum. They looked at each other with a warm, intimate look and exchanged a smile – knowing that they had created a success.

This intimate exchange was noticed by a woman standing at the far end of the entry gallery. Claire had decided to come to the show. She did not want to make an excuse and appear rude. But she was determined to be inconspicuous at the opening launch of Luce's gallery. Adam had talked to her about the party, and mentioned that Luce had suggested that she be included on the guest list. She had been uncomfortable about the whole idea, and wondered whether Luce knew about their affair, and this was her way of hitting back, by showing off her talent, and her role as Adam's wife.

However, she reluctantly agreed to attend the function and to make a brief appearance.

She had chosen an outfit that she hoped would blend in with the crowd. Her dark navy silk pant-suit had been chosen to be lost among all the colour on the walls, and the bright outfits of the guests. She had added a double string of pearls to her neck and large pearl studs in her ears, to break the starkness of her appearance.

The party gaiety surrounded her as she walked from one spectacular painting to the next. She realized that Luce had considerable talent as an artist and that the gallery was bound to be a success. This is what had been keeping Adam away from her for the past few months. He and his wife had obviously been engrossed in setting up this business venture together. As she turned to enter one of the smaller rooms she found Adam at her side.

"Thank you for making the effort to come. This has been part of my life during these past months and I wanted you to see what we had accomplished. I think Luce would like to meet you," he said.

"Your wife has an exceptional talent," Claire replied.

"She has, as you can see from her work. She has been very productive and creative since she came back from Paris. I think the change was good for her."

It was also very good for your togetherness, thought Claire as she answered. "Yes, I can see that. And you have given her a lot of support since then."

"I'm sorry that it has taken so much time away from our being together," Adam apologized. "Wait here and I'll fetch Luce to meet you."

Claire watched as Adam took his wife's arm and moved her from one group of guests to another; introducing her to those whom she did not know, and being introduced to Luce's art connections. They stayed close together, appearing to be the devoted couple who were launching a major venture together. However, Adam always acknowledged that Luce was the artist, and he just the supportive spouse. They touched each other often, Claire noticed, and the looks they shared sent a cold chill through her body.

He still loves her very much, she thought. They are sharing this time and this project together as nothing Adam and I have ever done. I wonder if we ever will, while he is so close to her.

She wanted to leave. She could not stay and watch their intimacy. A polite acknowledgement to Luce and Adam was necessary, however, and she would have to make the effort to smile and look pleased for both of them.

I need a fortifying drink first, she thought, as she put her hand out and took the proffered glass of champagne from a passing server. What I really need is a stiff shot of Scotch, but this will have to do, she thought.

As she looked up, she saw Adam looking at her intently over the heads of the guests. He smiled broadly and signalled that they were on their way to meet her. He bent to say something to Luce and his wife looked up at him. He gestured towards Claire and took his wife's arm to lead her to where Claire was standing. Claire put the champagne glass down and held her hand out to Luce as she approached.

The earlier conversation between Adam and Claire had been observed by Luce. She had seen the relaxed way in which they interacted; the way their heads met as they talked. There was an intimacy between them that was not usual between casual friends. Seeing this, Luce realized that the information she had received from the private detective, as well as the contents of the note was true. Her husband was certainly having an affair with this attractive blonde woman.

This relationship had to end, she decided coldly. She and Adam were husband and wife; they shared a family, and that was how the situation was going to remain. She had not made the difficult decision to return to Montreal and to forgive him, only to lose him to this woman. She had captured more of Adam's attention since her return. With the decision to open the gallery, he had become part of her life again, as they planned and worked on the opening. They were more intimate than they had been for years, and she was enjoying the revived closeness of the relationship. As she watched the two together, she decided to do everything in her power to put an end to this intrusion.

Luce stood with her hand held out to take Claire's, and took in the woman's appearance. She was very attractive, she conceded. Her skin was flawless and her blue eyes and blonde hair were eye-catching. She understood her husband's physical attraction to her.

"Congratulations, Mrs. Lambert, you have opened an extremely attractive gallery, and your work is most interesting," offered Claire as she took the outstretched hand.

"Oh, do call me Luce please; and thank you. But, you know people who call art work interesting usually do so to hide their dislike or lack of understanding."

Claire forced a soft laugh. "Sorry, I did not mean it as an insult. I'm sure the guests here tonight will appreciate your immense talent. Adam, thank you both for the invitation to join with you tonight, and may your gallery continue to enjoy every success, Luce."

With a smile she turned, making her way to the door where she exited the gallery, walking quickly to her car. She sat in the car for the next ten minutes with her head on the steering wheel, and wept quietly into her hands.

She did not notice the look that Adam and Luce exchanged as she made her hasty exit.

"That was very abrupt," commented Luce.

"Yes, she didn't seem to be her usual self tonight," replied Adam, trying to sound calm. He had wondered how the meeting between these two women would unfold. Mentally he thanked Claire for her quick thinking of being polite, but in exiting as soon as she felt she had done her duty. But her exit had almost been a rebuff. He had watched Claire leave, and knew that she would be experiencing very confused emotions as she watched him with the wife whom he would not, could not, ever leave.

Desperation

What is a man profited, if he should gain the whole world, and lose his own soul.
The Bible, Matthew 16:26

When Luce returned from France, Claire realized that Adam's wife had come back to stay. Her poison pen note had upset her, but had not driven her away from her husband and family. Maybe it was the children she had come back for, she thought. She had to be patient and wait to see if Luce was going to take the children and leave, or whether she really was home in Montreal to stay. The only way to find out was to monitor Adam's comments about his family life.

At night, lying alone in bed, she felt ashamed of her thoughts. She knew that what she was doing was thoroughly despicable by any standard, but she could not stop herself. Her obsession with Adam needed his constant companionship and, like heroin, the more she got, the more she wanted. She made a resolution not to do anything more to hurt Luce or the children, and that she would be satisfied with the time she could steal their father and husband from them.

However, when she awoke the next morning and thought about her day, she was again in a state of anticipation, wanting to see Adam as soon as possible; planning the times that she would be with him during the day. All good intentions it seemed, floated away with sleep; and the need to be with her lover was as strong as ever.

As the weeks passed, she realized that Luce had really come home to stay. She seemed to be involving herself in new, exciting projects, and Adam was talking about her activities with interest and enthusiasm. When he did this, Claire went cold with fear. She wondered if this meant that he was becoming less interested in her, and was moving back to the close relationship that he had once enjoyed with his wife. Was Luce trying to rekindle this passion? And if so, where did that leave *her* relationship with Adam? Her fears grew daily as she contemplated the possibility of losing his attention and love. She did not want to imagine a future without the man she loved as an integral part of her life.

Attending the opening of Luce's art gallery, she had watched the attractive woman in her own domain. She was a very elegant person, as only the French can be. Luce had looked magnificent that night, and Claire had noticed that Adam's gaze had constantly shifted back to his wife; that he was often at her side, as the devoted husband.

Claire recalled her own attendance at the party as a nightmare; the memory was a blur of watching Adam looking lovingly at his wife, his arm resting protectively over her shoulder. She tried to block the vision from her mind, but could not. It only spurred her resolve to take action again to lure Adam away from his wife.

Waking up one warm summer Sunday morning, she took her coffee out to the back patio, sat on a comfortable lounge chair and contemplated her life. She thought back to what it had been before she had met Adam at the conference in Toronto eleven months before. She remembered how hard she used to work; work had been her obsession then, and she had made a very successful career for herself. She had earned enough money to buy all the luxuries she wanted and she had been constantly busy. But, in reality, her life had been all work, exercise, and very little quality social time with friends, or even acquaintances.

Then her life had changed dramatically with one spilled cup of coffee. Instead of obsessing about her work, she now found that being with Adam was the drug she needed. Work still dominated her life, but now she took more time away from the office. She found time to be with her lover when he could get away from his family commitments. She was much happier than she could ever remember being in her life. Somehow, when she was with Adam she felt freer, more open, more communicative, more alive. She did not want her present lifestyle to change. That could *not* happen. She would have to find a way to make sure that Luce was not in Adam's life anymore; a way that would push her to leave permanently.

As she sat in thought, she stiffened. The most dreadful thought had crossed her mind. The only way to accomplish her wish was, somehow, to get rid of Luce. Luce had to be removed – whatever that involved. Was she prepared to do everything possible to ensure that the woman disappeared? Did that mean that Luce had to die? It probably did, she thought. And am I prepared to do that? Am I *brave* enough to do that? Am I *foolish* enough to do that? Am I *desperate* enough to do that?

She remembered the movie, *Fatal Attraction*, with Michael Douglas and Glenn Close in which the Glenn Close character becomes obsessed with a married man whom she meets on a business trip. The Glenn Close character torments the man and his family in order to lure him away from his family. In one scene in the movie, she boils the family pet rabbit in a pot. Claire wondered if she was bordering on some of the same destructive, obsessive behaviours. She shuddered at the possibility.

For a long time she sat with her eyes closed, trying to clear her mind of these terrifying thoughts. They were too horrible to contemplate. But in fact, she had thought them; and this both surprised and scared her. She would have to keep herself very busy to ensure that she did not follow this awful train of thought again. A long physical workout would help; she thought, so she left the patio, grabbing a bagel on her way through the kitchen. In the bedroom she changed quickly into workout gear, grabbed her kitbag and car keys, and headed out the door.

Two hours later she returned feeling refreshed and clear-headed.

Choices

Integrity has no need of rules.
Albert Camus

Claire and Adam had indulged in their time together while Luce was in Paris. With the housekeeper on call, they had managed to ensure that the children were well cared for. This meant that they had been able to enjoy dinner together at Claire's home frequently, to take long hiking days together, and occasionally Adam had stayed at Claire's home for dinner.

When Luce returned to Montreal and the family home, the time that the lovers now had together became more difficult to arrange. Adam was feeling drawn more to his family, with a vibrant Luce again a part of it. They had become a family again. After the party, they shared many discussions about the gallery, her work, as well as taking the children on outings together.

Adam began to realize that his life was becoming more complicated than was comfortable – with two very desirable women in it. Confused emotions left him constantly pulled in two directions. He was so comfortable when at home with Luce and the children now; but his passion for Claire and his need to be with her had not diminished. The time was coming, he knew, when he would have to make a choice.

One evening, sitting at home in the den, he and the children were watching a movie when Luce came in from the studio and joined them.

"I think I've had enough of acrylic paint for one evening, what are you watching?"

"It's Jim Carey in *Bruce Almighty*. Why don't you join us?" invited Adam.

"I will, but what if I make some popcorn first. It will only take a minute or two."

"Yippee," cried Juliette, "we love popcorn – with lots of butter."

Luce returned from the kitchen with two big bowls filled with buttery popcorn and handed one to the girls. She settled herself on the sofa next to her husband and smiled.

"Can you remember the last time we did this as a family? It seems like decades ago; but it does feel good, even if the movie is boring," she said.

"The movie is not boring," both girls yelled. "We love it."

Adam glanced at them and smiled. How good this felt to be relaxing with the family, and not feel torn about needing to be somewhere else. He put his arm around Luce's shoulders and, pulling her closer, kissed the top of her head.

As the family sat together Adam knew that this was where he was meant to be. He had to make a very difficult decision; but had to do it in such a way that it would not hurt the other woman whom he loved dearly.

The following week Claire told Adam that she was flying to Europe for some meetings with a company in Amsterdam. She suggested that it would be wonderful if Adam could find a way to join her for a few days, as they had not seen much of each other recently.

"I know that it's difficult to find time away from the family now that Luce is home, but this would be a very special time away with nothing pulling at us," she begged.

Adam promised to think about it, as it could provide the perfect way to enjoy her alone for a few days, without the emotional draw from home. Some time was definitely owed Claire after all the commitments he had made with the gallery. Also, their time together would help him confirm the decision he had to make.

Their work schedules were arranged so that they could be in Europe at the same time, agreeing to meet in Amsterdam and then fly to Copenhagen together where they felt they would be unknown; and in a city they both enjoyed.

Claire flew into Amsterdam where she met with European business associates from the company. The daily meetings were held in their offices on Sarphatistraat. Wanting to have more time with

Adam, she pushed for quick decisions. Her colleagues were intrigued with her efficiency, and her eagerness to come to conclusions; they did not guess at the true reason for her speedy efficiency.

Adam flew into Brussels where he had arranged some negotiations with clients on behalf of Stark, Nesbitt and Bouchard. When they had both completed their obligatory business arrangements, they met at the Amsterdam Airport, Schiphol, and boarded a KLM flight to Copenhagen.

As they walked into the reserved suite in the Admirals Hotel they looked at each other and laughed.

"Why do I feel like a schoolgirl who is doing something terribly naughty?" asked Claire.

"I hope you are going to be doing something terribly naughty; but with me," laughed Adam in response.

"Wait until I get you into bed tonight, Mr. Lambert; then I will show you just how naughty I can be."

"Put that purse down and come here to be kissed."

Claire walked into his arms and Adam bent his head and looked into the eyes of the woman who had so enraptured him for the past months. He leaned in and kissed her, softly at first, and then more forcefully. As she responded to his kiss, he felt a tightening in his loins. He needed her right then, not willing to wait until they were in bed at night. He gently led her to the bedroom, pulling off his jacket as they went. He stopped her at the side of the bed and started unbuttoning her blouse, button by button. As he did so he watched her pupils grow large with desire, and he was lost.

He removed her blouse and undid her brassiere, releasing her breasts. He cupped both in his hands and bent his mouth to one, running his tongue around the nipple. He heard her groan so he moved to the other breast and nipped it gently.

Her skirt came off next. He stood back and let it drop to the floor. Then he pushed her gently onto the bed and quickly stripped until he too was naked. Dropping his clothing carelessly onto the floor, he lowered his body to join her.

Kneeling over her, he slowly slipped his hand into her panties, running his fingers over the soft public hair under his fingers.

"I think we can do without this last barrier," he said hoarsely, as he slowly removed the garment.

"God, you are so beautiful," he said as he lay down beside her and bent his head to kiss her, feeling the softness of her lips. Very slowly he eased his tongue between them, and she opened her mouth to him.

"And I am so fortunate to have such an amazingly handsome man fondling my most private parts," sighed Claire. "Sometimes, with you, I feel like the world's best slut. You make me feel totally abandoned."

She was breathing hard, and wanted more of this man who had such a powerful effect on her body. He could take her to heights of lust that she had never experienced before.

Adam looked down at her and smiled. He adored the way in which this woman relaxed into the sexual joy of being together.

How could he ever have imagined being without her in his life, he thought later as he watched her slowly relax and turn to face him. They gazed at each other for a long moment, and he kissed her very gently, holding his lips on hers for a long moment of intimate connection.

"Was that naughty enough for you?" Adam asked softly.

"Very definitely," laughed Claire as she ran her hand down his chest, "and I think I can be just as bad later tonight."

"Oh, I do hope so," responded Adam. "In the meantime, why don't we go and explore this beautiful city."

The Admirals Hotel is a romantic waterfront hotel in a vast converted warehouse built in 1787. Many of its original features are still intact, such as a vaulted brick ceiling and enormous wooden beams. Adam and Claire had reserved a large room overlooking the Inderhavnen waterway.

During the next four days in their luxury accommodation they divided their time between passionate romantic interludes on the large king-size bed, or wandering around the varied sights that the fascinating city offered.

They often walked the two blocks to the picturesque Nyhavn, with its row of multi-coloured buildings lining the waterway. They sat at one of the outdoor tables in a restaurant and sipped on cold wine while gazing over the historic yachts moored in the harbour. They mingled with the tourists on the crowded streets; and one day joined a group on a boat to take the round trip through the harbour, down the Inderhavnen, past the opera house, and up through the Yderhavnen to stop and admire the Little Mermaid. Sitting on a boulder in the Inner Harbour, looking forlornly out to sea, is the little stone statue that is the city of Copenhagen's most famous symbol, an embodiment of Hans Christian Andersen's fairytale character.

One day, to escape the tourist crowds, they made their way to the quiet seclusion of the Disney-like fairy-tale palace, Rosberg Slot. The grounds of the palace provided a lovely place to explore the botanical gardens, and wander hand-in-hand. Looking at each other and smiling, they agreed to be tourists, and explore the interior of the grand red brick edifice, decorated with spires and towers and ornate Dutch gables. Inside they gazed in awe at the lavish Marble Room with its extravagant stucco ceiling, and the magnificent Long Hall containing the gilded coronation throne made from a narwhal tusk, as well as the three large silver lions standing guard over it all.

Turning to Claire, Adam commented, "No ruler in the western world would dream of pouring so much of its wealth into trinkets and extravagances like these. It's a wonder that the population of the time did not object to the decadent waste."

"I suppose they never got to see the interior of these huge palaces. Only the very rich, who were squandering as much as their rulers, enjoyed this finery. The poor just stayed poor as well as ignorant of all the waste."

Feeling awed by the magnificence, but depressed by the ostentatious decadence, they decided they needed a cheerful pick-me-up. They wandered down Oster Voldgade to find the Torvehallerne, the market. Food stalls of every imaginable edible delight filled the halls. Finding one that was offering wines, they sat on bar stools, and watched the crowded halls and the vendors selling a variety of Danish foods. This is Denmark's biggest and best food market. Its two long open-sided halls offered meat, cheese and fish in one, and non-smelly foods in the other; bread, chocolate, coffees. The smells tempted them to sit at one of the tables and indulge in *smørrebrød* smothered in sliced meat. They topped the meal off with what was purported to be the best coffee in town from Coffee Collection.

Replete from a busy day, they wandered back to the hotel where they enjoyed slow, lazy intimacy before dressing for a night on the town. They had hoped that they would be able to splurge and treat themselves to a meal in what was consistently voted to be the best restaurant in the world – Noma. However, when they phoned for a reservation, they were informed that the restaurant was fully booked for the next four months.

Looking at each other in surprise, they decided that they would have to make do with the next best. They chose a Michelin-starred eatery in Christianshavn, a few blocks from Noma. There they dined sumptuously on the restaurant's specialties; oysters, pork belly and beetroot. They both agreed that the food was heavenly, and after eating their way through the eight course menu, staggered back to the hotel where they curled up together and slept soundly.

"What would you enjoy doing on our last day together in this lovely part of the world?" asked Adam the next morning. They had enjoyed a leisurely room-service breakfast, and were now feeling restless; wanting to escape the room and the hotel.

"Why don't we see what's available outside the city, maybe to see some of the countryside and get away from the city crowds," suggested Claire.

"I'm sure the concierge downstairs will have some suggestions; let's see what he can tell us."

They wandered downstairs to the hotel lobby and explored possibilities with the hotel staff. After some thought, they decided to travel north on the train and visit the famed Helsingør where stood Kronborg Slot; the fortress that had inspired Shakespeare's Elsinore Castle.

"This is far more of a fortress than a castle," commented Claire as they walked up through the entrance to the large structure.

The stone building sat on a curl of land extending seawards into the Øresund. They were told, by a guide, that for hundreds of years, it had been the key control of that side of the ocean, and that Danish monarchs could extract a toll from every ship that passed through it.

With the connection to Shakespeare's *Hamlet*, the castle's interior displayed many mementos of performances of the play as well as famous actors who had visited the fortress. They wandered through the structure and then around the outside perimeter, trying to imagine what historic memories it held in its silent bricks. A small café down a side street in Helsingør provided a lunch of pickled herring with crusty bread, before they boarded the train back to Copenhagen.

Agreeing that their last night together should be a quiet intimate one, they chose to stay in the hotel. They dined in Salt, the hotel's fine restaurant overlooking the waterfront. When they returned to their room, they each felt very different emotions about the end of this time together.

Adam had been very quiet during the evening meal, and Claire had sensed sadness in his demeanour. It seemed to her that he was looking at her with sad longing, that made her hopeful that this shared time had led him to believe that his life should always be at her side.

She felt disconnected by her own inability to find words that expressed the nature of her response to this man: longing, warmth and lust; all these emotions that she felt as one single overwhelming passion.

"Times like this, together, help to cement our relationship," she began. "I feel that I know you so much better with each day that I spend with you, especially when we're enjoying experiences like we have just had for the past days. I feel I can relax with you; we can walk hand-in-hand out in public. There is no tension about being seen and recognized. Thank you so much for being here with me. I love you so much, my darling."

Adam looked back at her quietly and smiled. He leaned over and kissed her gently on the cheek. His silence was borne of a guilt that infused his entire self. He had enjoyed so much wonder with this woman. The two parts of his life were as separate as the two parts of a life could be. However, he had to reconcile himself to the fact that he could not continue to live a double life forever; he had a very difficult choice to make. He watched silently as the beautiful woman at his side smiled up at him with such love in her eyes, that his resolve melted and he took her hand and led her back to their suite and the welcoming closeness of the bed.

Decision

It is always thus, impelled by a state of mind which is destined not to last, that we make our irrevocable decisions.
Marcel Proust

Returning to Monteal, Adam felt that he had deceived Claire; which he had. He had agreed to their time together in Europe as a final tryst, knowing that he was going to have to end the affair; for his sanity as well as for the sake of his family. However, when he was with Claire in Copenhagen he found himself lost in the joy of being with her. He found that he could not broach the subject of ending the relationship. He knew that he had been a coward, so now that they were home, he had to find another venue and time for the difficult discussion he had to have with her.

Once he had made the decision that he would never leave his family, to be fair to Claire, he had to get away from her so that she could get on with her life, without him in it. Maybe this way, he reasoned, she would find another lover. She was a wonderful, attractive, sensual woman who would charm many men, but she would only be interested in them if he was not there. The thought of her lying in bed with someone else filled him with feelings of anger and jealousy, and he had to fight to hold to his resolve of ending the affair. He had to find the courage to take action before he made the wrong decision and regretted it for the rest of his life. In order to protect his family from hurt, he had to inflict hurt on a woman whom he loved dearly.

One evening, as he was leaving the office, he phoned Claire. They had not seen each other since their return from Copenhagen as both had been busy with work related commitments.

"Have you recovered from the jet lag yet?" he asked.

"Oh, hello, how are you? I miss you. Spending twenty-four-seven with you was good for me, but now I miss you twice as much. There is this huge gap in my life. When can I see you?"

"That's what I'm phoning about. Are you free on Thursday night? I've made a reservation at Restaurant Europa on Rue de la Montagne, so we can have a quiet dinner together."

Claire was taken aback, as well as surprised. They never went out dining in a public restaurant in case they were recognized.

"Yes, I can be free, but aren't you concerned about that very public venue?"

"For this one time I would like to be in a public space. Why don't I meet you there at seven-thirty, if that's suitable?"

"Yes, I can make it, and thank you, that will be a lovely treat. I look forward to it. There is so much I want to talk to you about; but it can wait two days. Good-bye darling."

When Claire closed her cell phone, she sat for a long while thinking about the unusual invitation from Adam. Why was he doing this now? She hoped that he was going to make it a special occasion and tell her that, after the wonderful time they had shared in Copenhagen, he had decided to leave Luce and be with *her* permanently. She did not want to have hopeful wishes, but she could think of no other reason why he was planning this event; especially after the intimacy they had shared in Europe.

Adam was already seated at a quiet table for two in a corner of the elegant dining room when Claire arrived at the Restaurant Europa. The waiter hovered around the table as soon as the maître'd had seated her.

"Good evening Mr. Lambert," he said to Adam formally as Claire sat down.

"Good evening to you. We will now have the champagne I ordered, please," Adam directed the restaurant staff.

Claire sat and looked at him as the waiter left. "Are we celebrating?" she asked.

"Yes, the wonderful time we shared in a beautiful city, and all the wonderful times that we have had together over the past many months," he responded.

When the waiter returned and poured a glass for each of them, they raised their glasses in a toast.

"To wonderful times," Adam offered. They touched their glasses and studied each other; each thinking very different thoughts about the tone the evening was about to take.

The restaurant menu was extensive and offered some of Montreal's finest offerings. Ordering from the menu, they passed them back to the waiter and turned their attention to each other. They smiled as they started sharing remembrances of their time together in Copenhagen. Adam also reminisced about all the times they had skied together, and about the moments they had shared at Claire's home.

They dined sumptuously on lobster cappuccino with truffle purée, followed by caramelized scallops with citrus juice, risotto and sautéed mushrooms. As their plates were being cleared, they ordered crème caramel and coffee to end the meal.

"That was a wonderful meal, Adam," Claire commented. "I am sure that I have added two thousand calories to today's intake, but they were worth every delicious bite."

Adam waited for the waiter to leave them alone, sipping their coffees. He sat with his hands on the table and looked at Claire intently as she smiled back at him. Then, leaning forward he took both her hands in his and held them tightly. Claire felt a wave of concern at the seriousness of his gaze.

"My darling, darling woman, I don't quite know how to start this conversation with you, but I have to say what needs to be said. Please forgive me for the hurt that I am now going to inflict on you. I only wish that it could be different, but it cannot be. You see, my love,

I cannot go on pulling myself apart in the way I have been doing for the past months."

Claire's heart stopped beating at the words she was hearing spoken. All the blood seemed to drain from her.

Seeing her distressed look, Adam continued quickly while he had the courage to finish what he had to say.

"I wanted to be with you for a last wonderful adventure, so I agreed to go to Copenhagen. And I loved every moment of it. But we cannot have any more of those times together. If I do, I will regret them for the hurt that I'll cause my family. You have been my lifeblood for the past months, and I will be a lesser man without you in my life. But I have to say goodbye. I have to free myself from this entanglement before I do something that I cannot undo. I cannot find another way, and I am so, so sorry for the hurt that this is going to cause you."

Claire had sat very still during all those words. Their meaning was not registering in her brain. She watched Adam's lips move as he spoke, the lips that she had kissed so many times; and now those lips were speaking words of betrayal that she could not comprehend.

"Claire, say something my darling. Do you understand what I am saying?"

Claire took her hands out of his, and put them onto her lap. She was beginning to shake. She had to hold her hands together tightly to stop their quivering. Her lips were moving, but no words were coming out.

She stared at him, feeling that he must be lying to her. She knew that he would never leave her. He would keep her as his lover, and maybe leave his wife, but he would never leave *her*, Claire.

"Claire, here, have some wine, you are deathly white. Are you all right? Oh, what have I done to you?"

Tears were forming in his eyes as he watched her.

"I am fine, Adam, thank you," she forced herself to say.

"Good, oh good, Claire." Then, getting to his feet he said, "I have to leave now so that I don't break all my resolve and take you in my arms. If we see each other again, please remember that I will always treasure the times we shared, but I have to be a family man. Please be happy, my love, and find someone who is right for you. This relationship was never going to have a happy ending."

He bent and kissed her on the cheek and Claire flinched as his lips touched her flesh. She felt totally betrayed. He had gone with her to Copenhagen, knowing that he was going to say good-bye when they returned to Montreal. He had invited her to this dinner in a very public place so that she could not react with anger or make a scene.

She knew that she had to get out of the restaurant, and find a place where she could let out a loud wail of anger, regret, and fear. She wanted to pound Adam on the chest and head until he changed his mind and apologized for the hurt he had just inflicted.

When Claire got home she felt shattered; thoughts of anger, regret and confusion were whirling around in her head. She could not believe that Adam had actually said good-bye. She had always envisioned him leaving Luce, and coming to live with *her*. This was not the way it was supposed to be. This was not the way she had been planning for the relationship to go.

Finally, exhausted, she fell onto the bed and passed a restless night interrupted by disturbing visions of her and Adam skiing together; and he was laughing as he skied past her, waving goodbye.

The following week passed in a blur. She had difficulty concentrating. She had difficulty sleeping. She was eating very little and colleagues were asking if she was ill. Some suggested that she take time off to rest; that she had been working too hard; that the work in Europe had been too much to fit into her busy schedule.

She spent the week-end at home, going nowhere, doing nothing but sit in the garden with either a drink of coffee or single malt Scotch in her hands. She concluded, sitting there, that if she *was* going to get what she wanted, she was going to have to take matters into her own hands. She was not going to accept the decision that Adam had made to end their relationship. That was not what she wanted; she had to do everything in her power to keep him interested in her, and with her. This meant that Adam would have to be free of the encumbrances that were keeping him away from her, particularly his wife in whom he had a renewed interest.

One morning as Claire sat at her desk with her head in her hands, Nathalie knocked softly on the side of the open door.

"May I come in, Miss Hardick? I would like to check some information with you please."

Claire lifted her head and looked at Nathalie. "Of course, come in Nathalie, sit down. What do you want to know?" She sat up straighter and tried to get her mind focused on the young woman now sitting across from her.

"Well," started her assistant, "I came across this transaction and it looks very strange to me. Did we really want to sell 5,000 shares of Norfolk Minerals for Mr. Poletier? I thought he said that he wanted to hold onto them and watch for an opportunity to buy more of the shares. Isn't that what you told me last week after you talked with him? Maybe I misheard what you said, but I just wanted to check before I processed this order."

Claire tried to clear her head of the fuzziness she felt. She was having difficulty focusing this morning. So far, she had done nothing but sit at her desk thinking about the break with Adam. She knew that she had to give herself a good shaking, as her father would say, and get on with her life. It was proving more difficult to do than to say. Work had always been her passion, and now she was feeling lost in the one place where she had always felt so comfortable.

"Leave that with me, Nathalie, and I will look into it. My memory is not working well right now and I will have to go back to my notes to remind myself of the conversation with Mr. Poletier. But, thank you for bringing your concern to my attention."

"Thank you," said Nathalie as she turned to leave. "Oh, Miss Hardick, I have to tell you my good news. Do you have time for me to share it with you?"

Taking a deep breath Claire smiled at her. "Of course, we have not had much time together recently. So why don't we walk down to the staff room to get a cup of the dreadful coffee they provide in this organization, and come back here and take some time to talk, and you can tell all your good news to me."

When they returned, and had settled themselves comfortably, Nathalie began. "You know that I had talked about the dentist that my parents liked and that I was not interested in at first?"

"Yes, I remember you telling me about him."

"Well, I was telling you that I was waiting to be swept off my feet by some thunder or sparkles from the sky when I met the man of my dreams."

"Yes," remarked Claire smiling. "I recall telling you that it seldom happens that way."

In her mind she could not help but think – yet it happened to me that way. With one cup of coffee that we never got to share because I covered him with it. That was how I met the man who has sent my body and my mind spinning, in a non-stop whirl of desire that I cannot control. Oh, Nathalie, if only you knew how simple, and how wrong, my advice was to you that day.

"Now," continued Nathalie, "I have discovered that there is no use waiting for the thunderbolt because I have such deep feelings for that same man, the dentist. He has been wonderful to me for the past months. He has spoiled me, taken me to places I never knew existed in Montreal. He knows the best restaurants where he treats me, orders for me, introduces me to wonderful wines that I have never sipped before. My family is overjoyed that we are now seeing each other regularly. I think that my mother is planning the wedding already, but we're still having such an exotic time exploring each other, and he is such a gentle lover – oops I did not mean to say that. I mean..."

Laughing, Claire responded, "I would be rather worried if you were not by this time, Nathalie. So, is he the one you have been waiting for?"

"I don't believe in thunderbolts for me anymore. I think I am going to be very happy with something more comfortable and stable. I feel I'll be a lot more contented with this kind of relationship; one that is predictable."

"I am very happy that you have found such a wonderful friend. Do you think he loves you?"

"Oh yes, and I think he is going to propose this weekend. We won't marry in a hurry as we want to get to know each other a lot better before we do. So my mother will just have to keep planning for a while."

"Congratulations, and do tell me on Monday if the happy event takes place."

She turned back to her desk to hide the tears that were forming in her eyes. Nathalie mistook this as a cue to leave, and walked out of the office.

When the young woman had left Claire alone, she thought again about her relationship with Adam and how unstable and unpredictable it was, compared with what Nathalie was enjoying with her dentist lover .

Exploration

Knowledge itself is power.
Francis Bacon

Thinking about removing Adam from his family, and actually accomplishing the act were two very different issues. Claire realized that making her wish come true was going to be a lot more complicated than she had envisioned. When she thought about her next move, she was not quite sure where to begin. Being a methodical person, she concluded that some research was required. She needed to find out about her enemy, his wife, before she could plan any further steps. How to do this could present some problems. She did not see the woman in the normal course of her day. She would have to find out how Luce Lambert spent her day, what she did with her time, where she went, and with whom. Maybe if she had all this information she would be able to formulate a plan.

Was it feasible to hire a private eye to follow Luce for a few weeks and report on her movements? However, she reasoned, if she did this, she would be leaving a traceable account of what she was up to. Whatever she did, Adam must never be able to trace it back to her, of that she had to be sure. She did not want to remove Adam together with his wife; that would be defeating everything that she was wanted.

The footwork had to be done by her alone. The first step was to follow Luce around and find out what her life looked like. Claire knew that, whatever it was that she was going to have to do, had to appear to be accidental, so that it could never be traced back to her. Adam would never forgive her if he knew what she was planning. In the same way that she knew that Adam would never find out that it was she who had penned the note to his wife.

Her thoughts and plans began to move in a logical manner. In order to stay unrecognizable she needed to rent a car. She did not want her own car's movements to be traced back to her. If she was going to rent a car, she needed to be able to do this without using her own name. That too, presented a problem. But in order to rent a car, she would need a driver's license and a credit card. Maybe she could pay cash for the rental fee without raising any alerts with the rental company. What she needed was someone else's driver's licence. The licence had to belong to someone who resembled her, and this could be difficult. She would either have to find a forger, or steal a licence. Her mind constantly revolved around the problems she was trying to solve.

But this last one proved to be easier than she could have predicted.

While sitting in a meeting at work she was running her options through her head, not listening to the topics of discussion at all, until Avery pulled her to attention.

"Claire, what do you think?" he asked.

"About what?" asked Claire, suddenly trying to focus on the discussion.

"The idea that Shelley has just presented to us about communication with clients," said an exasperated Avery. "You appear to have been doing some other problem-solving and not helping to solve ours. Are you all right this morning?"

"Oh, yes, I'm fine," lied Claire as she looked across at Shelley. "Shelley, I apologize, can you repeat your idea please?"

As Shelley outlined her suggestion, Claire studied the young woman closely. She had the same colouring as herself, her hair was a little longer, her eyes also blue. She was about the same height; a little shorter but that would not be noticed. Claire realized that she had never noticed Shelley much until now, when she was searching for a look-alike.

The discussion over methods of communication continued for the rest of the morning and the meeting broke up as everyone dispersed to their own offices and to lunch.

Sitting at her desk, Claire decided that she had to act while the idea was in her head. Thinking quickly, she picked up the phone and dialed Shelley's number. She suggested to the woman that they meet in the cafeteria to discuss another matter. Shelley agreed and Claire put the phone down.

She waited ten minutes, and then walked to Shelley's office. The surrounding offices were empty as it was the lunch break. Claire walked into Shelley's office and closed the door. She knew that she only had about fifteen minutes to act, as Shelley would not wait much longer for her in the cafeteria. She sat at Shelley's desk and opened drawers. She figured that Shelley would keep her purse in a closed space, and sure enough, in the left lower drawer she found the woman's purse.

It did not take Claire long to open the purse, extract the wallet and remove the driver's licence. She took a Kleenex from her pocket and wiped the purse clean of prints, to ensure that they were at least blurred, if not removed.

She returned the purse to the drawer, exited the office, and left the door open as she had found it.

Putting the card into her pocket, she went up to the cafeteria quickly and apologized to Shelley, saying that a phone call had delayed her. She apologized again for the fact that she could not stay, as the call had been about a meeting that she had to rush to. She knew that she would not be able to sit and look this charming woman in the eye after what she had just done, and the lies she had just told.

Her heart was beating fast as she walked away. Back in her office she tried to control her emotions and fears. Finding it difficult to concentrate, she left the office and went home. The best remedy for stress was always exercise for her, so she changed into her work-out clothes and headed for the gym where she worked up a sweat and exhausted her body of all negative thought.

When she arrived at her office the next morning, she discovered that there had been a theft in the building the day before. It appeared that someone had entered a number of offices and stolen money from many purses during the lunch break, Shelley's being one. The police were called and everyone was being questioned about their lunchtime activities the day before. Claire could not believe what she was hearing. If the thief had been wandering the halls the day before, they may have seen her enter Shelley's office. She would have to say that she went there to meet the woman, planning for them to go up to the cafeteria together.

When the phone rang it was Shelley on the other end of the line. "Claire, did you hear what happened to me yesterday when I was waiting for you in the cafeteria?" she asked.

"Yes, I have just heard. Did you lose much?"

"I had about fifty dollars taken from my wallet, and a credit card and my driver's licence were taken. I can't understand why they would want the driver's licence, unless they just got mixed up with the cards. It's such a nuisance to have to go and replace it. I have cancelled the credit card already; that was easy. Tell me when you can meet again and I will come up to your office."

"It's fine for now, Shelley. You have enough on your mind. Let's leave it until things quiet down," she quickly told the other woman.

The day passed very slowly for Claire. She expected the police to question her as they had others, but they never came. It was probably because her office was on another floor that she was above suspicion. This did not stop her from sitting in a sweat of fearful anticipation most of the day. She realized how easily she had accomplished this difficult theft, and how fortunate she had been that some other person was doing a nefarious deed at the same time. She persuaded herself that the gods, or whoever her guardian angel was, had definitely been on her side yesterday. Maybe, she reasoned, this was a sign that the heavens approved of her actions. Adam always said that the fates were on their side. Maybe they really were bringing them together again.

Renting a car presented no problem. Claire signed for a vehicle for a month using Shelley's driver's licence as identification. She paid in advance in cash, and chose a grey Honda Civic for its neutral colour and popularity. It would not be remembered or recognized if she had to follow Luce, she reasoned.

She requested a week's leave from work, and Avery gave it willingly as he thought she had appeared to be very tired and distracted recently. He felt that she needed a break, and some personal time to herself.

Her routine for the next week became one of arriving early on the Lambert's street and parking a few houses down from the house so that she could watch all activity. She had dressed in dark pants and sweat top, and had enclosed her blonde hair in a peaked cap. She hoped that she would be unnoticeable and unrecognizable from a distance.

Each morning she watched as Adam and the children left for work and school. An hour later, she watched as Luce got into her car and drove to Sherbrooke Street to her gallery where she spent most of the day. Claire got into the habit of parking the rental car and walking the sidewalk around the gallery to see if she could observe the activity inside. When she was out walking the street she donned a business jacket and let her hair loose so that she would blend in with the shoppers and business persons who made up the pedestrians on the upscale street.

One lunch time, as she was standing across from the gallery lost in a reverie of concentration, a voice interrupted her thoughts.

"Claire, what a nice surprise. What are you doing here? You looked as if you were ten miles away in your thoughts."

Startled, Claire looked up into the smiling face of Adam. Her heart stopped for a moment, and she had to swallow hard to force a smile on her face. She felt as if she was going to faint, so put her hand out on his arm for support.

"I... oh, I was just on my way to an appointment, and stopped to... make a phone call. I was thinking about what I was going to say on the call when you came up," she stuttered.

"What a wonderful surprise to see you in the middle of the day. I was just going to meet Luce for lunch. You will remember that her gallery is just across the road."

As they talked about the gallery and the children, Claire looked into Adam's eyes. He could not hide his feelings from her, and she knew for certain that he was still very much in love with her. She was convinced that she was doing the right thing trying to persuade him to come back to her, and only her.

"I can't invite you to join us for lunch. I think you understand that, but I am pleased to see you again, especially after our last time together. Are you sure that you are fine?" asked Adam.

"Yes, I am, and I do understand why we cannot lunch together today."

"Adam," a voice called from across the street. They both looked up and saw Luce standing outside the gallery waving at them.

"I must go," apologized Adam. "Keep well, my dear." He turned and crossed the street to join his wife, looking back to wave farewell to Claire.

Luce had come out of the gallery and seen her husband in conversation with Claire. She saw the woman's hand on his arm and she felt jealous anger growing. What was that woman doing here? Why was she right in front of her gallery with her husband? She was beginning to think that the affair was over. Obviously, they are still seeing each other. That has to be taken care of, she thought, as she waited for her husband to join her.

Claire watched, frozen to the spot as Adam joined his wife; as he kissed her gently on the cheek and together they walked away arm in arm. She had not realized that following Luce would cause her to feel so much pain; but this morning had reinforced her need to trail the woman and devise a way to remove her from her lover's life.

Chaos

I do not know myself, and God forbid that I should.
Johann Wolfgang von Goethe

Claire's life had become one of out-of-control chaos. She had always been a methodical person who liked her life to be predictable, ordered, and moving forward smoothly. At a very young age she had learned to plan well, to foresee possibilities in life; and this habit had made her very successful at almost everything she did. Her father had taught her the management skills that had made him a successful business man; rise early, plan well, execute thoroughly, and enjoy your successes. These learned skills had stayed with her after his death, and had proved their worth in her life. Her father would have assured her that she 'had life by the tail'.

Now she found that none of those skills worked. She was not sleeping well. She still woke early, but was exhausted when she tried to get her body moving in the morning. She was still planning, but she was not planning work related projects. All her thoughts and energy were now focused on a very negative issue. She did not know how she would ever be able to execute the plan she was working on. She felt as if everything she ever knew and believed in had suddenly left her.

Her distraction at work had not gone unnoticed. Nathalie kept asking if she was feeling well, or if she was ill. Avery had called her to his office and asked if she was seeing a doctor for her condition. Her condition? She had smiled. If only he knew what her condition was, he would be appalled.

She was going through the motions of life; eating, sleeping, waking, dressing. But most of the time she felt like an automaton, moving like a robot. She tried to concentrate on the purpose she had set herself, but there was no joy in what she was doing.

When she looked at herself in the mirror she could not believe that it was herself who was reflected back at her. She would stare at her image and wonder who the woman was who looked so hollow-cheeked and pale.

How did this get to be me? she wondered. How did I arrive at this place in my life? I know that sometimes good people do bad things, but not me. Am I still a good person? I don't know anymore. I don't know who I am or what I've become. This obsession has eaten into my very soul; it has been sold to the devil in my pursuit of this man.

But how can I live without him? Do I have the strength to move on alone? What if I have to, and he will never be with me again?

Her mind was on a treadmill of negative thoughts. Over and over she raced through reasons for, reasons against, actions to do, actions to avoid. But she never reached a conclusion.

Each night she fell into bed exhausted, only to toss and turn her way through haunting nightmares.

Re-connect

My soul is so knit to yours that it is but a divided life I live without you.
George Eliot

Meeting with Claire so unexpectedly on the street had created turmoil with Adam's emotions. He found that his heart was racing as he watched her walk away down the street, and he had to force himself to look away and wave back to his wife who was waiting for him outside her gallery, watching him and Claire together.

Crossing the street, he took Luce's arm guiltily, trying not to turn his head to see where Claire had gone. He thought that he had solved the problem of wanting two women when he had ended the affair with Claire. For the past weeks he had not seen her or talked with her. He had gone out of his way to focus all his attention on his family and particularly on his wife. They had spent more time together. He visited in the gallery to watch the customers come and go, to see their reaction to her work, and to watch her interact with them.

He was very proud of what she had accomplished, and excited by the new energy and enthusiasm for life that she had brought back from Paris. They were closer now than they had been for a long time, and he was enjoying the rekindled intimacy. They made love frequently, and he was enjoying the sensuality of their togetherness and felt that Luce was appreciating their new-found love life as well.

However, his physical reaction to seeing Claire surprised him more because of his closeness to Luce. He had tried very hard to get the other woman out of his life, so why had he been so stirred by seeing her again, and standing so close to her? He had felt aroused, had wanted to put his arms around her and hold her again, and never let her go. He knew that he had to get those feelings under control again; to put those desires to rest, and focus on his family as he had been doing for the past weeks.

He had turned to Luce, kissed her on the top of her head and walked with her to a local restaurant where they enjoyed lunch together. Luce seemed not to notice that Adam was distracted and she spoke animatedly of an amusing incident that had happened in the gallery that morning.

Sensuous dreams invaded Adam's sleep that night. He saw Claire, naked, lying on the lounger on her back patio. In his dream, she was suffused in sunlight and stretched out languidly, opening her legs as she did so; and she beckoned to him to come to her.

He woke from the dream covered in sweat with an engorged penis. He got out of bed quietly and went to the bathroom where he closed the door. Turning on the shower, he stood under cold water until he could breathe normally again.

Back in bed, he lay awake for the rest of the night, nervous to sleep in case the dream recurred. He was fearful of his reaction and did not want to wake Luce. His mind was a turmoil as he lay there. How was he going to cope with these feelings? He knew that he still desired Claire, and wanted very much to be with her again. Was it possible, he wondered, to continue a relationship with her, and still give his family the attention they deserved? Could he love two women equally and be fair to both of them? He knew that he was being selfishly indulgent, but he was finding it impossible to be without the closeness of Claire. She gave to him so much more than just exciting sexual encounters. There was a depth and strength to her, that Luce did not have. She had business experience that he could share with her, and their discussions were so much deeper and more complex than those he shared with his wife. He had missed this mental and emotional stimulation.

When the phone rang late one night, Claire answered reluctantly. She was not in the mood to talk with someone so late, especially just before she was ready to climb into bed.

"Claire Hardick here," she said sleepily.

"Claire, it's Adam. Is it too late to talk?"

Claire held onto the phone in silent panic. She did not know if she wanted to speak to him or not. Why was he phoning now when he had told her very clearly that he wanted to end the relationship? She had seen him when he was going to meet his wife, so she knew that they were close in their new togetherness. Seeing him accidently on the street had sent her senses reeling. First, there was the intense feeling of guilt that she had been caught trailing his wife; and then there was the intimacy she had felt being so close to him again.

She thought that she'd seen longing in his eyes when he had looked at her, and she was hoping that she had not been mistaken.

Maybe that was the reason for the phone call, she thought. She did not want him to accuse her of following Luce. That would be the end of their relationship and even their friendship. She could not live with that.

"Claire, are you still there?" Adam asked, wondering why there was such a long silence at the other end of the line.

"Yes, Adam, I'm here. I'm just surprised by your call."

"Well, I don't want to upset you, but I had to tell you that, since I saw you outside the gallery, you have been in my thoughts much of the time. I would like to see you again. Do you think that you could meet me for lunch tomorrow or the next day? We can go somewhere private if you like. Please say yes."

Claire's heart was thumping as she listened to his plea. He *did* want to see her again; he *did* want to be with her despite his closeness to his family. She wondered if she could risk meeting him and continue with her plans; but her desire to be with him won.

"Yes Adam, I can meet with you for lunch, but not tomorrow. What about Thursday? Why don't we go to St-Anne-de-Bellevue where we can sit by the side of the lake and still be private."

"Oh thank you. Yes, that's a good idea. I will meet you there on Thursday at noon. I really want to see you again. Please do come."

"I will," she responded, and put the phone back on the receiver.

That night she did not sleep much as she rolled around among the sheets, trying to settle her thoughts.

Her work schedule for the next two days was hectic, which was a good thing, as it kept her from thinking about the lunch meeting. She did not sleep well on Wednesday night, and on Thursday morning dressed with special care. Her outfit of choice was one that Adam had often admired, a short navy skirt with a soft patterned jacket and high-heeled shoes that he always commented were very sexy. She smiled as she wondered why she was doing all this preparation, but in her mind she knew it was to lure him back to her with an attractive appearance. Her freshly washed hair fell softly around her face instead of being tied back as she usually did for work.

She drove to St-Anne-de-Bellevue in a flurry of excitement, trying to stay cool and calm, but her feelings of anticipation were overwhelming.

When she arrived, Adam was already seated at a table close to the water. He rose to meet her and gently touched his lips to her cheek.

"Thank you for coming," he said as his eyes took in her appearance. "You look stunning today, but then you always do to me."

Claire thought that he looked nervous, and that put her on edge as well; waiting to find out what this pre-arranged meeting was going to produce. They both ordered light lunches, and when the waiter had left them alone, Adam looked at her intently.

"How have you been, Claire?" he asked. "You look as if you've lost weight."

"I am well, thank you," she lied.

She was not going to tell him how much she had missed him. How lonely she had been since they had parted. How she was not sleeping or eating well and that she desperately wanted to be back together with him. She could not tell him that she was working on a plan to get him back all to herself. Those things would stay secret from this man whom she loved and would not give up.

"Claire, when we met on the street the other day, I was overwhelmed with emotion. I find that you are with me all day; and at night you are invading my dreams. I wake up in a lather of lust for you. I know that I said good-bye weeks ago, and I really did try to get you out of my life, but I find that I cannot. This may be very unfair to ask, but, could we go back to how we were before? I am a wreck without you in my life. If you can forgive me for the hurt I caused you, I would take you in my arms and show you my need for you. Please Claire, my dearest darling, will you come back into my life?"

The joy that those words gave to Claire shone in her face as she looked back at the man who was pleading for her to agree to do just what she longed to do. What she was planning for and what she hoped would be a relationship that would last forever. This must be a sign that all her research and planning were the right things to be doing. They were meant to be together and now she could continue with her plans with renewed effort.

"Oh, dearest Adam, I have missed you so much, and would love to renew our relationship. We share something very special and it would be cruel to cause so much hurt to both of us. However, we should talk about what our relationship will look like," she prodded.

"I don't know that yet," Adam admitted. "Please let me see you, and I will think of how this will work with my family commitments. I won't let them interfere too much with our time together. I will work it out, but please let me be with you."

His plea was so genuine, and Claire knew that this time she would take away a part of him every time they were together. They agreed that Adam would come to her home the next night after work and they would enjoy time alone with each other again.

Their coming together was everything that Claire had hoped. Adam was conciliatory, and tender. He was determined to make her happy, and he appeared to be delighted to be in her company again. He asked if they could sit out on the patio and then gently pushed Claire down onto one of the lounge chairs.

He looked at her intently. "Claire, I had a dream the other night that sent me into a sweat of desire for you. I want to experience the dream in reality. Will you indulge my fantasy?"

Intrigued by this role-playing of his dream fantasy, she indulged his request with a broad smile on her face.

Adam lowered himself and slowly started taking off her clothing until she was lying on the soft cushion of the chair, fully naked. He looked down at her with dilated pupils and quickly stripped naked himself.

"Claire, please stretch out slowly and raise your arms," he requested.

She did so, languidly twisting her naked body and stretching her arms over her head, running one of her hands over each exposed breast as she did so, Adam let out a groan of desire and lowered himself onto the chair. He pushed her legs apart and entered her with a sigh of complete satisfaction.

"Oh, my darling, I don't know how I ever thought that I could not have you as part of my life."

When their passion was sated, they went into the kitchen where Claire produced a bottle of their favorite wine, the New Zealand Sauvignon Blanc from Martindale. It felt as if they had never been apart.

Stalking

Know what thou canst work at.
Thomas Carlyle

The surveillance of Luce had to continue if Claire was going to understand the woman's life. She was not going to rely on a private detective to do the work for her, so she had to accomplish the surveillance herself. She still had to be cautious about leaving a trail of what she was doing. Any indication that she was stalking the woman would be dangerous if discovered. This was new territory for her and she felt that she had to tread very carefully as she went about everything connected to her plan.

The house watching continued to occupy her time. She went early in the morning, as before, and watched Adam and the children leave. When she noticed that Luce was dressed for work, she tailed her until she saw her arrive at the gallery. That satisfied her that Luce would spend the day at the gallery, as she had observed that routine many times before. She could not risk waiting at the gallery again. Her accidental meeting with Adam, while she was tracking his wife, had been an embarrassment that she did not want to repeat.

Once Luce entered the gallery, Claire drove back home, changed for work, garaged the rental car, and drove her own vehicle to work where she attempted to focus on the issues of the day. She was trying to stay abreast with what was happening in the stock market every day, but was often not focused when she turned her computer on and scanned the screen.

One Wednesday morning, sitting in the car outside the Lambert house, she noticed that Luce came out dressed very differently from her usual elegant style. She was wearing blue jeans, a tee shirt, a casual denim jacket, and her hair was covered with a beret. She wore sunglasses despite an overcast day. Over her shoulder she carried a large black bag.

Claire was alert to the change in routine; she was intrigued. Was Luce going to the gallery just to paint today, and did not want to waste time changing when she got there? Or was she on some other mission today? She obviously was not dressed to meet clients in the gallery in her current outfit.

She watched as Luce got into her car as usual and backed out of the driveway. But, instead of turning right to go downtown, she turned left and drove down the street in the opposite direction. Claire switched on the engine of the rental car and followed, trying to stay inconspicuous.

Luce drove the car down Avenue Atwater, turned left onto Notre Dame Avenue, and then right onto Rue Charlevoix. She parked the car on Centre Street, got out, walked briskly down the street, and disappeared.

Claire quickly found a parking space and hurried after her. When she turned the corner she could not see the woman she was following. Where could she have gone to so quickly? panicked Claire. There was nothing here except – except the Charlevoix Metro Station. She must have gone into the station Claire surmised, and ran to the entrance of the station in time to catch a glimpse of Luce purchasing a ticket and walking towards the station platform. Claire walked quickly to the ticket counter, bought a return ticket and followed Luce onto the platform.

This station was not the most convenient one from the Lambert house, and Claire wondered why Luce had come here instead of going to Atwater Station, which would have been the closest. Maybe it was easier to park here; or maybe she did not want to meet anyone who knew her.

Claire stood back quietly and watched as Luce paced the platform, obviously impatient for the train to arrive. The platform soon became crowded with commuters at this time of the morning. Luce was standing close to the edge of the platform, scanning down the tunnel to see if a train was coming.

Claire, on an instinct borne of desperation, pulled up her collar, put her head down, and walked swiftly to where Luce was standing. She felt the draft of wind from the train in the tunnel, and heard the noise of its approach. If she walked faster she could get to Luce as the train was entering the station.

She was four feet from the woman when a man stepped forward, grabbed Luce by the arm and said in a firm voice, "Madame, vous êtes tout proche le train; c'est très dangereux."

Hearing the voice warning Luce that she was standing too close to the tracks, and seeing her startled face, Claire turned quickly and walked back into the crowd.

She stood at the back of the platform waiting for the train to stop, trying to calm her breathing. She had been one arm's length away from pushing the woman onto the tracks in front of the train. She had been about to commit murder in full view of a platform crowded with commuters. She wondered what had triggered that impulse. It was a spontaneous reaction that she had not planned. When she saw the opportunity, she had been ready to take it.

In a daze, she watched as Luce and the other passengers boarded the train. She stood frozen in her space on the platform. She was too terrified by what she had nearly done to move. Trying to get her mind back into reality, she stood breathing heavily.

A thickly accented voice asked, "Are you owright, mam? You look a mite pale. Can I get something pour vous? Mebbe you should sit down for a while until ya feel better?"

Claire looked up and saw a large black woman at her side. She was wearing a station attendant uniform.

"Thank you," breathed Claire slowly. "I think I am fine now, I just had a strange turn. I was giddy and thought I was going to fall. But thank you. I am really quite fine now."

"Okay then, but take care, you dinna wanna go falling on them tracks now. It's a mite dangerous down there you know."

Claire thanked her, stumbled her way back to the rental car and drove home.

It took a long time for her to stop shaking. The reality of what had almost happened scared and surprised her. Her quick reaction to the situation on the station platform terrified her. Despite all her research and careful planning, she had not known whether she would be capable of doing harm to Luce. The events of the morning replayed over and over in her mind. She imagined Luce falling onto the tracks, she saw the train approaching, she heard Luce scream. Then she witnessed in her mind, her own dilemma, as she was grabbed by the arms and dragged off to a police cruiser waiting outside the station.

In fact, she knew, that is what *would* have happened if Luce had not been pulled back in time. Not only would Luce's life be over, but hers would be as well. She would have been arrested and tried for murder; and her life, as well as her life with Adam, would have been over .

It took weeks for her to recover from the shock of the incident on the station platform.

Her togetherness with Adam was confusing. She tried to relax and enjoy his company and his body in the way that they had always shared. However, she found that she was stiff and awkward, often unable to get the sight of Luce falling onto train tracks from her mind.

Then she would look at Adam, melt into his arms, open up to his passion, and her resolve to be with this man alone, to have him to herself, was renewed.

These thoughts spurred her courage to go back to the Lambert house. She chose to go on a Wednesday morning, as that had been the day of the week that Luce had deviated from her usual routine. What if she had found something unusual in Adam's wife's life that she was keeping secret? Continuing to follow her could prove her suspicion true.

Consequently, she found herself waiting down the road from the Lambert house on a rainy Wednesday morning, watching Adam and the children leave. When Luce appeared dressed in the same casual clothing that Claire had seen her in before, she guessed that she had in fact been correct in her suppositions.

Again, she watched as Luce backed out of the driveway, drove to Charlevoix Metro Station, parked and walked into the station. This time Claire was alert to her routine, and was parked before Luce got out of the car.

Her ticket was bought, and she was waiting for Luce as she came down the escalator to wait for the train. Luce entered a packed passenger train car, and Claire followed. She kept to the opposite end of the car, but in a position where she could see where Luce was sitting. Claire stood, as she wanted to be ready to exit when she saw Luce move to leave the train.

They rode together for many stops and Claire wondered where Luce was going. They passed McGill Station and Place des Artes Station where she thought Luce would exit. However, she continued to sit in her seat as the train stopped at Beri-UQAM, Beaudry, Papineau, Frontenac, Préfontaine and Joliette. Claire was beginning to get concerned as passengers were exiting from the car at each stop, and there were very few left in the train car with her and Luce. She moved to the very end of the car and stood quietly, looking away from the woman she was following, but trying to keep her focused in her peripheral vision.

When she saw Luce move to get up and prepare to exit at the next station stop which was Pie-IX she was ready. This is very unusual, thought Claire, as she rose slowly to stand at the last door in the car to leave as well. She left the train with Luce, walking well behind her, but slowly so as not to attract attention.

Luce exited the station, turned left and walked three blocks down the road. Then she turned right and entered a street with many commercial outlets.

Following her, Claire saw her stop in front of a small service garage for automobiles. She stopped to speak with an elderly man dressed in work coveralls, who was rubbing down a car parked in the driveway. She shook his hand. The man gestured to the entrance of the garage, and they both disappeared into the service area.

Claire stood back, watching the exchange between the two, and was more perplexed than before. She wondered whether Luce was doing a series of paintings of workmen, and was using the mechanic as a subject. Maybe she was preparing for a special show, she thought. This would be something very different from her usual work, but Claire knew that Luce liked to push the edges of her art, and this new subject matter could be intriguing to her. She had noticed that Luce had been carrying a bag, but surmised that it was not large enough to contain all the necessary art supplies for a portrait. She could however, be making sketches only, which would mean that she would not require much in the way of supplies. If she *was* doing an art project, why would she not have driven here in her motorcar so that she could bring as much as she wanted in the way of art materials? The entire scenario was baffling to Claire as she waited on the sidewalk about twenty yards down from the garage.

She paced up and down, trying to appear interested in what was available in the neighbouring businesses. Finally, after half an hour, she went to a small café and sat down to pass the time with a cup of coffee. She was becoming too conspicuous on the street with her restless pacing.

She sat and mused about the entire exercise. It appeared to her that Luce was trying to hide this activity; that she was doing something very secretive in that car garage. Maybe Luce and the mechanic could be having an affair. The man had looked to be much older than Luce, but that would not deter some women. However, Luce was married to Adam, a handsome, young, virile man. So why would she want to have a sexual relationship with someone like the mechanic she had seen her with? It was not plausible. There could be a much younger, more attractive man in the back of the shop, but Claire felt that this was not the explanation either.

As she sat staring into space deep in thought, she suddenly saw Luce walk past the front of the cafeteria and head for the metro station. Claire quickly left a large note on the table to pay for the coffee and followed her into the station. Luce went through the turnstile and down the escalator to the train platform. She got onto the next train headed south where she sat quietly until the train stopped at the Charlevoix Station. She left the train, exited the station, got into her car and drove away.

Claire exited the train at the same time and watched her get into her car and drive off. She did not follow, as she suspected that Luce was on her way home and nothing would be gained by trailing her to the house.

As Claire drove home she was deep in thought, having no idea what she had just witnessed, other than to know that Luce had a secret that she did not want anyone to know.

To satisfy her curiosity she prodded Adam with questions about where they got their cars serviced. None of them went anywhere near the garage that Luce had visited. Claire also asked casually if Adam knew what projects Luce was currently working on, and he described the large semi-abstract landscapes that were capturing all Luce's time and artistic creativity.

All these answers negated the possible solutions that she had thought of, so Claire let the matter rest. She decided that it was a mystery that she would probably never be able to solve, unless she went to the garage and questioned the mechanic himself. This she obviously could not do, so she let the mystery remain a mystery.

Plotting

*He who does evil that good may come,
pays a toll to the devil to let him into heaven.*
Augustus William Hare

After all the weeks of trailing after Luce, Claire still tried not to think of this activity in terms of stalking. She concluded that there had to be a more convenient way to accomplish what she was planning. There had to be a more private way, a closer to home method. She was beginning to understand the daily routines of Adam's wife, but their life at home together was a mystery to her.

A good look at the Lambert home could offer some possible clues to this aspect of their lives, she reasoned. She had to get into their home and explore their privacy, as distasteful as it seemed to her.

Even if she managed to get into the house, what would she do there? Knowing what their lives were like did not help in her quest to get rid of Luce. When she thought of the woman, she tried not to think of her as Luce, or as Adam's wife, but just as *the woman*. It seemed to keep her at a distance, to make her a prey, rather than someone close to her.

Her mind kept thinking of ways one could use to get rid of people one did not like. She refused, in her thoughts, to use the word 'kill', but she knew that was what she was planning. What did she know about methods of dying? An accidental death was what she was searching for. After the scare at the subway station, she reasoned that she would not be able to physically kill Luce. She needed to find a way in which the woman could die an accidental death; but an accident that could never be traced back to her, Claire.

She toyed with the idea of poisons. How she could ensure that Luce ingested a dose of some poisonous substance. She explored this possibility with great caution as she could not accidently cause harm to Adam or the children as well. She would have to find out if Luce took any medications that the others never touched. The only way to find out would be to get into the house and search it for clues.

A television documentary caught her attention and provided some of the answers she was looking for. She listened to a commentary on the dangers of certain drugs, and the high incidence of death from doses of medications prescribed by doctors. These included painkillers such as oxycodone and fentanyl.

Claire sat up, alert, and wondered how available these and other drugs could be. She had not thought of this possibility, and wondered whether Luce took any medications that could be confused with strong painkillers.

The next few days found Claire sitting at a computer in an internet café doing research. Using her personal or office computer was too risky as these could be traced back to her. Dressed casually, so as not to attract attention, she frequented internet cafés that were distant from her residence.

She explored information on doctor prescribed painkillers first. There she found that oxycodone, a semi-synthetic opioid that was similar to morphine, could cause death in overdoses. The other commonly prescribed painkiller was phenethylamine. She read that doctors usually prescribed very low doses of these tablets, 5 mg, but that they were available in tablets with doses as high as 120 mg, and that these were purple in colour – very noticeable.

The internet also listed a host of other dangerous street drugs such as cocaine, LSD (known as acid), and MDMA, a pure form of ecstasy. All of these, she read, could increase the heart rate and blood pressure to the point of heart failure. Many of them caused respiratory failure as well.

The internet stated that cocktails of the drugs were the most dangerous. Mixtures of drugs such as painkillers, anti-anxiety drugs and or sleeping pills were very dangerous. These included RX combinations with painkillers and sleeping pills; or oxyContin, Xanax and alcohol. Such a concoction had killed the actor, Heath Ledger and possibly even the singer, Prince.

Claire found that the information she was gathering from her research was mind-boggling. She could not believe that, with all this information available, people still experimented with a host of these drugs. And they paid huge sums of money to get access to them.

There were more exotic drugs, she found, that were just as, or more dangerous, than those available on the street. These included drugs such as crystal meth, a very destructive drug that caused brain and blood vessel damage.

There was ketamine, an anesthetic and pain control substance. A fatal dose of this could kill in minutes by causing respiratory and heart failure. She found out about the Russian addiction, Krokodil, that was more dangerous than heroin; mainly because it was often home-made and included substances such as iodine, lighter fluid and industrial cleaning agents.

As Claire sat and absorbed all this information, she was horrified at the number of very dangerous drugs that were available; and how easily one could access them if one was desperate. She discovered that the internet was a pharmaceutical candy store for these drugs. As long as one had access to funds, they were available without any questions asked.

She went home from these research outings feeling very depressed by the dangers that lurked on the internet for vulnerable teenagers or those who were emotionally vulnerable.

Stealth

The searcher's eye
Not seldom finds more than he wished to find.
Gotthold Ephraim Lessing

Having decided that she needed to explore the Lambert house for possible answers to her problem, Claire planned on how to gain access to the house. This presented her with two challenges. Firstly, she had to find an entrance, and secondly, she could only explore the house when there was no one in it.

Getting in, the first problem, was probably the easiest. She could not see herself skulking around the house to find an entrance through a window or worse still, breaking a window or glass door to gain entrance. The easiest way for her to get in was to get possession of a key, and the only one she could possibly get was going to have to be Adam's house key.

She knew that he kept many of his keys together on one key ring. When he came to her house, he usually put the keys on the table in the hall so that they were within easy reach for him when he left. However, there were numerous keys on the key ring, and she could not be sure which one was the house key. The car key and the house key had to be on the same key ring she surmised. She had looked briefly at the bunch, but could not decide which key was the one she wanted. He would have to tell her himself.

One evening after he arrived, he placed the keys on the entrance table as usual. Seeing him do this, she leaned forward to kiss him in greeting, and ran her hand over the keys, knocking them onto the floor.

"Oh dear, wow, what a bunch of keys you have here, Mr. Jailer. Come in and tell me what they all open. You must have some secret hideaways somewhere for sure," and she walked into the kitchen carrying the keys.

Laughing, Adam followed her. He sat at the bar counter and took the keys from her as she prepared drinks, while watching him identify the keys on the ring.

"Well, my darling, here is the mystery solved. This, as you can see, is the key to my car. Alongside, is the key to the door from the garage into the house. On the other side is the key to my office at work, as well as the key to the records room at work, a very secret place. This large one is the key to our offices at work for when I work late. And finally, in the middle, this Yale lock key, is the key to my home. Does that satisfy your curiosity?"

"Well, I suppose so," responded Claire, making a special note of which key he had identified as the key to his house. "No great secret hideaways there. You are just an open book."

Later, when Adam excused himself and went to the bathroom, she took the key ring and separated the house key from the others. Taking the key she pressed it into the bar of soft soap that she had left at the side of the sink for this purpose. The impressed soap she hid in a drawer.

Her feelings of guilt stayed with her during Adam's visit. She begged tiredness and asked him to leave early. He was surprised and disappointed, but left her alone. She was feeling very uncomfortable about how she had to lie to the man she loved. She tried to rationalize that she was acting in his interest, even if he did not know what she was doing.

Not wasting any time to get the deed done, the next day she visited a key cutter with the impressed bar of soap and requested that a key be cut from the impression.

"What's with you, lady?" the store owner replied. "You know that they only do this in movies and on television. It's extremely difficult to cut a functioning key from an impression like this. I can try for you, but you may have a lot of difficulty opening the door with a key cut from an impression. Why don't you just bring in the real key and I'll cut a perfect one for you? What happened here? Are you going to rob your boss or something?" he joked.

Affronted and feeling quite uncomfortable, Claire tried to look the man in the eye and give an answer.

"Actually, it's none of your damn business why I need the key cut from an impression. For all you know, this may be part of a complicated game my friends and I are playing. You need to learn not to question your customers. Give the soap back to me, and I will find someone else to do the job that you cannot, or will not do for me." And, taking the soap from the startled man, she walked out of the shop.

Back in her car she found that she was breathing heavily. Oh Lord, what have I done? she thought. He will remember me now if there are any repercussions. Why did I not just let him try, and then toss away the useless key? I can't have a key that may not work or that will require maneuvering in the lock. If I get to the house, I will have to get in and out very quickly, so the key has to be a perfect fit. All these thoughts raced through her mind as she decided to give up on the exercise that was not going to work for her.

This still left her with the key problem. She would now have to get the original key off Adam's key ring and take it to a key cutter in order to have a duplicate cut. Or, she could just use Adam's key once she had removed it. When she imagined herself standing at the front door of his home with his own key, opening the door to his house, she knew that she would not be able to do it that way; the deceit she already felt would be magnified. If she *was* going to intrude, she would have to do it with a key that she had made for herself. The duplicity of her logic was baffling, but that was how her conscience was working these days.

On Adam's next visit to her house, she contrived a way in which to remove the key from his key ring. When she noticed that Adam had not left the key ring on the hall table, she figured that they had to be in his jacket, thrown over the couch in the den.

"Darling, why don't you pour drinks for us and we can take them out to the back patio while there is still some warmth and light," she suggested.

"Your every wish is my command," replied Adam, giving her a warm kiss on the back of her neck. "What is your pleasure, Madam?"

"I think I'll have a cold white wine. There is an excellent bottle of New Zealand Sauvignon Blanc in the fridge, the one from the Martindale vineyard. I was there a few years ago and was delighted with this wine. Join me if you like; I think it may be to your taste as well."

"Sounds good to me. I'll get the wine, you bring your gorgeous body so that I can sip the wine and lust after you," responded Adam as he rolled his tongue lasciviously over his lips.

Claire pushed him in the direction of the kitchen as she walked into the den. When she heard the fridge door open and Adam taking down glasses from the cabinet, she stuck her hand into one of the side pockets of the jacket on the couch. It took searching through three pockets before she found the keys in an inside pocket. Pulling out the bunch of the keys, she identified the house key, and using her fingernails opened the wire closing the ring. She took the key off the ring and left the ring slightly open, returning the rest of the bunch to the pocket of the jacket. She hoped that, with the ring not properly closed he would think that the key had slipped off by accident. Guiltily she joined her lover on the back patio.

"Cheers, my dear, this wine looks good. Here's to us and the good times we share together."

Claire raised her glass and took a long swallow of the mellow wine. She tried to relax as she sat back in the lounger to enjoy his company.

Adam looked at her lying on the lounge chair and came to kneel at her side.

"You look like a goddess lying there, waiting to be worshipped by her adoring fans. And this fan definitely adores every inch of your sensuous body." He leaned over and took the wine glass from her hand putting it on the side table. Leaning over he kissed her deeply on the lips and opened her mouth with his tongue, forcing her to respond to his advances.

Feelings of guilt suffused Claire. How could she respond to this man whose property she had just stolen? She opened her mouth and felt his tongue exploring her mouth hungrily.

His hand pushed under her sweater and found her breast, cupping it, caressing the nipple. She felt herself stiffen and tried to push his hand away, but he mistook the gesture, and took her hand and placed it between his legs encouraging her to feel his growing ardor. He was now obviously very aroused and she allowed herself to relax into his sexual energy.

It was the next day that Adam called to ask if he had dropped a key at her house as he could not get into the house the night before and had to wake Luce to open the door for him. He could not understand how the key had come off the ring. He'd noticed that the ring had not been properly closed, and he supposed that he had been careless and not closed it firmly enough.

Claire said that she would look around the house and driveway, and lied that she had not seen anything. That afternoon she took the key to a key cutter. She selected a different store so as not to arouse suspicions from the man she had been so rude to. She had a duplicate key cut at a small keyhole store in a side street just off Rue Montagne.

That night she took Adam's original key and dropped it into the side of the garden where Adam would find it on his next visit. Which he did, feeling quite perplexed, but pleased to have the key back in his possession.

Now that she had a means of entry into the Lambert house, Claire's next challenge to solve was *when* to get into the house. It had to be when the house was empty, and that was going to be a lot more difficult than stealing the house key. She prodded Adam about the family's movements. What time the children came home from school? What time the housekeeper arrived and left? Adam was amused by her interest in his family's life.

"It's all part of your life, and I want to know everything I can about the life you live when you are not with me. It's like you have all these secret things going on around you that I have no part of. So this is my way of trying to identify with them."

Adam smiled, kissed her, and gave her the information she wanted to know.

A phone call solved her problem.

"I won't be able to see you tomorrow, darling," said Adam's voice-mail on the phone. "We are going to give the girls a treat. It's Juliette's birthday next week so we're taking them to see *The Lion King* on stage. Being a Friday evening works well for us as the girls can sleep in the next morning. They are very excited about it. I will call you sometime on Saturday and we can figure out something to do together this weekend. Hope you're not disappointed. I love you."

Claire listened to the message on her cell phone. He had not mentioned the night out with the girls before, so she assumed that it had been a last minute surprise. Or maybe Luce had bought the tickets some time ago and surprised even Adam. Luce had really been working hard at proving that she was the perfect wife and it was making Claire nervous. She could feel Adam moving closer to his family and finding less and less time to be with her.

She needed to do something soon if she was going to turn things around, and maybe tomorrow night would be a good time to do some delving into the other possibilities that she had been contemplating.

Searching

Through the unknown, we'll find the new.
Charles Baudelaire

Friday night turned out to be cool and cloudy. Low clouds hung over the city, foretelling an early fall season. They provided a perfect cover to hide secret activities by someone trying to enter a property illegally, especially when the property was vacated by the residents.

Claire prepared for the task ahead. This was the opportunity she had been waiting for. The house would be empty. Someone moving about would go undetected.

Her preparation was meticulous. Making sure that all her clothing was tight fitting, she chose black tights, a snug black turtle-neck sweater, and a black toque for her head. A waist pouch around her middle held the front door key, snug cotton gloves, a flashlight, a pack of wet-wipes, and a small zip-lock plastic bag. On her feet she wore soft-soled runners. Standing back to look at herself in the mirror, she tried to imagine working at the tasks to come and could see no difficulties. Her heart was racing, and she was breathing heavily.

I feel like a criminal, she thought, looking at her reflection. I *look* like a criminal. Is this really me? Am I really going to break into someone else's home? But how can I not, when I have come so far? Her eyes responded to her questions with a steely gaze. Tucking her hair under the toque she left the house.

The rental car again provided her with a cover as she drove to the Lambert's street. The house was still bright with lights shining throughout, so she drove around the block and came back down on the other side of the street. Parking a few doors down from the house, she sat quietly in the car and waited. Adam's car was parked in the driveway. At seven o'clock the front door of the house opened and the two young girls came skipping out. Obvious excitement about the evening's treat showed in their movements, as they danced about the car waiting for their parents. Both were dressed in brightly coloured velvet dresses with wraps around their shoulders. Then Luce appeared, dressed very elegantly in a dark crimson evening suit, followed by Adam who stopped to lock the front door. He joined his family in the car, backed slowly out of the driveway, turned, and drove off down the street. None of them had given a glance in the direction of the dark grey Honda parked in front of a house some way down the road.

Claire watched as the car drove away and disappeared from view. She looked at her watch; it was just seven o'clock. She estimated that it would take the family at least twenty-five minutes to get downtown, to the Place des Arts, and more time to park and get into their seats. She did not want to risk the chance that they would return for something that had been forgotten. She sat quietly in the car, her heart thumping, and waited until it was ten minutes to eight.

It was time to move. She glanced first in the rear view mirror, then checked the side mirrors, and finally swivelled around to look in both directions. Nobody was in sight on the street. She took the pair of gloves out of her waist pouch and pulled them on. Taking out the duplicate house key, she held it firmly in her right hand. With a deep breath, she opened the car door, and stepped out.

Walking up the driveway quickly, she inserted the key into the front door lock. It turned easily and she let out a deep breath; Adam had not changed the locks when he'd misplaced his key. Now she was very relieved that he had not.

Entering the house, she turned and closed the door quickly, leaving it unlocked in case she had to make a quick exit. She stopped in the hallway to catch her breath. She was warm. Her blood felt on fire and she was trying to still her rapid breathing. The atmosphere in the house felt as if it was closing in around her and she gulped to fill her lungs. The family had left a few lights burning and these offered a soft glow filtering through the house.

This was Adam's space. This was where he lived, where he slept, where he ate, where he played with his children, where he made love to his wife. How was it that she was here, in *their* space? Why had she come? Her thoughts overwhelmed her, and turning, she moved back to the front door. Putting her hand out she steadied herself on the heavy wooden frame. A picture of Adam relaxing on her bed filled her mind. Yes, he belonged in her home as well. Why could he not? That was why she was here. She had come this far, and now she needed to finish what she had started.

Steeling her will, she retraced her steps and stood still, getting her bearings. The living room opened off on her right. Down the hall in front of her was the entrance to the kitchen. She could see right through to the glass doors leading out to the back deck and garden. To her left a passageway led to other rooms, and a curved staircase led upstairs. She stood still and took in the layout.

Slowly she walked through the house, stopping into each room briefly to look around. She started in the living room that was very elegantly furnished. Floral chintz love seats sat on a large Aubusson floor rug, and two pale green wingback chairs flanked a marble fireplace. She could see the hand of Luce in the room. With a shake of her head to clear the thought, she moved through an archway that led to the dining room. She moved quietly through the room with its mahogany table and sideboard, and into a large kitchen with adjoining family room at the rear of the house. Evidence of a hurried meal sat on the cluttered kitchen table, and soiled dishes were stacked in the sink. Claire's first instinct was to tidy up for them, and she had to shake her head to refocus on the reason she was in this house. It was definitely not to help this family with its chores.

Moving carefully into the den she found evidence of the children's half-finished homework; books left open on the table and couch. These brought a smile to her lips as she looked around at all the signs of the family and their life together. The house had a very elegant style that reflected Luce's artistic taste, but still retained a comfortable, warm feeling. It looked like a house that the family enjoyed living in. Strewn around the room were books, knitting, drawings, dolls' clothes. All signs of family life.

Down the hallway she stopped at a bedroom door. It appeared to be a guest bedroom as there was no evidence of personal items. Moving into the room she went to the window and checked the latches. These she found easy to unlatch and leave unfastened, which she did. This, she reasoned, could provide a possible exit if she was disturbed and could not exit quickly through the front door.

Leaving the room with a last glance, she moved quietly back down the corridor. When she reached the hallway, she stopped and listened for any sounds of activity around the house. Were the neighbours coming to check on who was inside? Had her entrance to the house been noticed? Only stillness answered her concerns.

And so she climbed the stairs to the upper level of the house. Two short passages led away from the landing. She turned right and walked past two bedrooms. These were obviously the children's rooms. There were clothes heaped on the bed on one room; she suspected that it was Michelle's room. She must have had difficulty deciding what to wear, Claire mused; just your typical little girl going out for a big night. The other room, Juliette's, was spotless. She is always so precise with everything she does, Claire thought; just the opposite of her sister. How well I know these girls already.

The other hallway led to double doors that opened into the master suite. She froze in the doorway. This was a very intimate space. This was the room in which she had to share Adam with his wife. She could not even think of her name; her brain was becoming numb. She could not allow herself to get close to this woman with her thoughts; because what she was about to contemplate would not allow for such thoughts. She glanced at the bed, noting which side of the bed appeared to be Adam's. A ski magazine was on the night table and a tie lay across the corner of the bed.

Very slowly she moved to the side of the bed and gently touched the pillow. She leaned down and drew in his scent. Instantly, Adam was with her, she could feel his arms around her and his head close to hers. She straightened up and quickly rearranged the pillows, hoping that they were in the same position as before. With renewed resolve she moved to the other side of the bed; the wife's side. She looked at the bedside table but there was nothing there but a French novel. She opened the drawer in the night table and realized that it was too dark to take in details.

Switching on the small flashlight she had brought with her, she carefully shone it into the drawer. It contained a small box of tissues and a roll of breath mints. There were no medications. She looked at the pillows on which Luce put her head. Running her gloved hand over the surface of the covering fabric she tried to feel their thickness. She tested their weight, wondering whether a pillow of this density would be firm enough to suffocate an adult. If the adult were drugged, with some substance such as acetone, it could possibly be accomplished. She picked up the top pillow, bunched it into her hands and pressed down hard onto the bed. She could feel the resistance of the pillow's softness on the bed. Gulping, she suddenly dropped the pillow, shook her head and walked away.

At the bedroom door she stopped and glanced back at the bed and blanched. How stupid. I cannot afford to be this careless. I have to be very aware of everything I do, everything I touch. Her thoughts were in a turmoil. She returned to the side of the bed, picked up the pillow, fluffed it up between her hands and gently placed it back into position alongside the pillow on which Adam rested his head.

Seeing the two pillows next to each other on the bed, tears began to well in her eyes. Shaking her head to refocus her thoughts, she moved purposefully into the en-suite bathroom. Carefully she opened one of the drawers in the counter. She found that they contained jars of creams, lotions, colour foundations, blushes with brushes, and other facial products.

Another drawer contained shaving needs including after-shave creams. This had to be Adam's personal drawer she thought as she lifted each item out gently and replaced it in the same spot. Everything she touched had to be returned to exactly the same position as before, and she was trying to be very careful.

In one small side drawer she found two bottles of prescription medications; one of Lipitor, a medication to control high cholesterol that she was familiar with. The other was labelled Lisinopril. She looked at the label for a long time trying to remember if she had ever heard of the medication. Both of them had *Mrs. Lambert* typed on them, together with directions for ingestion. Claire contemplated the two medications and was surprised that Luce needed them. Maybe it was the rich French diet she had been raised on, she thought. Then she remembered that Adam had told her that his wife went on medication after the death of their son. This had to be the one.

Being very careful, she opened her hip pouch and pulled out a small notepad onto which she copied the information from each bottle. Opening the containers, she extracted two capsules from each, and carefully put the four pills into the plastic bag she had brought, and returned it, with its contents, to her pouch. The bottles she replaced in the drawer. She completed her search of the bathroom by having a final quick check in the cupboards and other drawers. But she had found what she had come to find.

Walking slowly back down the hallway and then down the stairs, she returned to the kitchen. She opened cupboards and drawers, looking for the possibility of vitamin pills, or further prescription medications. There were children's chewable vitamins in one cupboard, but no further prescription bottles, or adult vitamin tables. These she realized would be too risky to tamper with as Adam may take them as well. The capsules from the bottles in the bathroom were a much surer bet.

There was one part of the house that she had not yet entered. She had seen the room's entrance door on her way through the kitchen; the entrance to Luce's art studio. Curiously, she walked to the door, opened it, and switched on the light. The first thing she noticed on entering the room was an enormous canvas resting on an easel at one end of the room. It was a half painted portrait of a man with his head turned away from the viewer. Claire walked up to the easel slowly and studied the portrait. As she stared, she saw Adam's face appear. Luce was painting a large portrait of her husband. Gulping, Claire stepped forward and peered closely at the painting again. This was the man they both loved and desired. She wished that she had the talent that his wife had; the ability to be able to capture his image, stroke by stroke, in this wonderful work. She stood and gazed at the outline of her lover for a long time.

Finally she turned away and started to leave the studio when her attention was caught by two small canvasses, unframed, hanging on one of the walls. They were delicately detailed portraits of each of the girls. They smiled back at Claire as she admired their likeness. She thought about Luce, spending time in the studio, working on a large portrait of her husband, and being watched by these two lovely faces from their canvas homes. This was not the image Claire wanted to take from the house with her. This experience was too painful. She felt hollow and lost. She began to shake and was having difficulty breathing. She turned again and looked at the half-finished portrait of the man she loved.

She had to get out of the house so that she could breathe again. Walking swiftly through the entrance hall to the front door she stopped and glanced back. She had found out all she could for now. This house was full of joy; but only searing pain for her.

Opening the front door slowly she glanced out to check the street. No activity was apparent, so she locked the door and walked down the driveway, got into the car and drove slowly away, hoping not to attract attention.

Perspiration soaked through her clothing as she drove. She was breathing heavily. This had not happened during her movements through the house; now she felt as if she had just run ten kilometres. Shaking badly, she had difficulty controlling the steering wheel of the car; her vision was blurring.

I must be having some sort of shock reaction, she thought. I behaved like a thief. No, worse than a thief; more like a criminal and my body is reacting to what I have just done.

Concentrating as hard as she could on the road, and steering rigidly, she managed to drive back to her house without causing any damage to herself or other cars on the road. She climbed out of the car on shaking legs and stumbled up to her front door, letting herself in. She made straight for the kitchen where she was violently sick into the kitchen sink. She clung to the edge of the counter as reality struck. Tonight she had actually taken a major step towards planning to kill someone. In a daze of disbelief at her own actions, she stumbled towards the bedroom where she fell onto the bed.

Light was shining in through the window when the telephone woke Claire the next morning. Lying very still she listened to it ringing. Her body was leaden, and her tongue felt swollen and dry. She heard the ringing stop and a voice leaving a message.

The voice said, "Good morning, my love, how are you on this bright sunny morning? I would love to see you today, so give me a call when you get in. I assume you've gone to the gym, or for a jog, so I'll catch up with you when you get back. We all had a wonderful time at the show last night. The girls were very excited, and managed to stay awake during the entire show. 'Bye, talk to you later."

Claire lay and listened to the voice she loved. The voice that belonged to the man that she wanted to be with forever, but could not be. This was the man who created these feelings of desperate need within her. The man whose portrait she had seen being painted by his talented wife.

Her thoughts were confused. I am obsessed by this feeling and this need. I don't understand who I am any more. I am slowly becoming someone I don't know, and don't like; but I cannot help myself. What would I call that? It is more than an obsession. He has become an addiction for me; like heroin. I cannot believe that I have spent weeks planning to kill his wife just to be with him.

It seemed like a game I was playing with myself. If I did commit this act, what would happen? Last night it became more than a game. I actually took action. In premeditated cold blood, I carefully went through her things to find her Achilles heel. How could I have taken that vital step, so that the thought was no longer just a thought in my head, but a plan I was putting into action with my deeds?

Slowly she rolled off the bed and, in a daze, walked into the bathroom. Turning on the water, she stepped into the shower and stood under the steaming spray, still clad in all the clothes from the night before.

She had to cleanse everything; every piece of clothing, including the hat and shoes that had been part of her dreadful plan. She undid the pouch from her waist, pulled the contents out one by one and dropped them onto the floor of the shower. The plastic pack with the capsules she threw into the sink to deal with later. Everything was soaked. Carefully she peeled off the wet clothing, and dropped the pieces in a heap onto the shower floor.

Standing naked, she scrubbed her flesh until her entire body was red and ached from the rubbing. She stood for a long time and let the steaming hot water wash over her until she could breathe normally again.

Stepping out of the shower, she dried her hair and body and slipped into a terry cloth dressing gown. In the kitchen, she brewed a pot of strong coffee. Her pounding head she tried to ease by swallowing two extra strength Advil tablets. Taking a large mug of coffee out with her to the back patio, she sat and thought about where her life was now.

She despised what she had become. She had changed so much during the past months. All of this had started with the spilling of a cup of coffee down a man's shirt front. At the start of the relationship, she had felt that she could enjoy his company and the sensual sexual experience. But over the months she had started to care too much. She had, she realized, become totally besotted – maybe even obsessed by this man whom she loved so deeply. She had never believed that a cool-headed woman that she knew she was, could succumb to such passion and such need. She had enjoyed the company of men before, but had never become so deeply entangled in any relationship.

Now she found herself in the strange space; a space where she was actually planning someone's murder to grab what she wanted. She acknowledged that a change had come over her during these many months with Adam.

Moving back into the house she opened the fridge and took out a yogurt. As she spooned the creamy mixture into her mouth, she knew that she could not face Adam today. In fact, she felt that she could not face anyone today; probably not even herself.

Back in the bedroom, she picked up all the wet clothing from the shower floor, tossed them into the dryer and then recovered the plastic bag with the capsules. Opening the bag, she took the capsules out and dropped each one carefully into the toilet. She pushed the flush lever and watched as each of them slowly disappeared down the drain. She flushed the toilet once more to make sure that they had all disappeared.

Walking to the bed, she dropped down onto it. She wanted to disappear into sleep for the day so that she did not have to face herself or anyone else. But sleep eluded her; she lay awake for a long time trying to calm her thoughts. Finally, she gave up, opened the bathroom cupboard and swallowed two over-the-counter sleep aids that relaxed her into a deep sleep, just as the telephone rang again. She slept for most of the day and night, not hearing the constant ringing of the telephone.

Intrusion

*Though a good deal is too strange to be believed,
nothing is too strange to have happened.*
Thomas Hardy

The Lambton household was bubbling with excitement. The girls were in a flutter. Their father had picked them up from school at lunch hour, excusing them from afternoon classes. This had given them an opportunity to have a short nap before sharing an early supper with their parents and then dressing for the evening event.

They were very excited about going to see a real live show on a stage. They chose their clothes very carefully, strewing many discards on their beds and floors before making a final decision. Luce had insisted that they wear dresses for the outing.

"You live in pants and jeans every day; I think you can be elegant for one evening and look like young ladies."

The girls did not even groan at this suggestion, but hurried off to their rooms to explore their wardrobes for something that could be classified as *elegance fit for young ladies*. And they tittered at the expression.

Luce had toyed with the idea of buying new outfits for them, but decided that they would not get enough wear out of more fancy dresses; so she let them choose something for themselves from what they had in their closets. She took the girls into her room and showed them what she was going to wear. They were impressed by the gorgeous outfit she showed them, and went off to their rooms with the challenge of selecting a dress.

However, when it came time to leave both girls appeared in charming dresses and fancy shoes. Luce knew that she had made the right decision to allow them to choose for themselves.

"I think we need to complete those outfits with a pretty shawl for warmth," she said. "Come with me."

She took them to her walk-in closet where she pulled out a number of pashmina shawls and other colourful wraps from which they could select. In delight, each girl found one that they liked and draped it around her shoulders, turning around in front of the mirror to admire their reflection with delighted grins on their faces.

The s t a g e show was a wonderful experience for all of them. The girls were enraptured by the music, the costumes, and the humour.

The clouds of the night before had disappeared by morning, and the autumn sun was making a valiant effort to warm the world below. Luce and Adam were sitting in the kitchen sharing thoughts about the night before, when the girls finally walked sleepily into the kitchen humming a song from *The Lion King* show. Luce was happy as she watched the girls. She felt that it had been a great success to do something like that as a family again. It had been a while since they had all been so close. She was beginning to feel more like Adam's wife these days, and she hoped that he was enjoying the intimacy as well.

The morning was spent putting the house in order again. The girls tidied up the clothing lying around their rooms and Luce insisted that they make a start at getting organized. She wandered through the house, making sure that all was clean and tidy. Feeling a cold draft as she passed the guest bedroom, she walked into the room to check the window. To her surprise, she found that the latch on one of the windows was unlocked and that the window had blown open. Closing the window, she checked to see that the latch was working. Finding that it closed perfectly, she stood and looked at the window and then carefully scanned around the room. She was sure that the windows in this room were only opened when they were expecting visitors, and that had not been the case for some time. She wondered why the latch had been opened, and so checked in the closet and chest of drawers, but found nothing out of place.

She was beginning to have a strong sense that someone could have come into the house through that window the night before while they were out. However, she could not understand how the window had been opened from the outside. She would check with Adam when he came back from his morning jog.

She walked through the living room, the dining room and the kitchen looking for signs of anything having been touched, or was missing. In the master bedroom she stood and looked around. The first thing she checked was the wall safe behind one of the paintings hanging on the wall. She took the picture down, and looked at the safe lock. It looked intact. However, she dialed the combination and opened it. Examining the contents of the safe, she found that all the items appeared to be in the same order as they were usually stored. Papers to one side, her jewellery boxes to the other. No one had been in there. She took out one of the jewelry boxes and opened it. The ruby and diamond brooch that Adam had given her when Juliette was born shone back at her. She sighed remembering how thrilled and touched she had been. It had been a wonderful gesture from the man who had loved her so passionately in those days. She replaced the velvet box, closed the safe, and reset the combination.

She must have been mistaken about the window. Maybe the housekeeper had opened it to air the room and forgotten to close it again. Then she remembered that she had checked the room a week before as a friend from Paris had emailed to say that she was thinking about coming to Montreal to see the art show at the Musée de Beaux Arts. Luce went back to the guest bedroom and looked around again. She knew that nothing had been touched. So, shaking her head in confusion, she went through to her studio, to spend some time working on the portrait of Adam.

Adam returned from his jog a worried man. He had taken his cell phone with him and had tried to call Claire to tell her about the show, and to arrange a time when they could get together either that day or the next day, Sunday. He knew that she always had her cell phone with her and that, if she saw his name on the call display, she would always answer. He hoped that she was not ill. He knew that she would not be upset about his going out last night with the family. She was always understanding about his home commitments. That was one of the things that he loved about her; she was so undemanding of his time.

He left a number of messages for her to call him, each one sounding more urgent than the last. If he did not hear from her by Monday morning he would go to her house and check, to make sure that she was not ill.

That evening, as they were sitting in the den, Luce mentioned the window latch to him.

"I am sure that we always keep that window latch closed as we don't go into that room very often. We don't ever want to forget that it's open. So why is it open now, especially after we have been out for the night?"

"Do you think we had an intruder?" queried Adam.

"I don't know, I've walked through the house and I don't see anything missing or moved. I even opened the safe and checked the contents and everything's there. Maybe I am just being touchy about nothing. But, I did go into that room two days ago to air it out as Simone emailed to say that she may come for a visit. I am sure that I locked the window again, but I suppose one can forget things if one gets busy."

"Of course we can," agreed Adam. "You were probably just excited about Simone's visit, and about taking the girls to the show. You say you haven't noticed anything missing, so there's nothing to get worried about. I am sure we don't have ghosts in the house."

Later that same evening, when Luce went to take her daily tablet of Lipitor she opened the drawer and stopped for a moment. She looked at the bottles carefully. She thought that she always had the Lipitor on the left side, and the Lisinopril on the right side. She always did this so that she did not get them mixed up and take the wrong medication, the wrong amount, or at the wrong time of day. Now they were switched. Really, what with the window latch being forgotten, and now the bottles in the wrong place, she must have been very mixed up yesterday to do two careless things in a row.

She stared at the bottles in the drawer again, and wondered if she had really made an error with the medication that she was always so careful about. Then she opened the other drawers and cupboards in the bathroom, checking each carefully. She opened her clothes closet and checked through her wardrobe. She could not see that anything had been moved or taken.

While she was examining the clothing, Adam came into the room.

"What are you doing? I thought you were going to bed, not checking your outfits," he joked.

Surprised by him, she muttered that she was just thinking about what to wear to another gallery opening later in the week and walked into the bathroom where she moved the pill containers back into their correct position and swallowed the dose she usually took in the evenings.

Lying in bed she tried to think about the strange events. If vandals had come in through the window they would have trashed the house, and thieves would have taken something valuable, but she could not see anything missing. Perplexed and wary, she tried to fall asleep.

Adam sensed that Luce was restless, so he turned to her in the bed and whispered, "Are you still worried about intruders?"

"Maybe I am, but I think I am just being paranoid."

"Would it help if there really was an intruder?" Adam responded softly.

"Oh, no we don't want our privacy invaded!"

"Not even this privacy?" questioned Adam as he ran his hand down his wife's thigh and gently touched her pubic hairs, running one finger between the folds of her private parts.

Luce was surprised, as they had not had intercourse for some time, and now Adam was feeling romantic. She was delighted and felt herself responding to his advances. She turned to face him as she felt his fingers exploring her sudden wetness.

"I welcome that intrusion any time," she whispered back to him, and reached up to touch his face, kiss him, and open her mouth to his response.

They made love slowly and then relaxed in each other's arms. "Are you still nervous about intruders in the house?" Adam asked.

"Well, it depends on who's doing the intruding; some intrusions are more welcome than others. And this one was one most welcome," laughed Luce in response.

They curled up in each other's arms and slept.

Commandments

Thou shalt not covet thy neighbour's... wife...
Bible: Exodus 20:17

Claire sat bolt upright and wondered if she had really called out aloud in the dark, or just imagined it. In the silent aftermath, she listened for any sounds. All she could hear was her own rapid breathing and the throbbing of blood in her ears.

Her body was wet with perspiration, so she pushed the comforter aside and glanced at the bedside clock. It was only five o'clock and the first rays of morning light were working their way through the window. Her head felt as if it had been pounded by a large mallet. Her temples ached, and when she staggered out of bed to the bathroom, the mirror confirmed that her eyes were bloodshot and her skin was pasty. Her hair was plastered onto her head. She opened a drawer and pulled out a bottle of pain killers. Taking out two tablets, she swallowed them with water, hesitated and then took another one. She felt as if she was going to need all the help she could get to make it through the day.

She pulled on a hooded sweat shirt and casual jeans, slipped her feet into brogues and went through to the kitchen where she brewed a pot of strong coffee.

Taking a cup out to the back patio, she sank into a lounge chair, slowly sipping on the dark brew.

As she relaxed in the lounger she looked out at her garden. The sun rose slowly in a burst of red and orange behind the trees along the fence line of the property. A large chestnut tree hung over the fence at the back of the property and several pines ringed the perimeter; together they created a green surround. The dappled shade of the large branches provided cool shade. Under the trees, a natural meadow garden turned from grey to soft yellow as the sun rose in the sky. The unkempt rustic look was pleasing to look at, and the space needed very little care and attention. Bird life was abundant among the trees and garden plants. Watching the birds, and hearing their morning songs, Claire slowly began to unwind. She loved this space at the back of her house. It was her refuge, her place to think, and the privacy cut off the sights and sounds of the city.

As she watched the sunrise of a new day, she felt ashamed of her actions of the night before. It had taken her months of careful planning to devise a plot to rid Adam of his wife, and yet, when it came to the execution of the deed, she found that she lacked the courage. Maybe it was not a lack of courage, but her innate moral fiber that was getting in the way. This thought brought a sense of relief. For weeks she had felt as if she had been walking in the shoes of a stranger, planning and plotting to kill another human being. And she had been prepared to do all this because of her obsession with a man; a man to whom she had no right. He was legally and morally bound to his family. However, this did not stop her from wanting him desperately. So desperately, that she had been prepared to commit murder – or had been planning to do so. She knew that she could no longer even contemplate such an act. And as she sat outside and listened to the birds in the trees, she knew that she would never be able to lose her center, her core again. She heard her father's voice chiding her, 'Always be true to what you believe in, my girl!'

She knew that she had to make sure that she never got to the stage in her obsession where she was being pushed to the edge again. However, it was easier to think that, but far more difficult to do. When she was with Adam her longing became all-consuming and she suspected that she would be lost again.

She needed fresh air to clear her head. Maybe if she took a walk, or even a jog, she would feel better. Her body was feeling so fragile, that she knew she would have to ease into the exercise. Putting on comfortable running shoes, she left the house at a slow jog. Moving took a major effort for her exhausted body, but she pushed herself for three miles, and then slowed her pace to a walk.

She found herself on Avenue des Pins. Turning down University Avenue, she walked a few blocks, head down, trying to catch her breath again. She turned onto St. Catherine Street and joined the Sunday morning strollers. Wandering aimlessly, lost in thought, the sound of singing caught her attention. She looked up, startled from her reverie, and noticed that she was in front of the St. Patrick Basilica. The hymn-singing of the congregation was what she had heard. The quiet, slow melody drew her towards the doors to the church. Hesitantly, she opened them, and walked into the vestibule. The church was full of worshippers, and in the pulpit stood a priest dressed in full Sunday vestments. It was years since she had attended a church service; in fact, she could not remember the last time she had been in a church or a cathedral, other than as a tourist admiring the architecture or the stained glass windows.

Moving quietly to a back pew, she sat down, and waited. A quiet time in a place that was there to provide succour and healing may be just what she needed for a short while. She closed her eyes and listened to the closing of the hymn and the rustle of the congregation settling themselves back onto the pews. The loud voice of the priest startled her and she opened her eyes and looked at him. He was an elderly man with grey hair and a surprisingly unwrinkled face. He had a voice that was clear and calm; that resonated through the building.

"The first reading today is taken from Deuteronomy 5, and I will condense the text in the interest of time," he intoned loudly.

"Moses proceeded to call all Israel and say to them: Hear, the regulation and the judicial decisions that I am speaking in your ears today, and you must learn them and be careful to do them. You must not walk after other gods...

you must keep the commandments of Jehovah your God... that God concluded a covenant with them... saying I am Jehovah your God, you must never have any other gods against my face. You must not make for yourself a carved image any form like anything that is in the heavens above or that is on the earth underneath or that is in the waters under the earth. You must not bow down to them... You must not take up the name of Jehovah your God in a worthless way... Keeping the Sabbath day to hold it sacred... Honour your father and your mother... you must not murder, neither must you steal, neither must you testify to a falsehood against your fellow man, neither must you desire your fellowman's wife, nor selfishly crave your fellowman's house."

The priest looked at those gathered in the pews in front of him for a long while. Then he intoned, "The second reading is taken from the second book of Samuel 11, verse 2."

Looking down at the bible in front of him on the lectern, he read,

"And it came about at the time of evening that David proceeded to rise from his bed and walk about on the rooftops of the king's house, and from the rooftop he caught sight of a woman bathing herself, and the woman was very good in appearance. Then David sent and inquired about the woman and someone said: 'Is this not Bathsheba, the wife of Uriah?' After that David sent messengers that he might take her. So she came in to him and he lay down with her. Later she returned to her house. ... And the woman became pregnant..."

The priest paused, and then continued.

"And now I read from verse 14: *And it came about that David proceeded to write a letter to Joab and send it by the hand of Uriah. So he wrote in the letter, saying, 'Put Uriah in front of the heaviest battle charges, and you men must retreat from behind him, and he must be struck down and die.'*"

The priest closed the bible in front of him. He leaned forward and looked intently at the people sitting in pews in front of him.

"This morning," he said, "I invite you to join with me in examining our lives. To take a look at what we believe, and how these beliefs play out in our daily routines. I am going to use two stories from the bible as illustrations of using guiding principles in our lives. My theme will be – where is your life right now?"

Claire sat in the pew, mesmerized. Did this man know that she was in the church? Did he know that was exactly the question she had been asking herself all morning as she sat in her garden, and as she walked the streets of the city? She watched the priest intently as he continued with his message.

"The two readings from the bible provide the illustrations for us. In the first reading, we have Moses, coming down from Mount Sinai where, in a hail of fire and smoke, God has spoken to the Israelites with a strong message on how to conduct themselves if they are to be true to Jehovah, their God. These ten commandments Moses then chisels into two stone tablets that he places in the Hebrew's Ark of the

Covenant. These are words that God has sent to guide their lives."

He looked out at the congregation and said, "And now I will tie those commandments to our second story of the morning. In the second reading we find one of the central characters of the Old Testament, King David. King David was raised knowing what was written on those tablets in the Ark. In the passage I read, we see an adult King David, the powerful ruler over all the kingdom."

In a quiet voice the priest continued to talk to the congregation, pulling their attention in with his telling of the biblical stories.

"This is the same David, who as a boy, put all fear aside and bravely faced the enemy when no other man would, or could. The Bible tells us a wonderful story of this bravery. Do you remember the story of David and Goliath? When the Philistines sent forth their biggest and strongest man, a veritable giant, and challenged the Israelite army to send out a man to fight him in single-handed combat, they all quaked with fear. Only a young man, David, not quite fully grown, stepped forward and said that he would like to try. He, who was not even a soldier; in fact, he was only the armour bearer for King Saul."

There was a shuffling from the congregation in the pews as the priest continued.

"Yes, you can imagine the reaction from the enemy. They burst out laughing and scoffed at them for sending a boy to do a man's job. But David, probably full of fear, overcame any doubt he had and stepped forward. He looked at the large man facing him, this man called Goliath. What David saw was a man who wore a copper helmet on his head, and was clad in a coat of mail with overlapping scales. The Bible tells us that there were greaves of copper above his feet. I think we can assume that these were metal plates on his sandals. And, the scripture goes on to tell us that he had a javelin of copper between his shoulders. The blade of his spear was made of iron. This giant taunted the Israelite army by saying, 'Give me a man and let us fight together.'"

The priest paused to let the tension in the story of the battle to build up.

"Now, we have all heard this story before," the priest stated, looking down at the congregation. He was sure that he was capturing their attention by telling them details they may never have heard in the telling of the ancient tale.

In a back pew Claire sat and listened as the priest unfolded the biblical story. She had heard this story as a child, but was engrossed in the retelling. She leaned forward to follow the story.

"Yes, we know that David slew the giant, but how? Just imagine this. The Bible tells us that when David looked at the giant he could see only the lion and the bear that he had killed to save his father's sheep. This man, he reasoned, he would treat in the same way as the animals he had slain before. He knew that God had delivered him from the paw of the lion and bear, and had faith that He would deliver him from the blade of this Philistine. David did not have any armour, not being a soldier. So, Saul put *his* armour on David to prepare him for the fight. But David, just a young lad, could not move in the heavy equipment that he had never worn before."

Someone in a side pew coughed loudly. The priest paused, looked at the man closely and remarked. "Yes, I am sure that most of King Saul's army was ready to give a nervous cough as well. They did not have much faith in the outcome of this lopsided battle. But David, instead of armour and sword, chose for himself five of the smoothest stones he could find from the valley floor and placed them in his shepherd's bag. In his hand was his trusty sling. The Philistine came towards David taunting, 'Just come to me and I will give your flesh to the fowls of the heavens and to the beasts of the field.'"

This last taunt from the giant was shouted out by the priest, mimicking the giant in the story. The congregation gave a start and someone giggled. Claire sat forward and listened. This story of the bravery of the very young man had been told to her by her father. He used it as an example of what could be achieved if one believed that one could accomplish any difficult, challenging task. Her father had constantly reinforced this message; and she smiled now, as she sat and listened to another elderly man tell the congregation the same story.

"And," the priest continued, "David answered the giant with his own brave words. 'You are coming to me with a sword and with a spear and with a javelin, but I am coming to you with the God of the battles of Israel whom you have taunted. This day God will surrender you into my hand, and I will strike you down and remove your head, and give the carcasses of the camp of the Philistines to the fowls of the heavens, and to the wild beasts of the earth, and the people of all the earth will know that there is a God belonging to Israel.'"

Stopping to catch his breath, the priest then looked down at those in the rows of pews in front of him.

"Can you imagine the courage of this man/boy to say these words to the enormous, armour-clad man coming towards him?"

He paused for effect. Then, in an effort to keep the excitement of the story alive, he spoke rapidly.

"Then, the Bible tells us, David ran towards the man, put his hand into his pouch and pulled out a stone, placed it into his leather sling, and slung it hard, so that it struck the Philistine in his forehead. The stone sank into his forehead, and he went falling upon his face to the earth. David then ran and stood over the man, took up the man's sword and put him to death when he cut his head off with the sword."

The congregation gasped, despite the fact that they all knew how the story of bravery ended.

"Yes, a brave lad indeed," continued the priest with his message. Then his voice became very soft, and serious, and he continued in a sad tone.

"However, years later we see an adult David. We see David who has become king, who rules wisely, leads armies into battle, is an accomplished lute player, who writes numerous psalms praising the Lord. Then, a change. We see the David in the reading from the Second Book of Samuel. A David who forgets the commandments that Moses wrote into the stone tablets. He forgets the words from God that should have guided his actions. We see, in that second reading how David has changed."

The priest's now spoke slowly.

"The Bible tells us that, one evening, David was walking on the flat rooftop of the King's house. He sees a beautiful woman taking a bath. He asks who she is and finds out that she is Bathsheba, the wife of Uriah, one of his army officers. This does not deter David, however. In his lust for this beautiful woman, he sends his servants to fetch her to him, and, the Bible tells us, he lay with her. Yes, another man's wife."

There was absolute silence in the cathedral as the priest looked out at his listeners.

"When Bathsheba falls pregnant by him, he tries to cover his sin by sending for the husband so he could lie with his wife to make the child legitimate. But the loyal officer chooses to stay with the King, in his service. Now David is in the proverbial pickle. What can he do? And what *does* he do?"

Now the priest raised his voice in anger.

"There is no bravery here, no standing up for what is right; he has to hide his sin. He orders his officers to put Uriah in the front line of battle so that he should be struck down and die. And Uriah dies. King David kills the husband of the woman he covets."

The priest dropped his voice again to a sadder tone.

"How David has changed from the boy who slew the giant. God was not pleased with David's actions, and He shows His displeasure by letting the child born to Bathsheba die a slow death. David is punished for his actions; actions that violated the commandments given to Moses on Mount Sinai."

The priest relaxed for a moment and let the impact of the punishment sink into the minds of the people sitting in the congregation, listening to the story of David's punishment.

"The last commandment of the ten carved in the stone tablets by Moses on Mount Sinai, told the Israelites very specifically not to covet your neighbour's wife," continued the sermon. "Not only did David covet his neighbour's wife, he also broke the sixth and seventh commandments: thou shalt not commit adultery, and thou shalt not kill. David forgot about the words given to Moses and written on the stone tablets. David forgot who he had once been. He had lost the part of him that was the core of the brave young man who fought Goliath, the giant. This was a weak David, one who could not fight his desires as he coveted someone else's wife."

The priest then continued his lesson on the moral lapse in society, but Claire did not hear much of what he was saying. She sat very still and felt the guilt of what she had thought, planned and executed wash over her. She too, like David of old, had broken the tenth commandment, and both she and Adam had broken the sixth. Was their punishment to be the death of a child? She felt fear creep over her as she contemplated the possible punishments that they could bring down on themselves and their family.

What had led her to enter this cathedral today? What fate, or power, existed to guide her walk, her need for a quiet time in a cool church? And then, to have the priest's message be spoken as if it was meant especially for her. She had felt as if the man could see her sitting in the back pew; that he could feel her guilt and was speaking directly to her. It had felt as if he had been delivering the message to her alone. As she sat in the pew, she knew that she could not ignore this warning that had been given to her. There was too much coincidence, right here in this house of God, to ignore what had just happened.

Like King David, her obsession with Adam had led her down a path of destruction. She had to find a way out of it; she had to get back her self-respect, her truth, her honesty. She was horrified at what she had been doing over the past months. She felt ashamed of the time and energy that she had spent planning the death of a woman who has done no harm to her. How could she have sunk so morally low? She knew that she had to deal with the feeling of despair that was overwhelming her.

Quietly she stood up and left the pew in which she had sat frozen as she listened to the priest's message. Leaving the cathedral, she walked home very slowly, overwhelmed by what she had just experienced. Was this a guiding hand being held out for her to take? If she took the hand, where would it lead? She tried to think of various scenarios that could result. She could tell Luce that she was in love with her husband, and that she wanted him. She could be prepared to take a piece of what Adam was prepared and able to give her. And, most drastic of all possibilities, she could walk away from Adam and never see him again. This last act she knew, would save her soul.

With her head pounding and her heart racing, she walked home where she fell onto the bed, exhausted, and let her body drift into a deep dreamless sleep.

Escape

The man does better who runs from disaster than he who is caught by it.
Homer. *The Iliad.*

The sound of bird song woke Claire the next morning. The sun was shining through the window, casting a yellow hue over the room. As she slowly opened her eyes, she lay in the glow of the warm colour walking its way up the walls and ceiling of the room. She heard the musical noise from the feathered singers coming in through the half-opened window.

She stretched lazily. She felt refreshed after what was the first restful sleep she had enjoyed for weeks. Then she remembered what had taken place in the last two days of her life, and she crawled back under the warmth of the comforter. She knew that this had to be a new day. This had to be the day to make changes in her life. Today was the day that she had to make some very difficult decisions. Yesterday she had realized that she was suffering from an addiction, and that she had to deal with that addiction as any other addict would. Alcoholics have to stop drinking, drug addicts have to stop imbibing. She now had to follow the same treatment.

However, *her* addiction was human. Adam was going to have a mind of his own, and would want to be with her. So, she knew, she had to remove herself from the addiction. She had to get away; and far enough away that Adam could not find her until she had the addiction under control. Unless she took this drastic step now she may be capable of doing something very drastic that would ruin her life, as well as that of others. She had to get herself far from Adam's wife as well, so that she was not captured again by the idea of ridding her from this triangle in which they were enmeshed.

She wanted to get away. She needed to get away. She did not trust herself or the control that the obsession had over her. She needed help, and the only way she could think to get it, was to get far away from all the temptation. Yesterday had been a wake-up call. She now knew that she had to act, and act quickly.

The clock in the kitchen told her that she was going to be late for work, even if she hurried. Leaving a message on Natalie's work phone telling her that she would be in later in the morning, she dressed for work, but did not leave. Instead, she sat at the computer and searched for quiet places in Canada that were as far from Montreal as possible.

Searching the internet, she explored places on the east coast. There were picturesque spots like St. Andrews by the Sea. Alternatively, there were smaller fishing villages where the ocean would be the only noise one would hear, other than the lilting accents of the Newfoundland fishermen and their families.

Then she searched the west coast possibilities in British Columbia. She explored Vancouver and decided that, however beautiful and interesting the city was, it was just too big for the quiet time she needed. She googled to explore Whistler Mountain, the large ski hill just north of Vancouver. She decided that being on a ski hill would remind her too much of skiing with Adam.

Moving further west she explored information about Vancouver Island, the large island lying off the coast of British Columbia with the city of Victoria at its southern tip. As she checked out places on the island she found, on the Pacific Ocean side of the island, a small town called Tofino. She could not get any further away from Montreal, she thought, than the western most sea-shore of Canada.

On the computer tourist site, Tofino was described as a town of two thousand residents with wild, natural scenery; lakes, and inlets and ancient rainforests. The town sprawled on a peninsular that provided long sandy beaches for residents and visitors. Together with the rugged beauty, the town also provided luxury lodges, hotels and spas; things you would not expect to find in a remote village. Claire decided that it sounded like the perfect spot to hide away in, and still be very comfortable. On the computer screen it looked and sounded idyllic. Picking up the phone, she made a reservation at a resort nestled on the shores of one of the long sandy beaches just south of the town of Tofino.

Wasting no time in making a decision, she phoned Air Canada and booked a reservation on a direct flight to Vancouver for that same evening. She had no intention of delaying, or of giving herself an opportunity to change her mind. She packed a suitcase with casual but warm clothing, cleaned out the fridge, and left a message on her answering service that she would be away. She parked her car in the garage, closed the door, and drove the rental car back to the agency before taking a taxi to her office.

Nathalie was surprised to see her when she walked into the office.

"I thought you were going to be away for most of the day, Miss Hardick. But I am glad that you're here. We have a few clients wanting to speak with you." Then she hesitated, "How are you feeling? You look tired today. Are you okay?"

"Yes, I'm fine thank you," replied Claire with a sigh, thinking about the clients waiting for her to solve their investment problems. This is not what she needed when she wanted to get away as soon as possible. "I will need some time alone first to clear up a few things, and then come in and we'll talk about the clients who called."

Entering her office she closed the door and sat at her desk. Her workload was a different sort of issue that she had to solve. She had not been at her best during the past few months, and now she was planning to leave it all behind for a while. Avery would not be pleased, but she would have to deal with the consequences. She opened her computer and starting making detailed notes to leave with both Avery and Nathalie.

With these tasks completed, she picked up the phone and called up to Avery's office.

"Avery, I need some time to talk with you as soon as possible please."

"What's up, Claire? I called your office earlier and Nathalie told me that you probably would not be in today?"

"That is what I need to talk with you about."

"Well, I have a meeting in ten minutes, but come up after that; give me an hour."

"Thank you," responded Claire with relief. At least she would get that difficult meeting over with early.

Calling Nathalie into her office she told her that she was planning to be away from the office for some time, and that she was relying on her to keep things on track until she came back.

"How long are you talking about?" Nathalie wanted to know, feeling nervous about the responsibility she was going to have to handle.

"I'm not sure, but I suspect it will be for at least a few weeks. I will contact you regularly to help problem-solve. I know you can handle the day-to-day run-of-the-mill work. You are very competent, Nathalie, and I trust you to keep things on track."

Nathalie had a million questions about where her boss was going, and why, but she felt that as Claire had not provided any details, it had to be very private. She did not want to pry.

"Thank you for your confidence, I won't let you down."

The conversation with Avery was a lot more difficult than the one with Nathalie.

Avery did not understand why she had to leave in such a hurry, and why she would not say where she was going, or for how long. He became pushy and angry and this did not help the tone of the conversation.

"What the hell's going on here, Claire? I have a company to run and I need my money managers to be here, and be at their best. You have not been at yours recently. And now, you want time off! To do what exactly?"

Claire had no option but to push her cause, so answered back in a very firm voice.

"Avery, I am going, and I am not going to be here tomorrow morning. So we had better start sorting out what needs to be done to fill the gap while I am away. If you want to fire me for going, so be it, but this is a decision I have made, and I am not changing my mind."

Avery looked at her in surprise. She had always been firm but never so forthright. He wondered if Claire was in some sort of trouble and needed support, not harassment. He looked at her closely, and then asked tentatively, "Can I help with whatever is sending you away, Claire?"

Taken by surprise, Claire responded, "Thank you, no. This is something I am going to do on my own. I will let you know when I'm ready to come back. Now, let me fill you in with the business that I'd like you to help Nathalie with."

When she left his office she felt as if a weight had lifted from her shoulders. She knew that she could leave and that her clients would be well served; that between Nathalie and Avery, she would retain her role at the company when she returned.

Back in her office she took an hour with Nathalie, ensuring that all the current projects were up to date. She agreed to telephone her as regularly as possible, but that, if there was an emergency, Nathalie was to go to Avery.

"But he's a very scary man," muttered Nathalie.

Claire laughed. "I agree, but he will be expecting you to go to him, so he won't feel bothered. This will be good for you to build up your courage. If you are going to advance in this business, Nathalie, you are going to have to develop nerves of steel. But thank you for doing this for me."

After Nathalie had left her office, Claire picked up the telephone and ordered a large bouquet of flowers to be delivered to the young woman the following morning, together with a thank-you card.

Sighing deeply, she then sat and pondered how she could tell Adam that she was going away. She pulled out a sheet of paper and wrote a note to him. She did not want to use the computer. This note had to be personal, and she did not want to leave any trail. She had become so accustomed recently to keeping every movement she made secret, that it had become second nature for her.

She wrote the short note, inserted it into an envelope and decided to send it on her way out of the office.

Leaving the building, she wished Nathalie well and to her surprise, the young woman came up to her with tears in her eyes and gave her a hug.

"I hope you come back well again, Miss Hardick," she said through her tears.

Confusion

The discipline of desire is the background of character.
John Locke

The ring on the end of the line continued for some time, and then an electronic message said that the person was not available. This was the sixth call that had resulted in the same message. Adam had been trying to phone Claire for a day and a half without any success. He was beginning to get worried. She had never had her cell phone off before; now there was only silence when he tried to contact her.

He wondered if she had been in an accident or if she had been cross about his going to *The Lion King* show with his family. Maybe she had wanted to go to the show with him, but that would not have been like her. She was always understanding about the commitments he had with his family.

However, she had been different recently. Maybe the change had started about the time that Luce had come back from Paris. He knew that they had enjoyed a wonderful few months together without his wife in the city; but now that Luce was home again his loyalties had, of necessity, been split.

His relationship with Luce was much closer now than it had been for a long while. Maybe her being away had made him realize just how much he still needed her in his life. The opening of the art gallery was a project that they had accomplished together. As well, Luce had been more warm and open since her return, and her welcome to his sexual overtures of the night before brought his feelings of desire back. However, those feelings were tinged with guilt as he realized that he was thinking of his night with Luce as he was worrying about Claire.

How many men could admit that they enjoyed the company of two beautiful women, both of whom, he knew, loved him? He acknowledged that he was being very selfish. To be honest with himself, he knew that he loved both of them, but very differently. Claire was a wonderful joy and bonus in his life. He had never imagined that he would meet a woman like her; one that he would share such passion with, and be able to open up to in the way that he did with her.

His worry about her silence made him decide to take a detour past her house on his way to work, to check to see if there was anything wrong. Stopping in front of the house, he first noticed that her motor car, which she usually left parked on the driveway, was not there. He speculated that she could have parked it in the garage, but that would be unusual for her. If it was not in the garage, then she had to be out somewhere. That would be a relief, he realized, as she had to be unharmed if she was driving around.

Further exploration was required, so he drove to the end of the block, parked and walked back to the house. He scanned the house carefully and saw that all the blinds were drawn. This surprised him, as Claire never closed everything up. She was fanatical about letting light into the house, so seldom closed the drapes or blinds. The street was very private, and she used to comment that if some Peeping Tom wanted to peer into her windows, he deserved to see what he did. Sometimes, she had said, the view was not worth seeing. He used to smile when she made these comments, as he knew from experience that the view usually was very worth seeing indeed. To see all the blinds pulled down at every window worried him.

Walking up the driveway, he saw that the daily newspaper was still on the front doorstep. He went to the front door, rang the doorbell and heard it echo hollowly through the house. Claire did not answer the ring. Puzzled, he walked around to the back of the house and noticed that there too, all the blinds had been drawn. Feeling very concerned now, he rang the doorbell again and waited. When there was still no response, he turned away and walked back down the drive.

As he did so, a woman appeared from the house next door and walked up to him. She stood in front of him with her hands on her hips. Her body language made Adam feel nervous. Suddenly he was feeling very guilty about being at Claire's house in broad daylight.

"Can I help you?" she asked in a firm voice.

"Yes," Adam responded. "I'm trying to find Claire Hardick. I tried to phone her but she was not picking up and I started to worry. I decided to come around and check to see that all was well, but she's not home."

"Oh, I think she has gone away for a while. She asked me to keep an eye on the house," the woman told Adam.

"Gone away? Did she say where? On business, suddenly?" asked a confused Adam.

"Oh, she didn't tell me, and I don't pry. But I think she'll be away for a while. That's all I know."

"Thank you," muttered Adam, and turned away so that she could not see the consternation on his face. In confusion, he walked down the driveway, and down the road to his car. He drove to work feeling as if he had been punched in the stomach. This was so unlike anything Claire had ever done before. He could not understand why she would go away without telling him. She usually checked to see if he could join her for part of the time when she was travelling.

When he got to his office he closed the door, and dropped his head down onto his arms on the desk. He felt like sobbing, but that would not solve the mystery. He had to try to find out where she had gone, and why she had left without telling him. As he sat trying to solve the problem, a knock on his office door roused him.

"What is it?" he asked.

"I have a courier package for you, Mr. Lambert," a staff member told him from the other side of the door.

"Come in then."

"It has just arrived, so thought I'd bring it right in."

"Thank you," said Adam, taking the small package from her hands.

He looked at the courier package. There was no information on the outside other than his name. Opening the wrapping he found an envelope inside addressed to him in Claire's handwriting. Surprised, he tore the envelope open and read the short message on the note.

Adam,

I am going away for a while. I need to be alone to find out who I am again. I have not been well during the past months, and this will be my way to heal. Please do not try to find me. I will return when I am well again.

There was no signature to the note but he knew that it was from her. He read and reread the message. He had been aware that she had not been herself recently but was reluctant to talk about her problems, so he had never been able to find out what it was that was bothering her. He wished now that he had pushed her more to find out what the issue had been, and to help her with it. It could not be health related as she never mentioned going to the doctor or undergoing any medical tests. He supposed that is had something to do with a work issue, and he hoped that it would resolve itself quickly for her sake, as well as for his own.

As he reread the note, the thought crossed his mind that maybe the issue was their relationship. He wondered why both the women who were close to him, had felt the need to run away and leave him. First, Luce had gone away to Paris for months, and now Claire had left for, who knew where, and for an indeterminate time. What was he doing to these women to chase them both away? He felt that he was to blame somehow, but could not find the reason.

He had always gone out of his way to be very discreet about the relationship with Claire and felt sure that Luce did not know that his friendship with her had progressed into a passionate love affair. And Claire had always known, from the first time they had met, that he was married with children, and that he could not give her any more of himself than what he could steal from his family's needs.

For the rest of the day he suffered in a state of torment, trying to imagine where Claire may have gone. Would she go back to a place where they had been? Would she go to the Manoir in the Eastern Townships again? Probably not, as he could easily find her there. Would she go back to Europe? That would make it more difficult for her to deal with any business issues. Over and over, his mind raced to different scenarios, but he could find no solution.

By the middle of the afternoon he finally gave up trying to work. He informed his staff that he was leaving for the day and he went home. Luce was working at the art gallery, so he was alone in the house. He poured himself a large drink of single malt scotch and went out to the back garden. As he sipped, he found that his confusion had not lessened during the morning. He had no option but to abide by Claire's wishes. He would not be able to find her, and she did not want him to look for her. Obviously, she did not want to be with him. She wanted to be alone to deal with whatever the problem was.

He had to force himself to relax and get on with his own life without her until she contacted him. The dreadful thought occurred to him that she may never contact him again. A dozen questions, none of which he could answer, tormented his mind.

What if this was her way of saying that the relationship was now over? What if she felt that the relationship had run its course, and she had to be free again? Maybe she was tired of playing second fiddle to Luce and needed to be on her own? Maybe, he thought, she was thinking that she needed a full time partner, and that he was not the man for her; despite all the things she had said to the contrary?

That she loved him he was certain. Not only had she told him that on numerous occasions, but had demonstrated that love in a million ways. So what could be her motivation for ending the affair?

When he thought of his life without Claire he felt despair. Over the past many months she had become an integral part of his life, essential to his wellbeing. She was the one to whom he took his fears, his woes, his problems. She was the only one to whom he could open up totally and show his vulnerable side. She was the only one who seemed to sense his moods; when he was feeling low, and how to share his highs.

He knew that, if she had gone for good, he would be a lesser man. Being with her had made him feel strong; had given him the wherewithal to cope with some of the challenges he faced at work. He knew that the children would miss her as well. They had come to like her immensely, and enjoyed time with her on the hill as well as their dinners together while Luce had been away. Would they ask where she was? And if they did, what would he tell them? Would Luce be curious about his ski friend's absence?

He wondered if he was perhaps just a very shallow human being. A selfish, narcissistic person who took everything he could, whether it was right and moral or not. He was aware that he was committing adultery every time he was with Claire. Somewhere in his memory, he thought that one of the Ten Commandments said something about adultery. He could not remember what commandment it was, but he was sure that it was one. Maybe it was one of the Seven Deadly Sins; he could not remember them either.

As a lawyer, he knew that adultery was a cause often cited when one partner was suing for divorce. Luce, however had never gone that route, not even when she had left for France. Suddenly he wondered if Luce did know about his affair with Claire and that was why she had left so suddenly for Paris. Had she been thinking about leaving him for good then? She had probably missed the children too much and decided to come home to them, not to him. She had been much closer to him since she'd returned; much warmer, more sexually inviting than before.

These thoughts brought out acute feelings of guilt as he imagined the possible hurt he had caused his wife, and the hurt he had caused his children to experience when their mother had left. Had he really been the cause of her departure? Was he now the cause of Claire's departure as well? Had he just been a blind fool in his selfishness; taking what he wanted when it was offered to him?

No, Claire had not offered herself to him; he had pursued her. He had wanted her from the moment he had seen her on the stage at the conference in Toronto. He had not been able to keep his longing for her under control, and had gone out of his way to capture her attention.

However, he had not chosen the erotic passion that had resulted from that relationship. What had started out as an enjoyable friendship had developed into an all-consuming desire for both of them. They wallowed in the sexual pleasure they shared; they feasted on the mental stimulation they enjoyed. These were the result of that casual meeting in Toronto.

The full consequences of his actions were only now becoming clear to him. He knew, from the feeling of numbness inside him, that part of his life was over.

Solitude

The best thinking has been done in solitude.
Thomas Alva Edison.

The direct flight to Vancouver was scheduled to leave Trudeau Airport at six that evening. Claire took a taxi to the airport and boarded the flight. Wanting to blot out the world for a while, she ordered the quick meal service that was available in business class so that she could eat early and sleep for the rest of the five hour flight.

When the plane landed in Vancouver, she was feeling somewhat refreshed. The quiet time alone in her seat with her eyes closed, sometimes dozing off to sleep, had left her feeling more positive about the move she was making. The Fairmont Hotel, connected to the Vancouver Airport, provided her with comfortable accommodation for the night, before setting off the next morning.

The air was cool as she checked out a rental car and drove away from the airport terminal. A clear blue sky created a bright canopy for the grey mountain shapes she could see on the horizon. Turning the car north, she headed towards the ferry terminal at Horseshoe Bay to cross the channel to Vancouver

Island. The scenery was spectacular. The ocean fell away to her left, a calm blue under the clear sky, with polka dot islands intersecting the waterway up the coast.

She boarded the car ferry at the Horseshoe Bay Terminal and enjoyed the view from the upper lounges as they sailed across the Strait of Georgia to the port city of Nanaimo. The sky promised a clear day and calm waters. Standing on the outer deck of the vessel, Claire looked back at the skyline and admired the jagged line of mountains on the mainland. What beautiful country, she sighed, as she climbed the steps down to the lounge area and settled into a comfortable seat to watch the ocean through the sealed window.

Disembarking from the ferry in Nanaimo, she turned on the GPS in the car and headed north to the town of Parksville, and then west onto Highway Four, heading to the coast of Vancouver Island.

The two hundred and thirty kilometre drive took her through tiny picturesque hamlets, past horse ranches and small farms. The terrain and vegetation were so different from the Montreal area that the time passed quickly. She stopped in Port Alberni for a quick lunch, and then continued driving east towards the town of Tofino.

Arriving at the coast, she drove up to the Pacific Shores Beach Resort where she had a reservation. The receptionist was welcoming, and very efficiently had Claire checked into a two bedroom beach house in a row of buildings along the shoreline of Cox Bay Beach.

The interior of the beach house delighted her. It was more than she had expected, and she quickly decided that she would be very comfortable in these luxurious surroundings. A fully equipped kitchen with adjoining dining room led to a living area with fireplace. A large comfortable couch and two wing back chairs faced the sea. Sliding glass doors led to a cedar deck overlooking the ocean. Upstairs she found a smaller bedroom and bathroom, as well as a large master bedroom, with an adjoining bathroom with low windows. One could sit in the tub and look out over the ocean in total privacy.

Not wanting to waste time with unpacking her few belongings, she changed into sturdy walking shoes and left the house, heading for the beach. The sandy shoreline was just steps away from the front deck and stretched as far as the eye could see. A long sigh escaped her lips as she took in a deep breath. The sea air was so fresh that she could almost taste it.

She walked the length of the beach and back again, focusing on her body, and easing the tension that had built up in her muscles during the past weeks. Then, feeling exhausted from the long drive, and now more relaxed, she returned to the beach house. It was only then that hunger pangs struck, and she realized that she had not stopped to buy supplies on the way to the resort.

Oh well, she thought, I will have to face the crowded restaurant at the resort this one time; or maybe they would prepare something for me to take out. She was not ready to meet strangers yet; and she certainly did not want to have to tell her life story to some nosey traveller about why she was here alone. The restaurant was most obliging when she made enquiries and they agreed to deliver a cheese and fruit plate to the house.

Feeling more relaxed after eating, she lay down on the couch and listened to the ocean noises as the waves pounded onto the rocks. It was not long before she drifted off into a restful sleep.

It was dark when she suddenly woke, feeling cold and stiff. Looking around she did not know where she was. Is this a nightmare? she wondered, and she lay very still hoping the dark would clear. Then she heard the soft splash of waves as they broke gently onto the shore. With a sigh, she recalled that she was at the ocean in British Columbia, away from the stresses of Montreal. The noise of the waves calmed her as she lay on the couch and thought about the next weeks. Rousing herself, she stumbled up the stairs to the bedroom where she fell onto the bed, fully dressed, and pulled the comforter over her cold body. She tried to empty her mind of all thoughts; to clear the past few weeks from her memory.

At some point during the night, without any sense of where it had come from, she thought of something that her father had often quoted to her. *Be true to yourself; the only thing we have to fear is fear itself.*

These words stayed with her throughout that first long night, endlessly repeating, like a mantra, until she finally fell into a restless sleep.

The morning broke with grey skies and a light rain falling. Claire stretched and lay for a long time listening to the dual water noises; the pattering of the rain on the roof combined with the sound of waves breaking onto the shore of the beach.

The words of wisdom from her father that had guided her through many of her life's difficulties still repeated themselves in her head. They would guide her through this difficult time as well, she knew. She had to make an effort to get herself settled so that she could be alone and quiet to heal her emotions and to find again some semblance of calm for her soul.

A trip into the town of Tofino was required to buy supplies. The town was an interesting mix of restaurants, souvenir shops, art galleries as well as businesses advertising whale watching, fishing and other outdoor activities. She found a small supermarket where she bought basic needs; a fish shop where she went overboard buying a variety of fresh fish such as salmon and halibut as well as two large crabs.

A town resident directed her to The Common Loaf Bake Shop where she enjoyed a cup of delicious coffee and stocked up on their homemade muffins, wholegrain breads, as well as soups. Laden down with these supplies, she returned to the car and made her way back down the coast road to the resort.

She stocked the fridge and freezer, unpacked the few items of clothing she had brought with her, and decided to take stock of where she was, and how ready she was for this time alone.

She had enough food in the fridge and freezer for a few weeks, and she could always go to the restaurant if she ran out of supplies. She stood at the sliding glass door in the lounge and looked out at the ocean and the beach. She felt that this place would provide a haven for her to find her true self again.

Donning a waterproof hooded jacket she went out to walk on the beach as she had the day before. The beach stretched far into the distance in a gentle curve around the bay. Scattered logs were strewn along the shore, washed up by the crashing waves.

She established a routine during the next week. She woke early, took a long shower, dressed and sat for a time on the front patio of the beach house with a large mug of coffee and a muffin, and watched the waves roll in onto the beach. There were a variety of birds on the seashore; gulls, and terns, as well as large eagles. She was not knowledgeable about birds, but decided that she would buy a book on bird species when she next went into the town.

A long walk on the beach filled what time remained of every morning. This was the most recuperative time of the day for her. She found that, being alone with the sound of the waves, walking and breathing the salty air, made her feel alive again. On most days, after lunch, she enjoyed the unusual luxury of lying on the couch and dozing.

Before her evening meal she would venture outdoors again. This often included clambering over the rock outcroppings that projected out into the ocean at one end of the beach. The vegetation growing along the shoreline was fascinating. She often stood and watched the crows and gulls as they pulled mussels off the rocks, dropped them from a height to open the shells, and then swooped down to eat the soft flesh that was now exposed.

She wondered how she had managed to live all the years she had in Montreal, and not realized how physically healthy it was to breathe such fresh air. How restful the silence was; not to hear the roar of traffic or overhead jet engines. The thought of returning to the big city caused her to break out in a cold sweat. She did not know what life would hold for her when she returned.

Thoughts of redemption occupied her mind constantly. She was haunted by the depths to which she had sunk. Disbelief that she had stalked and plotted against another human being who had caused her no harm filled her thoughts; she had not forgiven herself. When she forced herself to examine her feelings towards Adam, she was at a loss to focus. She knew that she still loved him; that she would find it very difficult never to see him again. It would take time, she realized, to cleanse him from her soul.

After two weeks, she felt that she should make contact with the office. She used her cell phone to make the call, as she did not want the call to be traced by anyone, not even the office. When she spoke to both Nathalie and Avery, it appeared that there were no crises, and that they were coping in her absence. They both wanted to know when she was returning to Montreal but she would not give them an answer; she *could* not give them an answer. She did not know herself when she would be ready to return to the city.

The fog in her mind slowly began to clear with the walks on the long, sandy beaches, breathing the salty air. The days were often wet and cloudy in this place – one of the wettest places in North America. One day the wind strengthened to a strong gale, which whipped the ocean up to a fury. The unprotected coast bore the brunt of hurricane force winds, torrential rain and massive ocean swells. That day the ocean was a frenzy of white froth and spinning driftwood.

Claire was fascinated. She covered herself up in a bright yellow anorak and ventured out onto the beach. She wanted to be right in the middle of the fury. Fighting against the wind that howled in from the ocean she made her way down to a large spruce tree whose branches were bending under the onslaught. Wrapping her arms around its trunk, she hung on as the storm buffeted about her. She was experiencing one of the ocean storms for which Tofino was famous. Clinging to her tree anchor, she watched in fascination as the furious ocean threw up waves metres high, to crash down onto the sodden sand of the beach.

Finally, the clouds grew darker as night approached and the waves began to calm their frantic dance up the beach. Claire released her hold of the tree and staggered back to the safety of the house.

The storm had an unusual effect on Claire. The fury she experienced in nature seemed to drive the fury and confusion out of her body as well. She felt that she had been washed clean by the rain and the crashing waves. The experience was cathartic; she felt energized.

Footsteps on the deck the next morning alerted her to the fact that someone had come to the house. Expecting to see one of the resort staff, she was surprised to open the door on a gentle worn face and large mellow eyes.

"Good morning, my dear. I am Aaron. I have a small house further down the beach," the elderly man opened the conversation to Claire's surprised stare. "I watched you on the beach yesterday, clinging to your tree. These storms are wonders to behold, but can be extremely dangerous. They are best experienced from the safety of your house."

"Oh, yes, thank you," stammered Claire in surprise. "Would you like to come in?"

"Well, that is very kind of you. Yes, that is very kind of you." And he strode into the house.

Claire made a pot of coffee and together they sat and watched the ocean calming down after its furious performance of the previous day.

"I have seen you walking the beach alone every day. As I said, I am Aaron. I own a house at the end of the beach. A very quiet spot. I too like to be on my own. Is this a time of recuperation for you? I have watched you getting stronger every day."

Claire relaxed back into the comfortable deck chair and looked at the kind face watching her. How did he know why she was here? Maybe he thought that she was physically ill. Maybe he'll tell me his story before I open up with mine.

"My name is Claire. Pleased to meet you, Aaron. Yes, in a way this visit is a healing one for me. But, how long have you lived here on the beach?"

"I came here when my wife died of cancer fifteen years ago. I could not face the hurry-up attitude of Calgary on my own, so packed up and found refuge and sanctuary on this wonderful ocean. It has washed my grief and my city exhaustion away, and made me a very contented human being who is quite at peace with himself and his place in the world," Aaron explained.

"What a wonderful place to live – a life so close to nature. I have found that it has relaxed me, washed away my negative thoughts as well, especially the storm yesterday. Standing in the middle of the ocean's fury last evening was cleansing."

The old man smiled back at her and leaned forward to take her hands.

"You have been through a difficult time. Close your eyes and relax into the fresh, salty ocean air with deep, cleansing breaths. It will always work miracles."

Claire did as he suggested and felt herself sink into a space of utter contentment; the first she had felt for months. The old man's soft voice was hypnotic, and her body responded to his low, calm voice.

They sat together for a long time, watching the waves break their foam onto the wet sand and ripple gently up the beach. Banked clouds created huge clumps of white froth in the sky, as the sun made an effort to push through their mass to warm the water and sand below.

"You know that Zen masters would retreat to a distant mountaintop far away from the distractions of town and urban centres, and there they would do solitary meditation. I use this beach as my mountaintop."

Looking at Claire the old man sat back and slowly told Claire of his beliefs. "I practice Zen sitting every day. It helps me to focus on being mindful of every moment of every day. You know the Sanskrit tells us that there are over six billion moments in a single day," the old man continued. "And if you think about that, every moment provides an opportunity to re-establish one's will. Every snap of your fingers provides you with sixty-five opportunities to choose activities that will provide beneficial karma and turn your life around."

Claire sat and listened as the soft voice continued.

"Self-awareness and knowing how you spend every moment of every day will teach you to focus on that which is true to you."

Where did this man come from? Claire's mind was spinning as she thought again of the messages she was getting from elderly men recently. First, the priest in the pulpit spoke directly to her need. Her father had talked in her dreams all night when she had first arrived at the beach, and now this wonderful old man, who had held her hands so gently in his, was giving her a method by which she could refocus her life.

"Can I come and sit with you one day?" she asked tentatively.

A broad smile greeted her words. "I think I would enjoy the company of a fellow traveller on the same Zen path. We can start this evening as the sun goes down. I will watch for you as you walk to the end of the beach. Wear something warm."

He took Claire's hands again and held them firmly between his own. "You will heal, I can see the focus in your eyes."

Then, sitting up straight, he released her hands and stood.

"But you have not seen the real beauty of this corner of the world yet, I think. Have you seen the large visitors of the ocean we get at this time of the year? Or the giant trees that have been here for generations, and will be here long after we are forgotten? Have you explored the peninsular at all?" he asked.

Surprised at the sudden turn of conversation, Claire responded, "No, I'm afraid that I've been holed up here on my own trying to get my head into a sane space. I was not very well when I arrived some weeks ago, but I feel that the solitude, the contemplative walks, and finally the storm, have restored me. I am feeling more enthusiastic about life this morning."

"That's a good sign, my dear. Would you like to join me on an adventure? I sometimes volunteer with a company that does a short tour to see the wildlife. It fascinates me, which is why I do it. Interested?"

"But what…" began Claire.

"A surprise, but you will enjoy it, I guarantee."

With a laugh at the fun her companion was having, she dressed warmly as he suggested, and together they drove into Tofino.

As they drove, Claire realized that it *was* time that she left the beach house to explore the wonderful natural beauty of the area. Her companion stopped at a company that advertised wild game watching. He suggested that she join the group that was leaving to watch black and grizzly bears eating along the shoreline. Now full of energy, she agreed, and climbed into a small power boat with five other tourists as well as her elderly companion. Aaron, she discovered, was a tour guide and he worked with the captain of the cruiser.

The boat had to get to the sheltered inner waters, away from the stormy waters of the ocean. The ride took about thirty minutes to go through the tranquil inside passage to the north-east side of Meares Island, and then into Fortune Channel. There the boat, with its passengers, meandered slowly down the shoreline looking for the bears. Aaron, sitting in the front of the small vessel explained to the passengers that, emerging from hibernation, the bears were usually very hungry and needing to feed. It was too early for the summer salmon runs, so they came to the shorelines searching for shore food.

As the group watched, the bears, with their huge paws, turned over rocks and boulders searching for crabs and other seafood. The old man described for the tourists the hibernation practices of the bears, how they foraged for food until the salmon runs started, and pointed out the species of bear they were observing.

As the group in the boat watched, two large black bears lumbered out of the forest and made their way to the shore. They stopped, gazed out at the ocean and the boat, waved their heads in a sideways motion and then, undistracted by the sight of the tourists, began to turn over the rocks. Finding crabs, they scooped them up in their paws, stuffed them into their mouths and chewed. Claire, sitting in the boat, could hear the crunch of the crab shells as the bears chewed. She was fascinated by the sight of these huge animals feeding at their leisure, unperturbed by the visitors.

On the way back to Tofino they were followed by a large sea lion who curiously lifted its head out of the water to get a look at the boat and passengers, as they all stared back at it. Their guide pointed to two large bald eagles in flight, high in the sky above their heads. Cameras had been clicking all around Claire as she sat in the boat; but she felt that she wanted to burn every moment of these experiences into her senses and hold them there, not mask them through a lens.

She returned to the beach house in a daze, quite overwhelmed by what she had experienced by being so close to the natural wonders and beauty of the ocean, the wildlife and the stillness. She thanked her new-found companion who suggested that she explore more of the coast before returning to Montreal. Tofino, she was discovering, was a fascinating blend of luxury and wilderness, and she wanted to share in all of it.

As promised, that evening she walked to the end of the beach where she found Aaron sitting on the front deck of a small clapboard house painted bright blue – to blend with the ocean he commented as he saw her standing on the beach admiring his home.

"Come up to the deck, Claire," he invited. And together they spent time in quiet contemplation. Claire found that the silent time, close to the calm lapping of the waves on the beach, together with the companionship of the old man, was restful and restorative. After that first evening together, it became a ritual to join with Aaron for a Zen sitting, either on his deck or on the sand of the beach.

She had not given up her desire to explore more of the surrounding areas, so two days later she took another long walk, but not on Cox Beach this time. She had read about the Big Tree Trail that was renowned for its old growth trees of spectacular size, and had seen pictures of these huge trees. She decided to examine them for herself. So she drove into the town where she boarded a small boat. This small water taxi took her on the ten-minute ride through a maze of small islands, sand bars and channels to the start of the walk. The boat dropped her and two other passengers off, right up onto a rock outcropping. The boat skipper directed them to climb up onto a large log and to follow the wooden boardwalks into the forest to the start of the hiking trail.

Claire stopped when she reached the boardwalk and stood, marvelling at the work it must have taken to construct the walkway out of hewn logs, in the middle of this huge forest. The wooden boards were quite slippery in places, and she had to tread carefully on the steps as she clambered up and down and over large tree roots, on her walk along the path. At the end of the boardwalk was a large western red cedar tree, nicknamed The Hanging Garden, because many other trees and plants were growing from it. A plaque at the base of the tree estimated that it was two thousand years old. She walked the wooden boardwalk wrapped around the base, looking at this strange gnarled tree from all angles.

Leaving the boardwalk, she stepped onto the muddy dirt trail leading into the forest. Following the trail she passed huge, gnarled trunks that were twisted into strange shapes. The towering hemlock and cedar trees were interspersed with tree roots bulging from the ground, as well as ferns, and hanging moss. Old Man's Beard lichen draped over the tree branches.

One of the short trails led to the coastline, where she stood gazing out at the breathtaking view across the sound to the tip of Meares Island. She took a moment to sit on a rock outcrop and take in the beauty of what lay before her. As she sat, she remembered Aaron's words about being aware of how one spends every moment of every day. How healing contemplation was in a setting as peaceful as this. She carried this thought with her as she made her way back to the passenger pick-up rock, clambering over and under tree roots and fallen trees to the waiting water taxi that took her back to Tofino.

She was at peace the next day when she awoke to find the sun streaming in through the windows. How appropriate, she thought, my life is suddenly beginning to feel bright as well.

Now firmly acquainted with the elderly Aaron, they would sit together on her deck sipping on a glass of wine, watching the waves and sharing stories of their lives. Claire did not relate the details of her nightmarish behaviour, but talking about Adam and their relationship with another human being was cathartic. Her listener never advised or criticized, but prodded her thinking with questions that she found helped her to focus on how she saw her life and the person she wanted to be in the future.

A phone call to the office assured her that everything was in good order there. She informed Nathalie and then Avery that she would probably be returning to work the following week after being away for a month. She felt renewed by the rest she had enjoyed; the time to be alone, without being pulled by needs and obsessions. When she thought about Adam it was with warm, gentle memories of what they had shared together. She felt that she had found a good friend in him, one who was undemanding and supportive. She now accepted the fact that he would always stay with his wife and family, and if she still wanted to be part of his life, it would have to be just that; only a part.

She had tried to imagine what their lives would be like if they were to continue as lovers. How would she feel about having to share only a small part of his life? She wondered how *he* would feel about continuing their relationship when he was now closer to his wife than he had been when they had first met.

Aaron knocked on her door that morning.

"The sun is shining, all is well in the world, and you have one more adventure to experience before you leave," he prodded.

"How do you know that I am getting ready to leave?" Claire asked with a smile.

The old man looked at her knowingly. "You have had a get-up-and-go city look about you these last few days, my dear, so I assume you are girding your loins in preparation for your return to the big smoke."

Claire just looked at him and burst out laughing. She stepped forward and put her arms around this man who had provided so much succour during the past weeks.

"Yes, I have to get ready to go home. I am going to miss you, Aaron."

"Ditto," he replied. "But before we miss each other, let's enjoy another adventure together. The giants are visiting I hear, and we should go and welcome them to our ocean."

"I get it," said Claire, and turned to pull warm clothing from the closet. "How much of this will I need?"

"All of it, better too much than being cold and wet."

In Tofino, they joined an aquatic safari on a cabin style cruiser. The boat headed out into the ocean, through the famous Broken Islands, looking for whales. On the way out the group spotted otters surfacing the water, watching curiously as the boat went by.

As they sat looking at the ocean, the guide called out, "Everyone look to the port side, there are two humpback whales surfacing." Everyone moved to the port side and looked out over the ocean in time to see an enormous grey shape break the surface of the water. It was an unforgettable sight. Claire gasped in surprise at the size of the marine mammals.

"These are some of the largest whales that come up this coast, so enjoy the sight," the guide continued. "We will stay here at a safe distance and watch for a while, and then move on and see what else is passing through these waters."

Cameras clicked non-stop as they watched these giants of the ocean. The boat then moved on to find a school of orcas that were reported being in the area. The boat rode swiftly through the water, chasing the route the whales had been seen taking. As they bounced over the waves the guide called out, "Found them," and he slowed the boat to a comfortable speed and pointed out to the port bow of the cruiser. Again, cameras clicked as the school of orcas surfaced, giving the tourists a distinct sight of their black and white markings.

"These whales are often referred to as killer whales because they eat seals, working as a group to dislodge them from ice floes. However, they can be very friendly towards boaters and often come up alongside the craft to check us out as much as we check them out," the guide explained. Everyone laughed at the commentary and the sight of the playful whales.

That evening she and Aaron decided to celebrate their new-found friendship by dining at the Wickaninnish Inn restaurant, The Pointe. The famous resort served up delicious fish dishes; halibut and sablefish that they enjoyed with a summer salad.

As she stood at the door to her suite to say goodbye to the old man who had been so supportive, she felt tears form in her eyes.

"You will be fine," was all he said as he looked at her. "Believe in yourself, my dear, and all will be well." He turned and walked down the beach back to the blue house.

"That's what my father always said to me," she said aloud as she watched him walk away. How did he know that? He never really told me much about his personal life, and I only saw where he lived. She watched as her elderly companion disappeared in the mist of the evening.

It was with a relaxed mind and body that she boarded the airplane in Vancouver, sat back in the seat and thought about how her relationship with Adam would unfold after she arrived back in their home city.

Return

*It's not what happens to you,
but how you react to it that matters.*
Epictetus

The relaxation at the ocean-side resort, and opening up of herself to the natural world, had given Claire a fresh look at life. She had come to realize that her relationship with Adam, and the tension that it had created in her personal and business life, was a very small part of the greater universe, of the world in which they both moved. She knew that her contribution to the shaping of the future was miniscule. However, her share of what unfolded was as important as each wave breaking on the shores of Long Beach in Tofino. As important as each human being in his own space was; as every action taken by every human being was.

She had read about The Butterfly Effect, the core of Chaos Theory. This scientific theory asserts that a single occurrence, no matter how small, can change the course of the universe forever. It suggests that just the flap of a butterfly's wings can change the air around it so much, that a tornado can occur two continents away.

If she believed this theory, then she needed to ensure that *her* contribution was the most positive it could be. She knew that the obsession that had gripped her a month ago had been very destructive; not only destructive to any positive energy she could have contributed to the world, but destructive to Adam, his wife, and his children as well – much closer to home.

As the airplane flew the thousands of miles back to Montreal, she sat back quietly in her seat and vowed that the focus of her life would now be positive. She swore that she was going to take a different road, and journey down a path of reconciliation with herself and the way in which she saw Luce, Adam's wife.

She had no specific plan to implement for when she saw Adam again, but she knew that she would feel no anger towards Luce, or the time that she took her lover away from her side. There would be no negative thoughts about planning for Luce's disappearance. There would be no more stalking, no more plotting, no more jealousy. She felt at peace with her new resolve.

As the plane flew over Winnipeg, she dozed off and arrived at Trudeau Airport feeling refreshed.

A wonderful sense of belonging swept over her as she opened the door to her house and felt instantly at home. She had missed her personal space while away and it now felt good to walk through the rooms, becoming familiar with the intimacy of her own world again; the things that she had surrounded herself with over the years. There was a sense of being swaddled in the warmth of the familiar, and she relaxed into the sensation.

The next morning brought with it renewed energy and enthusiasm to start anew; to find her old life again, whether it be with Adam or alone. She had some immediate actions to take to cleanse all memories of the dreadful mental state she had been in a month before.

Her first action was to get rid of the stolen driver's licence card. She knew that she would never be able to return it to its rightful owner, and this she regretted. She would like to have taken it back with an apology, but doing so would scar her reputation at work permanently. Standing at the kitchen sink with the card in one hand and a pair of large scissors in the other, she methodically cut the card into small pieces and dropped them into the kitchen garburator. A turn of the switch and they were minced into nothing as she washed them down the drain.

The house key, which she had cut to fit the Lambert house, was more difficult to dispose of. She turned on the barbecue outside and adjusted the heat to the highest possible gauge. When it was almost white hot, she dropped the key into the heat, hoping that it would melt away, as she wished her previous actions could melt away.

She planned to take a day away from the office, and a quick phone call to Nathalie assured her assistant that she was now back in Montreal, and that she would be in the office the next morning. Nathalie was delighted to hear that she would be working with Claire again the next morning. This relieved her fears that her boss may have left for good; a situation that the young woman could not have borne.

Claire phoned Avery Heap. "Avery, hello, this is Claire. I am back in Montreal."

"Claire, what good news. How are you feeling?" cooed Avery, surprised and delighted to hear her voice again.

"I am well, thank you, Avery. I just wanted to let you know that I will be in the office tomorrow. Maybe we could meet later in the morning. I need to do some catching up, and the sooner the better for me."

"For me as well, and for the company. Call when you are ready. And, welcome back, Claire."

Putting the telephone down, Claire thought about her return. After an absence of a month, there was much to do to get back into a routine again. The rest of the day was filled with the chores of picking up her mail, stocking the cupboards and fridge, contacting the house cleaning company for a thorough cleanse of the house, and checking on the condition of the garden.

That evening, she finally collapsed in the den with a glass of wine, and relaxed into thoughts of her day at the office the next day. The sound of the doorbell roused her from her reverie.

I wonder who that could be? I have not told anyone except Nathalie and Avery that I've returned, she mused. Opening the front door, she found Adam standing there, looking at her with joy and surprise on his face.

"You're home; how wonderful!" he exclaimed.

"Adam, what are you doing here?" she asked, not sure whether she was ready to invite him in or not.

"May I come in?" he asked meekly.

Hesitating, she looked at him. He looked tired, as if he had not slept in a long time. He was watching her with such pleading eyes, that she relented and invited him in.

"Would you like a glass of wine?" she asked as they went into the den where she had left her glass.

"I – I – just want to put my arms around you, not drink wine. I have been riding past your house every night to check if you were home. I saw your car parked in the driveway and was so overjoyed, I had to come and see if it was true that you had returned."

"Yes, I'm home to stay," responded Claire, smiling at his devotion. She knew that she now had to have the conversation about what their friendship would look like in the future. She was not sure whether she was ready, and did not want to be pushed into making the wrong decision by Adam's persistence.

Without waiting for further response from her, Adam stepped closer and wrapped his arms around the woman he had missed more than he could have imagined. He rested his head next to hers and gently stroked her hair. He stood very still, holding her close, not saying anything. Claire could feel his emotion. She sensed that he was overwhelmed to have her back. Gently, she pushed him back and looked at him. She saw that tears shone in his eyes as he looked back at her.

"You cannot imagine how much I have missed you. Please don't ever go away for such a long time again. I don't think that I'd be able to survive if I had to go through that agony a second time."

His words melted the hard core of resistance that had been building inside her head. She wondered how she had imagined that her life could ever exist without the presence of this man as part of it. She smiled at him, held out her arms and welcomed him back into her life.

As the months followed, Adam and Claire established a routine for finding time together. This involved taking business trips together. These they planned very carefully, so that their time together did not invade the time Adam needed with his wife and children. He was home in the evenings with Luce, and they enjoyed dinners around the table as a family.

The lovers' sojourns away from Montreal together meant that they could relax more, enjoy a few days as a couple, be seen in public, and the greatest joy for both of them, was being able to curl up in each other's arms together in the same bed at night. The pleasure of waking up and seeing each other first thing in the morning never failed to delight them both.

Claire was resigned to the fact that she would only ever have a piece of Adam; that she would be his mistress, and only that. To her surprise, she found that she was quite content with that role. She was free to spend long hours in the office, to travel on assignments, and even to enjoy the occasional evening out with other men. Adam was still the centre of her life, but the new arrangement left her with space for her own personal, selfish pursuits.

Adam did not have this luxury. He continued to live a busy life, torn in two directions by the lovers in his life; neither of which he was prepared to discard. Because of their limited time together, he and Claire enjoyed them to the fullest. They both made sure that, when they were together, there were no other distractions. They agreed to turn their cell phones off, and devote their full attention to each other.

They did however, continue to enjoy their public time together on Mount Tremblant. When the winter snows fell again, and the ski season started, they became known on the ski hill as a twosome, two who were good friends, and work acquaintances. They enjoyed lunches together in the ski lodge, and restaurants in the village, sometimes with his children. They often went to the hotel and had drinks in the public bar together, and then walked away from each other to reinforce the public perception of the relationship as being only platonic.

There were times however, when Adam would enter the hotel, sit at the bar for a while and enjoy a quick drink, speak to a few acquaintances, then excuse himself and leave, taking a diversion to the elevators and go up to Claire's suite. There, they would steal times of intimacy and passion, to appease the lust that they had felt all day during their skiing together.

Occasionally Adam would be able to join Claire at her home. He always parked his car on the next street so that it would not be recognized by neighbours. They would cook meals together, sit on the couch and watch movies, or just talk.

And so the months passed in quiet enjoyment of each other's company and bodies. Adam always returned home to Luce, the children and the comfort of his family at home.

Luce had been living an emotional roller coaster for the past months. She had sensed that something significant had changed in her husband. They still enjoyed the new closeness, but he often appeared stressed and distracted. Numerous times she and the children had to repeat questions they had asked him, and he responded as if mentally far away. She felt his distress and tried to ask him about it, but he did not want to discuss his feelings, so she suspected that there could either be difficulties at his work place or his relationship with his mistress.

She was not satisfied as the situation continued and Adam's distress became more apparent. Even the children questioned him about his health, and kept asking if he was tired or if they had done something to make him sad. Luce wanted to explore the causes for his change herself. Knowing where his lover lived from the detectives report, she drove past the house wondering if she would see any evidence of a change. What she did notice was that there was no car in the driveway as the detective had indicated. As well, the house looked unlived in. All the blinds were drawn, and even when she checked at night, there were no lights shining from the interior. She concluded that Claire had left town. She sincerely hoped that the woman had left for good, but was cautious about feeling too confident.

Disguising her voice as well as she could, she phoned Claire's place of employment and asked to speak with her. The woman at reception told her that Miss Hardick was away for an undetermined period, and that she could speak with her assistant if she wished. Luce thanked her and put the phone down with relief. Now she knew that the woman was away, and the reason for Adam's distress.

Knowing that the absence of his lover was upsetting her husband did not provide any comfort for Luce. Whether Claire was there or not, Adam was obviously missing her. Luce had hoped that the relationship had run its course, but now she knew otherwise. Her only response, she reasoned, was to be a comfort to the man she loved, wait for him to forget about the affair, and then return to his family.

Everything changed suddenly when Adam came home late one evening. He was whistling as he walked into the house from the garage, went to the drinks cabinet, poured a large drink of Scotch, and collapsed onto the couch in the den. He sat with his head resting against the leather back, his feet up on the ottoman, his eyes closed as he sipped at his drink

Luce watched him carefully. It seemed to her that a different man had come home that night. She was curious as to what had brought about the change. If, as she suspected, his lover had returned to the city, she would have to deal with the affair in a more proactive manner than she had before. She would have to find out if her fears were founded.

The next morning Adam awoke early, and was in the kitchen making pancakes for the children when Luce came down from the bedroom. She stood at the door and watched him as he chatted away with the girls, looking relaxed and happy. A knot tightened in her stomach as she took in the scene. Her husband was back to his usual cheerful self, and something had definitely happened to bring about that change.

She feared for herself, she feared for her children, she was very afraid that her marriage was in danger.

Accident

Those who have courage to love should have courage to suffer.
Anthony Trollope

"Is the water boiling yet?" asked Adam as he peered into the pot over Claire's shoulder. "These lobsters in the bag are pretty active still. They don't know what's awaiting them – two minutes of torture in boiling water. It really is quite cruel, this so-called gourmet eating habit."

"Just about ready," Claire responded as she stood at the kitchen counter, tossing a green salad to accompany the lobster.

This was how they were ending a day of enjoyment. They had hiked in the hills around Mont Tremblant. The weather had been warm and the sky clear all day. The foliage on the trees along the trails had been a shimmering cover in multiple shades of greens and gold. They had circled the lake, and worn themselves out before collapsing on the bank of the shoreline to enjoy a light picnic lunch.

On the way home they had stopped at a fishmonger and picked up three live lobsters that had wriggled in a brown paper bag all the way back to Claire's house. A slow, hot shower together had resulted in their falling onto the bed to share an intimate time together; a slow exploration of each other's bodies.

"Do you think those lobsters are still alive and watching us from their bag?" Adam had laughed as he pulled on his clothes. "I'm starving, let's get at that pot, chef."

Claire dressed and followed him into the kitchen where she placed a large pot of water on the stove to boil. Adam opened a bottle of what had become their favorite white wine, a Sauvignon Blanc from New Zealand, and they sat on bar stools at the kitchen counter, sipping, as they watched the water in a large pot come to a boil.

"Can you get the butter out of the fridge so I can spice some for dipping the lobster into. The butter has to run down our chins to really enjoy the flesh," Claire requested.

"Sure," said Adam as he opened the fridge and searched around on the shelves inside.

"There is only a small piece of butter in here. Do you have some more hidden away?" he asked.

"Oh no, I thought we had lots," moaned Claire aloud. "How are we going to enjoy lobster without decadent butter slopping all over it? If you watch the pot, I'll go down the hill and get some – it won't take more than ten minutes," Claire suggested.

"No, you are much better at getting the meal prepared than I am; I will go down and get some butter. Salted or unsalted?"

"I think unsalted to keep the flavor of the lobsters. I'll add a few mixed herbs to the butter instead. Take my car, it's parked in the driveway as usual and will be quicker than walking over to your car. I'll get the keys for you; I think I left them in the drawer of the hall table."

"Just don't drink all that great wine before I get back," retorted Adam.

Claire picked up the keys, tossed them to him and gave him a quick hug and a kiss on the lips.

"And no speeding down the hill; the lobster will wait until you get back," she ordered.

She stood at the door and watched him get into her car. She always backed the car into the driveway so she could then drive straight out and not worry about oncoming traffic. She smiled as she remembered the warning Adam had given her months ago about not leaving her car outside. He thought that it would just encourage vandals. Nothing had ever happened to the car, and lazily, she kept leaving it parked on the driveway. This was one of those times, she thought, when it was just easier having it outside, than having to open the garage and back the car out. It did save a lot of time this way.

Watching the car disappear down the hill she turned back into the house, and continued tossing the salad and setting the table. She decided to light candles, and make the evening more romantic as it was the end to a very enjoyable day. She set the table with a blue and white cloth that she had bought in Copenhagen, added blue china candlesticks with white candles, and put out matching blue napkins. She stood back and admired the table. It did look lovely, she thought. Now all they needed was butter.

She went back to the pot and added more hot water to the boiling pot. She checked on the lobsters. They appeared to be calming down, instead of trying to claw their way out of the paper bag. Everything was ready, so she sat down at the table and poured another glass of the Sauvignon Blanc and sipped slowly.

She glanced up at the clock on the kitchen wall. She could not remember what time Adam had left, but she was sure that he had been gone for at least thirty minutes. She decided to try his cell phone to see what the delay was. She dialed the number and heard it ring six times and then a message came on that he was not available. Strange, she thought, he must be in the shop and not able to answer. The store must be busy; or maybe he couldn't find unsalted butter at the small store and decided to explore other places to find it. She was beginning to feel a little irritated by the delay. What was keeping him? He had known that everything was ready for the dinner, and now he was taking his time.

Annoyed at his tardiness, she walked outside and glanced down the hill but saw no sign of him or her car. She returned to the kitchen, threw the lobsters into the pot of boiling water and put on the timer to track their cooking time. Sitting on a bar stool at the kitchen counter she poured another glass of wine. When the kitchen timer rang she picked up the tongs and removed the lobsters from the pot, placing them onto a large oval plate. They looked delicious. She took the small pat of butter and melted it quickly over the boiling water. Adam had still not returned.

She decided to take a chance and call his cell phone again. She dialed the number and heard it ring and the message that he was not available was repeated.

He must have been called home on an emergency, she decided. That was why he could not call her and explain his delay. She hoped that the children were not in trouble, or that Luce was ill. She would just have to wait for him to contact her when he was available.

She looked at the lobster and decided that she was very hungry. All the exercise of their hike, and the sight of the lobster had more than whet her appetite. She put one lobster and a generous helping of salad onto a plate, drizzled butter over the lobster and took it to the elegantly set table. She lit the candles and had a one-way conversation with an absent Adam as she ate.

"Cheers, Adam, wherever you are," she started to tell him. She continued conversing with his empty place.

"Thank you for sharing such an enjoyable day with me. These stolen times together mean so much to me. Being with you completes my psyche. It's as if my other half is walking, talking, lying next to me, and making me whole."

As she filled her wine glass again, her conversation became more intimate.

"I have to tell you how much I adore your blue eyes, your hairy chest, your long lean legs, your erect penis."

She giggled to herself as she realized how ridiculous this conversation was.

"You don't know what you're missing Mr. Horny Adam Lambert – romantic meal with a beautiful woman, and then, if you're really lucky, another sexy roll in the proverbial hay."

She sat back in the chair. Suddenly, she felt very lonely. She had wanted to end the day with him. They had enjoyed perfect companionship during their walk, their intimacy in the shower, and the meal preparation. Now he had to leave her to attend to the needs of his family.

This was a scenario, she acknowledged, that was going to be a frequent occurrence in their future as the relationship continued. They had both admitted that they would be together forever, and that only a crisis could separate them now. They had suffered too much during their month of separation to end the affair. Luce, they realized, must know of their affair and seemed to be prepared to look the other way.

With a sigh, she rose from the table. Carrying the dirty dishes to the kitchen, she put them into the dishwasher and turned on the wash cycle. As she put the two left over lobsters into the fridge, she decided that she and Adam could enjoy them cold at another time.

Walking through to the bedroom to prepare for bed she realized that she was feeling very tired. She had enjoyed quite a few glasses of wine; could not remember how many, but the bottle had been almost empty when she left the table. It had all made her feel very sleepy. She was brushing her teeth when she heard the doorbell ring.

"Well, about time," she said aloud. "I hope he doesn't want some of that great wine because I slugged it all down, greedy me."

She opened the front door saying, "Too late, I ate all the lobster and drank all..." and stopped in mid-sentence when she saw two men standing on the doorstep.

"We are sorry to disturb you, ma'am, but are you Claire Hardick?" one of them asked.

"Yes, I am," replied Claire, looking confused.

"We are police officers, Miss Hardick. May we come in?" one of them asked.

"No, I'm afraid you can't. Not until you tell me what this is all about. I do not let strange men into my home in the middle of the night."

"Miss Hardick, there has been a bad accident and your car was involved," the officer replied as he pulled out his identification and passed it to her. "I am Detective Inspector Sam Mullen and this is Detective Michel Giroux. We need to talk with you."

Claire looked at him blankly as she registered what he was saying, and clutched onto the doorframe for support. She felt light-headed with shock and fear. The wine and the tiredness were not helping her to focus. She turned and walked into the house, collapsing into a chair. Detectives Mullen and Giroux followed her, closing the front door behind them. They stood in the living room and looked at her.

"Are you all right, Miss Hardick?" Mullen asked. "Can we get you a glass of water?"

"Please tell me what has happened," Claire asked quietly, shaking her head, not wanting anything other than information. She felt a cold fear gripping her heart, and was horrified to think of what may have happened to Adam who had been driving her car.

"First of all, do you own a dark blue BMW with the license plate Y83 CHY?" asked Detective Mullen.

Claire nodded a confirmation, and the detective continued.

"We found your automobile registration in the glove compartment in the car. It appears that the driver of your car lost control, and could not stop the car on the way down Harlow Drive. He drove right into the oncoming traffic on Côte-de-Neige. The result was not pretty. I am afraid there is not much left of your car."

"And the driver? Is he hurt? Is he in hospital, can I see him …?" stuttered Claire.

"All we can share at present is that he was taken to hospital. However, the crash was very bad; the front of the car was crumpled in completely. The driver had to be taken out with the 'jaws of life'. I am sorry to have to tell you that the paramedics did not give him much chance of surviving the accident."

Claire froze. She stared back at the two police officers, hoping for some softening of the facts. When none were forthcoming, she rose to her feet unsteadily, and stood for a moment looking at them.

"Do you mean that he could be dead?" she murmured. "No, he cannot be dead. It's not possible."

She put her hand to her mouth, gagging as she spoke. She felt overwhelmed by emotion. Bile rose in her throat as she ran out of the room to the kitchen where she leaned over the sink and was violently sick. She stood there heaving, trying desperately to rid herself of the terror, the fear, and the guilt that she was feeling.

The two detectives came into the kitchen.

"Sit down, Miss Hardick," Detective Mullen suggested, taking her arm. He offered her a paper towel from a roll to wipe her mouth. He poured a glass of water and handed it to her. Claire sat on the chair and sipped at the water. Her body shook and she could not control the tremours.

"Please tell me everything you know," she whispered.

The men described what they had witnessed when they had arrived at the scene of the accident. They told her how the paramedics had not been able to get the body out of the car and that eventually, when the 'jaws of life' had opened the car door, they had gently moved the body of a man into the ambulance, shaking their heads. They had thought that he had probably died instantly. A police detachment had stayed at the scene, and eventually had towed the wrecked car to the police compound for examination. Their first suspicion was that the brakes may have failed, but they needed to check the car before they came to any conclusions.

"That cannot be. I am very good about maintenance of the car, especially the brakes, because I live on this steep hill. How could they have failed? I just don't understand."

"That is what we will have to find out. We will let you know when we have more information. Will you be all right now, Miss Hardick? You do not look well."

"I will be fine, thank you. I just need to be alone now to try to understand how this could have happened."

"First we have to ask about the driver of the car. If he was in your car, we need to assess whether you gave the keys to him, or whether the car was stolen. Did you know the driver?"

"Yes, yes, he is a …" and she hesitated, "a friend – oh, *was* a friend. We were going to have dinner together. He went down to the store to buy some butter…" and Claire could not finish the sentence. She could not hold back the tears any longer, and they found their way onto her cheeks.

The two detectives watched her carefully, saying nothing, but waited for her to continue.

"I am sorry, but yes, I gave the keys to him," she finally managed to say. "I feel so guilty about that. I wondered why he had not come back. I assumed that he had been called away to his family and that was why he did not come back."

"His family?" questioned Sam.

Claire told them who Adam was, that he was married with two children and where he lived. They thanked her.

"We did not find any identification on his person, only some cash stuffed into one of his pockets, and a cell phone."

"He left his jacket here, and I assume his wallet must be in there still. He left in a hurry as he did not think it would take long to pick up some butter."

Claire remembered those last minutes together as she had teased Adam about hurrying back or she would polish off all the wine; and how she had tossed the keys to him. As these thoughts crowded in on her, she sobbed softly. Guilt overwhelmed her. *I cannot even go to the hospital to see his body. That is the right of the wife and family, not the lover.*

The two detectives recorded the details she had given them about Adam. They took his jacket and identification with them when they left, and assured her that they would return to talk with her as soon as they had more information.

"Miss Hardick, can we get a female officer to stay with you for the night? It may make you feel more comfortable."

"No, thank you. I will be fine on my own. I need to come to terms with what has happened. It is all such a shock, and so horrible," she assured them.

When they finally left the house she was relieved. Locking the door behind the departing men, she turned and walked into the bedroom. There she stood in the middle of the room and howled. She yelled, she shrieked, she sobbed until her throat became dry and hoarse and she could cry no more.

"Oh, Adam, how could you do this to me? How could you?" she whimpered over and over.

"Did I do this to you? Was my car the instrument of death? How can you ever forgive me for encouraging you to take my car? I am so sorry, so sorry. I did not know that the brakes were a problem. You know that I would never have hurt you, my darling. Come back, come back, come…" and finally she sobbed herself into a restless sleep.

A nightmare woke her in the early hours of the morning. Bathed in sweat, her clothes clung to her body. She lay still, panting from the fear that the dream had conjured up in her. She had seen Adam coming towards her, his body covered in blood, his head was misshapen and blood dripped from his mouth and eyes. He was looking at her and saying, "Why did you want to kill me in your car? I did not want to die. Why did you do it, do it, do it…?"

She sat up on the edge of the bed in the dark, trying to pull herself out of the nightmare, and into reality. The house was very silent. The only noise she could hear was the occasional car passing down the street. The sound of the cars disturbed her more than the silence, and she covered her ears to block out the sound of the engines.

Stumbling into the bathroom, she splashed her face with cold water. Slowly she surfaced from her sleep state and looked down at her clothes. She was sweat-covered and rumpled from sleeping in the same clothes from the day before. She tore at the garments, pulling them from her body as fast as she could. She threw the bundle into the corner of the room, stepped into the shower and stood under the stream of hot water until she felt that she had managed to cleanse the nightmare from her mind.

Pulling on a terry cloth gown, she walked through to the kitchen where she brewed a pot of coffee. She sat at the kitchen counter on a bar stool with her head in her hands, sipping at the strong liquid, trying to get the reality of Adam's death to register in her mind. Understanding of how such an accident could have happened would not penetrate. She always had her car checked very carefully when she had the BMW serviced. She was aware that, living on a hilly street, she would always need a well maintained car.

Questions crowded her brain. What if Adam had been correct when he warned her not to leave her car outside on the driveway, instead of parking it safely in the garage? Maybe vandals had come and tampered with the car during the day, or the evening. The police had said that they were only surmising that the brakes or the steering could have failed. What if there was another reason for the accident? Maybe the car had been hit by another as it entered onto Côte-de-Neige. She felt at a loss as to what to assume. She wondered how Luce and the children were reacting to the news. They would be stunned, and heartbroken. The girls loved their father dearly and this loss would not be easy for them to accept.

Her body felt restless. She could not sit still. Sitting still forced her to think about what had happened. She needed to move. She paced around the house, trying to calm the thoughts that were racing through her head. She felt hollow inside, devoid of feeling, numbed by the events of the night.

"I will have to learn to live one day at a time," she thought. "Each day that goes by without Adam will be torture; but I will have to survive. He would want me to survive. He told me that he was going to come back and that he would never leave me. But he did not keep that promise; or *could* not keep that promise. It will be up to me to keep him alive in my mind, and my heart, through my memories. We drank a toast together to all the good times we had enjoyed together, and I will hold those very close."

With those thoughts, she started to weep again, realizing that there would be no more of those good times to share with the man she loved. She staggered back to the bedroom, crept under the bed covers and fell into a deep sleep.

The Investigation

Discovery consists of seeing what everybody has seen and thinking what nobody has thought.
Albert von Szent-Grorgyi

The police station was a typical older building in the inner city, with chipping stucco and graffiti vulgarities scrawled on the walls. Black and white police cruisers parked in front of the door where a sign read, Division des Enquêtes sur les Crimes Contre la Personne. The two plain-clothes detectives came in together, hardly noticing the throng of police and suspects filling the main hall. The sergeant at the front desk was arguing with an obviously drunk derelict about the charges against him. Leaning casually on the counter, the arresting officer watched the proceedings with some interest. A middle-aged woman sat on one of the benches sobbing loudly, being comforted by a female officer.

The two men looked at each other, shrugged, and continued through the corridor to an office at the rear of the building. There they took off their raincoats and hats, and settled themselves behind connecting desks. Sam Mullen pulled a folded newspaper out of his raincoat pocket and opened it.

"Did you see this report? Some reporter felt that he had to make hay out of what was, to all intents and purposes, just a bad car accident. They always get to the scene of these accidents like vultures after carrion."

He read from the paper,

"Driver killed in freak accident. What appeared to be loss of control, sent a car hurtling through the evening traffic of Côte-de-Neige and straight into a store window, killing the driver instantly. The cause of the accident was not initially apparent, but police suspect some malfunction of the vehicle."

"How could they write that when we have not said a word about the cause of the accident to the press? These media types can drive one crazy. They set up a bad scenario for the family to cope with. Mon Dieu, how can we work around these guys?" responded his partner.

"Yea, but that newsman may be right on the money for all we know."

"But I still don't like to over-guess until we do more digging into what was going on here. This seems to be a liaison-à-trois to me; one that got too tangled for safety," suggested Michel.

"You know what I think. The wife knows the husband is having an affair. The lover knows the wife knows, the husband thinks that nobody knows, so carries on. A mixed up affair, you know," responded his partner.

"Too many knows there, Sam, but I get the gist. Now, if they were all aware of the situation, how did he die? Was it really an accident? Want to take a guess?"

"Well, I talked with a guy who works in traffic and he says the lab boys went over the car again. It appears that there was something strange with the steering shaft. They also thought that one or more of the tires had been tampered with. It was very strange. They suspect that there's going to be an investigation. They don't think the guy just couldn't stop; they know why he couldn't stop with awkward steering and flattened tires. At first they thought it was the brakes being worn down. That was an older car, even if it was a BMW. But there should not be steering problems."

"So what? How could this have happened to the car? Is it just wear and tear, do you think?"

"I will check with the lab boys, but I think those cars have rack and pinion steering, and to purposely make it dangerous, the pinion would have to be disconnected from the rack. I don't know enough mechanics, but I will find out."

"Would the damaged tires cause the problem alone, or would the steering present enough of a problem?"

"Well both, I guess."

"Could a regular guy cause the problem with the steering? Any punk could damage tires, but what about the other?"

"If someone knew what they were doing, I figure they could do the job in short minutes, ten or twenty at the most. If you know where to look, it's just a matter of having the tools and getting under the car, or possibly into the front or under the hood. Also, the woman who owned the car lived on that hill, so she must have been very careful about checking the brakes constantly. If the car was damaged it was probably done the day or night before," offered Michel.

"So you think there was someone lurking around who could have done the job the same night of the crash?" questioned Sam.

"That would be my guess. Or that the car had not been used that day. We did not ask her if she had been out in it during the day."

"Maybe we should go and talk with the folk who live around there and see if they saw anyone lurking around, or saw anything suspicious."

"Sounds like a plan. Remember, nobody is treating this as a crime yet. It's still on the books as an accident, even if we do have a dead body."

"You know the thing that baffles me? Why did the guy not just take his own car? Why drive *her* car? And, if her car was tampered with, then she was the one who was meant to have the accident. So do we look to see who would want to hurt her – or kill *her*, not the guy who died?"

"Let's go and see what we can find out. It's all still a mystery to me."

The next morning Detectives Mullen and Giroux took off to find out who would want to kill the attractive blonde who owned the car.

Their first stop was to go to Stark, Nesbitt and Bouchard, Adam's place of work. They introduced themselves to the receptionist and asked if they could speak with someone who worked with Adam Lambert.

"Mr. Lambert is not in the office today, sirs. I can contact one of the partners for you if that is whom you would like to speak with. Can I tell them what it is about please?"

"No, we would prefer to speak to the partner first," said Sam. Michel nodded in agreement.

The receptionist phoned through to the managing partner, and showed the two officers through to his office.

"Good morning, gentlemen," said the man who rose from his chair behind the desk and held out his hand in greeting. "To what do I owe this visit? You told Valerie that it was to do with Adam Lambert, but he is not in the office yet this morning I gather; how can I assist you? I am Derek Porter, the managing partner of the firm."

Sam and Michel introduced themselves. Both shook the hand offered in greeting, and then told the partner the news.

"It appears that you have not heard the bad news yet, sir. Mr. Lambert died in a motor car accident last night."

"What!" said a surprised Derek. "He was in the office on Friday looking hale and hearty. But this was an accident you said." He moved to his desk and sat down. He looked taken aback, and had turned pale.

"Please sit down, gentlemen, and tell me what happened. This is quite a shock to me."

"It has been to all concerned I can assure you. He was having dinner with a friend and it appears that he took her car to go to the store for something, and the car went out of control and ran into heavy traffic; it was not good for him, the driver. We are following up on all avenues right now, trying to get to the bottom of the accident. May we ask you some questions about your colleague Mr. Lambert?"

"Certainly, but I'm not sure that I can tell you much. He was a very private man. I know his family of course. I have met his lovely wife a few times, as well as the children, at our Christmas events. They don't socialize much with the business staff. His wife must be absolutely shattered. A lovely woman. They are a perfect couple together; sorry, *were* a couple, that you could not but notice. Both very attractive people and they were absolutely devoted to each other."

He did not notice the look that passed between the two detectives as he made the comment about the state of the marriage of the dead man. They had both had the distinct impression that the dead man and the beautiful woman who owned the car were lovers. So much, they thought, for being a devoted husband. Appearances can be very deceiving.

"I saw them together at the opening of his wife's art gallery. She's a very talented artist, you know. They hosted a wonderful opening party for her gallery. Yes, a very elegant and very talented woman. She's from Paris you know, and it shows in the way she dresses. A delightful French accent to her English, and of course she speaks real French," continued the partner.

"If I can interrupt for a moment, sir. Can you think of anyone who would want to see Mr. Lambert dead?" asked Sam.

"Want him dead? Do you mean this was not an accident?" asked the partner in surprise.

"We are just following every avenue in case the accident was not an accident. Did he have any enemies? Anyone here at work that he did not get on with? Anyone who held a grudge against him maybe?"

"I can assure you that there has been no hint of animosity here in the office towards Adam. He got on well with everyone, and we all had to work with him at one time or another. He was one of our resident lawyers you see, so his work touched all of us. No, Inspector, you are barking up the wrong tree there."

Watching the partner very carefully, Sam decided to try another tack to see what reaction he would get from the man.

"He was not driving his own car when he was killed. He was dining at the home of a friend, Claire Hardick. It was her car that he had taken out and was killed in. We suspect that maybe her car was damaged."

"Claire Harkick?" said Derek surprised. "I know that he knew her. They met at a conference I think. I saw them together a couple of times up on the ski hill, Tremblant, where they both skied. I did not know that they were very friendly. Was Adam's wife dining there as well?"

"We don't think so. They were alone," replied Michel watching the man carefully.

Derek Porter blushed and looked away. He took a moment to compose himself before turning back to the officers.

"Are you suggesting that there was something inappropriate going on between them? I would be surprised, but then…" he tailed off, trying to look as if he was totally shocked by the revelation.

The sly bastard kept his affair very quiet and secretive, thought Michel as he glanced at Sam. They nodded to each other.

"We are only asking questions, sir. We are not drawing any conclusions about any one's private life. It is only the cause of the accident that we are investigating, nothing else. If you feel that there are no issues to follow up here, we will thank you for your time. Is there anyone else you think we should talk to while we're here?"

It was suggested that they not ruffle the waters in the office any more than was necessary. Derek Porter agreed to contact them if he heard anything more and they left the office and headed back to the station.

"So, what do you think?" Michel asked Sam.

"I think this guy was pretty clean; no enemies that are going to jump out at us, and he was very good at keeping his private life private. I think the guy we just talked with knew about the affair. Maybe a lot of them in the office did, but he was not going to tell us. Did you see how red in the face he got when I opened the topic of the Hardick woman? He covered it up very quickly. You know, office policy must be to keep any scandal as low a profile as possible. And I think he really liked the guy's wife – a protection job there maybe."

"Well, let's go and see what else we can find," concluded Michel.

Detectives Mullen and Giroux decided that the next stop on their trail of discovery had to be the offices of the woman who owned the car. They suspected that she was the person who was meant to get into the damaged car. This was where they had to start looking for possible enemies.

Arriving at Claire's office they asked to see her boss. They were told that Claire was not in the office, but that her immediate superior was a man called Avery Heap. They asked to see him, and were shown to Avery's office.

"Yes," barked Avery, "what is it you want? We are trying to run a place of business here. This had better be important."

Trying to keep his cool Sam replied.

"Let me introduce ourselves to you, sir. I am Detective Inspector Sam Mullen and this is my partner, Detective Michel Giroux. We are here investigating a possible murder."

I'll put the fear of God in you to keep you quiet, you rude bastard, thought Sam, as he added the last phrase.

He saw Avery blanch at the mention of murder, and seat himself quietly back into his chair.

"Do tell me what this is all about and what it has to do with our business?" he asked politely. He did not want any scandal inside the office. Whatever these two wanted had to be kept strictly private.

"The car of one of your staff was tampered with at her home the other night, and we were wondering if you or any of the staff could shed some light on possible motives," Sam explained.

"What do you mean? Which staff member are we talking about?" questioned Avery.

"I mean," responded Sam, "the car belonged to Miss Claire Hardick. Is there anyone that you know of who would want to do her any harm? Does anyone have a grudge against her? Was she on bad terms with any of the staff? Did she ever talk to you about problems she was having?"

"Claire's car? That is strange," offered Avery. "No, I don't think that she has any enemies, but she did have a very rough time some months ago. She seemed to be a nervous wreck and had to take a leave from the firm. She went away for a month; when she came back she was her old confident self again, and she seemed happy. I don't know what her problem was. We all thought that she was working too hard and was strung out. Now, I don't know whether there was something else bothering her. She never mentioned anything or anyone to me. Maybe you should talk to her support staff; a lovely young woman called Nathalie. She may be able to shed some light on the matter."

"That would be most useful, thank you. Did she ever mention a man called Adam Lambert to you by any chance?" questioned Michel.

"Lambert? I don't think so. Was he a friend?"

"Yes, he was in her car that we mentioned had been tampered with. The car was involved in an accident that resulted in his death. We just want to know if she had ever mentioned him to you."

"The name is not ringing a bell. But if he was in her car, he must have been a close friend I suppose. He is dead you said?"

"We think he was a close friend. Now is it possible to speak with her staff please?"

"Come with me, I'll take you up myself. Claire has not been at work for a few days. She phoned in sick, but now I know what her problem really is. Thank you for letting us know. If she has just lost a good friend she will need our support."

The guy still has a few soft spots, mused Michel as they followed Avery to Claire's office.

A very surprised Nathalie watched as Avery and two men came towards her office. She jumped up quickly and stuttered, "Good morning, Mr. Heap. Is there a problem?"

"No, Nathalie, but these two men are police detectives and they would like to ask some questions.

Please take them into Miss Hardick's office for the interview."

Very nervously, Nathalie led the men through to Claire's office and stood waiting for them to follow. They told her to sit and then sat themselves.

"Thank you for giving us some of your time, Nathalie, and please don't be nervous. This has nothing to do with anything you might have done. I am Detective Inspector Mullen and this is Detective Giroux. You may not know, but a friend of Miss Hardick's was killed in a motor car accident the other day and we are trying to find out how the accident happened. You see, the friend was driving *her* car; that is why we are asking questions."

"Oh no," blurted out Nathalie. "I hope this was not her special friend. She will be so upset if it was."

"Her special friend?" enquired Michel, looking pointedly at Sam.

"I don't think I should say anything about that. It was a very private conversation that we had."

"Well, maybe in this case it would be fine. But, let me tell you first that the accident may not have been an accident. There is a possibility that Miss Hardick's car was tampered with, and that's what caused the accident. If it was, then this could mean that someone expected Miss Hardick to be driving the car, and she was the one meant to have the accident. Do you see what we mean?"

"You mean that someone was trying to kill Miss Hardick?" stammered Nathalie in disbelief.

"Maybe," responded Michel.

"Nobody would want to kill *her*. She is too kind and thoughtful to everyone. No, she was not the one they wanted to kill I am sure. There has to be a mistake."

"Now, if someone was trying to hurt her, who do you think it could be? Was there anyone in the office that she was not on good terms with? Anyone who is very jealous of her, maybe? Was there a competitive rivalry between her and another person in the company?"

Nathalie listened to all of this open-mouthed. She could not comprehend that someone could possibly have tried to kill her boss, the woman who was so kind and thoughtful to her.

"If there is someone like that I would like to get my hands on them, because they are so wrong," she blurted out sharply.

"I know that it is an upsetting thought, but think for a moment. Was there anything during the past months that gave you cause for concern? Was there anything unusual in Miss Hardick's behaviour, or anything she said, or a telephone conversation you may have overheard that seemed to be different, or unusual?" prodded Sam.

He looked at the young woman who obviously adored her boss, and he suspected, would do anything to protect her. He had to keep prodding to find out as much as he could because he was sure that, if this was a deliberate act, it was Claire Hardick who was the intended victim.

"I don't think I heard anything unusual," said Nathalie slowly. "Miss Hardick was away for a month but she has been very happy since she came home, so I'm sure that she didn't have any enemies."

"Oh, she was away for a while. Was she away on business?"

"Oh no, she took some time off as she was very tired and needed a rest. She was looking very stressed, and I noticed that she was getting thin, so she needed some time on her own."

"Can you remember when this was, Nathalie?" prodded Michel.

"Yes, she has been back for about six months I think, so it would have been in the spring."

"And do you know where she went for this rest cure?"

"No, she would not tell anyone. She said that she didn't want to be bothered, so she didn't want to be found. We all thought this was very funny, but it worked. She would phone in to check with me to see how everything was going, and we would problem solve. But that was all. We all agreed to leave her alone. She came home looking very refreshed and full of energy again, just like she always used to be."

"So you can say that you don't know of anyone who would wish her harm?"

"Certainly," replied the young woman emphatically. "No one at all!"

Sam and Michel looked at each other and stood up. They knew that they were not going to get anything more out of Claire Hardick's support staff.

As they were leaving, Sam turned back and asked, "By the way, who was the special friend you said Miss Hardick had?"

Nathalie opened her mouth to answer, and then thought that he was trying to trap her into giving away the secret that she shared with her boss.

"I don't know of any special friend, Inspector," and she looked straight at him. She was definitely not going to let Claire down, especially not in these circumstances.

"Thank you for your help," said the detective. He joined his partner and they both left the office.

As they got back into an unmarked police vehicle, Sam commented, "I think it's time to talk to the woman herself again. She will be over her initial shock by now, and will be a lot calmer. That's our next place of call."

Detective Michel Giroux nodded in agreement.

Intended Victim

Question everything
Learn something
Answer nothing
Euripodes

"That was quite a turnout at the funeral. I did not realize that the guy was such a well-known figure. His family seemed to be pretty cut up," commented Inspector Mullen as he sat back in his chair at the station. He rested his feet on the worn desk in front of him, and gazed thoughtfully at his partner. It was now the day after the funeral, and they were still investigating the accident. Canvassing the homes in the neighbourhood of the accident had turned up no leads. Nothing unusual had been noted. However, the car belonging to Adam Lambert had been found close to the Hardick house and had been returned to his wife.

"Sure, Sam, but did you notice the other woman was there as well. I wonder if the wife knew about the affair they were having? Je pense que la femme était courant de l'intrigue amoureuse."

"Yes, Michel, surely she must know by now. She knew that he died in the other woman's car, so he had to be with her just before he died. What a bummer for the family; to lose their dad in his lover's car. Did you see the look that passed between the two women at the end of the service? I figured they both knew what was going on, and that the lover knew that the wife knew, if you know what I mean."

The two detectives sat in the back office at the station and went over the information they had from their two visits. Sam looked at Michel thoughtfully.

"There wasn't much to learn from any of those folk in their places of employment was there? I don't know if they were just keeping mum, or whether there really is nothing there to follow up on. They appear to be squeaky clean, both of them. But I would bet a chunk of dough on the fact that those two were lovers, and had been for quite a while. I would love to know when they first met. It may have been lust at first sight. She's a very attractive woman." And he smiled broadly at his partner as he said this.

"Oui, très jolie. I think you're right. We may be able to get her to tell us more about the relationship when we go back for the follow-up visit."

This time, the door was opened by a more polite Claire who ushered them into the den. The detectives had called ahead and requested an interview, which Claire had agreed to.

"It's more comfortable to sit here," she remarked as she invited them to be seated. "I've just made fresh coffee, can I offer you a cup?"

The offer was accepted by both men. Feeling that it would give her something to do while they talked, and hopefully would relax her responses as well, Claire moved into the kitchen. Both men followed her and sat on bar stools at the counter as Claire poured three cups of coffee and offered cream and sugar. She went to a cupboard and removed a packet of cookies.

"Sorry, I don't do home baking, so this is the best I can offer," she apologized.

They both accepted the offered cookie, thinking that they were a lot better than the stuff they had back at the station.

As Claire sat herself at the counter with them she asked, "I hope that you have more information for me this time, Detectives. I was not in a state last time we met to take in much of what you said."

"We are here to give you as much as we know to date and can share, and we also have some questions we'd like to ask, if that's all right with you."

"Certainly," said Claire with emphasis. "I want to get to the bottom of this accident for which I feel so responsible." Her voice caught in a sob as she said this.

"Miss Hardick, you do not have to feel any guilt about this accident," comforted Michel. "When we give the details to you, you will realize why."

"Please tell me," urged Claire.

Sam began to outline the suspicions that the police were following. He knew that he had to be cautious, as he did not want to scare the woman and make her feel that her life was unsafe.

He started with some of the basic facts first.

"The police lab thinks that the steering on your car was purposefully tampered with. It is not a difficult thing to do, but you have to know what you're looking for."

Claire went white when she heard this detail.

"Adam told me that I should not park on the driveway; that someone could come and vandalize my car if I did. He kept encouraging me to park it in the garage, but it was such a nuisance, and I suppose I just got lazy. Now I'm paying the price of that laziness. No, Adam is paying the price for me. Oh, what have I done to him!"

Again she felt the tears start and had to lift the coffee cup with a shaking hand and take a large gulp to calm herself.

"Will we ever find the vandals do you think?" she asked.

"If it was vandals; no I don't think so. The car is being swept for fingerprints, but I am sure there will be so many on the car that it will be difficult to isolate one alone."

"A pity," she sighed.

"We need to mention another possibility to you, however."

"What is that?" she asked.

"When your car was damaged, whoever did it knew that it would be dangerous to drive the car, and that it could result in a bad accident. That would be very obvious. Because you live on a hill, one would not be able to control the speed well. The vandal would be anticipating that *you*, and not a friend, would be driving the car. They would assume that you would be the person to be involved in a bad, possibly fatal, accident."

Claire looked at Detective Giroux with wide eyes as the reality of the situation dawned on her.

"Do you understand what we're saying, Miss Hardick?" Sam asked.

"You – you – you mean that someone could have purposefully tampered with the car in order to cause me to have an accident which could have been fatal? That would have been setting me up to be killed. Isn't that murder?"

"That is why we thought we should ask you some further questions. In a nutshell, who would want to kill you, Miss Hardick? I know that's a blunt question, but that may be how it looks."

Claire was now thoroughly taken aback by the turn in the conversation. She could not comprehend the fact that someone may have tried to kill her, and instead had killed her lover.

"I don't know of anyone who would want to try and kill me. I don't think I have any of those kind of enemies. But why would they do that?" she responded, nonplussed.

"We have to explore every possibility. Is there anyone at the office that is very jealous of your work? Anyone who would be promoted if you disappeared, or who would take over your clients if you were dead?" prodded Detective Giroux.

"Oh well, I'm sure we all would like to inherit a sound client base from someone else, but none of us would go to those lengths to get them. No, there is no one that I can think of."

"What about your personal life? Can we ask about your relationship with Adam Lambert?"

"What do you need to know? He was a very close friend and we saw a lot of each other. We skied together at Mont Tremblant, and he came for dinner occasionally. When his wife was away I went out with him and his two girls. They are both delightful. He was here for dinner the night of the accident, and he offered to go to the store for something that we needed, some butter in fact. I suggested that he take my car as it was parked in the driveway and was closer than his car."

She paused in her explanation and gazed off into the distance. "And he never came back," she whispered.

"We are sorry about that as well," sympathized Michel, "but it would help if we knew a little more about your relationship."

"Can you tell us where his car was that night, and why he did not take his own car instead of yours?" questioned Sam.

Claire was now feeling flustered. Was she going to have to admit that she and Adam had been lovers for a long time, and that he was more than just a close friend? Would it make any difference to them solving the crime if they knew? She wondered if she was breaking any law if she withheld information like that.

"He always parked his car further down the road, and not in front of my house," she offered.

"And why was this?" Sam prodded.

Claire looked at the detective for a long time and then at the other man. She realized that they both already suspected that Adam had been her lover. They were just waiting for her to confirm their suspicions.

"I think you both know the answer to that," she said and stood up. "Would you like another cup of coffee? I need another about now."

The detectives refused the coffee.

"We cannot act on a suspicion, lady, we would like confirmation please," Sam Mullen prodded.

"Yes, Adam and I have been lovers for quite a while. We did try to break off the relationship, but we got back together again. The friendship did not interfere with his marriage or his family life. He gave me what time he had, and we had no intention of ever hurting either his wife or his children. That was how the relationship stood when he was killed by someone who wanted to kill me – maybe." Her tone was terse and matter-of-fact as she told them the truth, hoping they would be satisfied.

"Did the wife know you were her husband's lover?"

Claire turned away from the two men and looked through the glass door to the back deck. She noticed the loungers on which she and Adam had often made passionate love and she felt a heavy loss course through her body.

She had never told anyone else about her love affair with Adam, but it did not matter anymore that it be kept secret. With his death she had lost all that she had held so dear with her time with him. If it helped to catch the vandal, she would open up to these men who were making her feel so uncomfortable.

Very softly, she answered the question the detectives wanted her to answer.

"I am sure that she knew; but she never said or did anything – either to him or to me. When they were together they were a happily married couple. I think he truly loved her; but it was me he wanted to be with. He was very torn between the two relationships, and it sometimes tortured him that he could not be with one of us alone. I felt for his torment, but I could not be without him in my life either."

She turned back and looked at them. They were obviously not surprised by what she had told them. In fact, they looked pleased with the details she had just given them.

"And I do not think that there was anyone who wanted to kill my lover either," she added. "Now, if that is all, I need to be alone to digest what you have told me. Am I in any danger do you think? Should I get protection from the nutcase who tampered with my car?"

She was beginning to feel very angry, and wanted these prying men out of her house.

"No, we don't think so, but I would be careful for a while."

Sam Mullen was not sure that the statement was true, but he did not want to scare the woman. He and his partner would request a police patrol on her street for a week to monitor any unusual activity; just to make sure that she stayed safe. This case was a mystery, and they still had no clues as to how or what had really happened.

Suspicion

If you would be a real seeker after truth, it is necessary that at least once in your life you doubt, as far as possible, all things.
Rene Descartes

When the two detectives drove away, Claire watched the car as it disappeared around the corner of the street. She stood at the window for a long while, lost in thought. Was everything they told her true? she wondered. How much were they not telling her? Maybe they had someone in custody already and could not share that information with her.

She should have asked them if they had met with Luce, and what she had said to them about her husband being involved in an affair with another woman. Her thoughts jumped around randomly, searching for answers. Would Luce admit to the detectives that she knew about the affair, or would her pride prevent her from opening up? Would she show them the poison pen letter, if she still had it? *Would* she have kept it? Claire was not sure. Adam had never said a word about it, and she did not know whether Luce had ever told Adam about the note.

What she did know was that Luce had come back from Paris a very different woman, more out-going; more full of interest in life, and in her husband. It was as if she had come back to Montreal determined to have her husband back. Claire wondered whether writing that note on the spur of the moment, as she had done, was the worst thing she could have done to get Luce to leave. It had worked for two months, and then the intent had totally backfired on her. She deeply regretted sending it. She had regrets about all the negative thoughts and actions she had taken during that period, when she had seemed incapable of controlling her obsession with Adam.

Now that disaster had struck, she could only wonder whether the gods, that she and Adam had joked about so often, were finally punishing them for their torrid relationship. They had both imagined that they had their lives sorted out. That Adam, Luce, and the children had settled into a comfortable family life; that he could share with her the time he could find away from them. Their relationship had mellowed into a close, loving sharing of time and interests that had been very satisfying for both of them. They had felt no need to push for anything more. They had been content with how things had evolved. Adam had often remarked that the two parts of his life were as separate as the two parts of any life could be.

Had Luce been content with how things had turned out? Claire did not know. She was reasonably sure that Luce knew about the affair. She could not have been unaware of Adam's constant absences from the house; and often at very unusual times. She must have questioned the numerous work travel trips he had taken. Luce was an intelligent woman, and, if she had been aware of her husband's infidelity, what reaction would she have had? When she had received the hateful note from Claire, her reaction had been instantaneous; she had reacted immediately. She had obviously been very upset by the knowledge that her husband was unfaithful. So why had she then been so placid about their affair – if she had known?

Claire paced through the house trying to find some answers. She walked around the garden hour after hour, trying to think about what *she* would have done if she were Luce. The possible answers that came to mind made no sense to her.

She tried to imagine who would want to damage her car? Who disliked her? Would some vandals have chosen her car randomly? Why select *her* car to damage when others parked outside on the street as well?

What if this had not been an accident? she pondered. She was aware that the police were exploring the same possibility; that they had talked with her colleagues at work, trying to find a motive, just as she was.

Finally, she settled into the lounger on the back deck and sipped at a scotch on ice with no answers coming to mind. It was all so tragic.

"I do my best thinking out here," she said aloud. "Adam always said that this was a very calm place to cogitate on the world's problems."

She relaxed and closed her eyes and almost fell asleep. As she did so, her thoughts ranged over who would want to harm her. She thought of her colleagues, her clients, her friends; people she interacted with in other venues like the hotel on Mount Tremblant. Nobody came to mind as a potential enemy. She was sure that she had irritated some of these people from time to time; she was sure that some of them had been very angry with her occasionally; but none, she felt, would ever intentionally go out of their way to harm her physically.

Whoever it was had to have some knowledge of how a car worked to be able to get under the car and know something about mechanics. She curled up on the chair and dozed. In her sleepy mind she wondered how much one needed to know to be able to sabotage a car. She was not sure.

Feeling ignorant and confused, she rose from the chair, picked up her now empty glass, and went inside. She poured another Scotch on ice, and walked into the den, settled herself at the computer and searched the internet for *automobile sabotage*. She sat there for forty minutes reading about the various parts on cars. How they worked. What constituted the steering, the brakes. She found out where they were located. The computer diagrams looked very complicated. There were pictures of auto mechanics working on cars, and pointing out various components.

Sitting and looking at a picture of a mechanic, she thought about the mechanic that she had seen Luce talking with outside the car repair garage. She sat and stared at the computer for a long time, feeling a cold chill pass through her body. She could not comprehend the thread of an idea that was beginning to curl through her mind. She did not believe that it could possibly be fact. Just the mere thought of it sent waves of fear and disgust through her.

She knew that she would have to explore this new possibility further. However, it was too late to deal with it that evening; but she promised herself that she would answer the question first thing in the morning.

Sleep did not come easily that night. He mind kept racing over possibilities. She kept coming back to the ultimate horror of what had happened, if her suspicions were true.

The next morning found her at the Charlevoix Metro Station riding north. She rode all the way to Metro Pie-IX as she had done before when she had followed Luce. She exited the station and walked the two blocks to the location of the garage where she had seen Luce talking with the mechanic. There was no one in sight, so she walked up to the entrance.

"Bonjour. Est-ce-qu'il y a quelqu'un ici?" she called out.

Hearing no reply, she walked further into the service bay and called louder.

"Bonjour messieurs."

A voice replied, "Oui, ici. Que voulez vous?"

Claire replied in French, "Je cherche le mechanicien. Can I speak with you please? I won't take a lot of your time."

"Wait a moment, I'll be right out," came the reply in French.

Claire waited as a young man came out from the service bay. He was wearing a workman's overall and wiping his greasy hands on a rag. He was not the man Claire had seen talking with Luce some months before, and she hoped that she had not made a mistake by coming here.

"I am very sorry to bother you," she began. "A friend of mine was coming here on Wednesday mornings. I would like to talk with the mechanic she met when she was here."

"Oh yes," the young man smiled. "I remember that lady. She was great fun to have around, and she learned so fast. We had a good time when she was here. Do you want to learn as well?"

"What was she learning?" asked a puzzled Claire.

"Oh, motor mechanics. She wanted to show her husband that she could fix her car if it broke down. We do not know if she ever had to do any repairs, but she knew how to do a lot of the basic things."

Claire just stood and looked at him, nonplussed. The man stared back at her.

"Are you all right, lady?" he asked.

Claire shook her head to clear her thoughts. The possibility of the impossible was now a reality.

"Yes, yes, I think I am," she stammered.

"We can sign you up if you want lessons. We will charge you of course, and we will make the lessons go fast. You will be changing a tire in the first lesson."

"No, thank you. I mean, maybe in the future. Right now I think I need to just sit down for a while."

"You are not well, Ma'am, come into the office. I will get a glass of water for you."

Claire allowed herself to be guided to a chair where she sat and looked out at the service bays. She saw a car up on the car lift and she saw, in her imagination, Luce walking into the garage.

She sat in the garage until she felt that her body had stopped shaking and her thoughts were clearer. Thanking the young mechanic, she stood up unsteadily and made her way back to the metro station.

The train ride back to Charlevoix Station was a nightmare for her. She now knew that the accident had in fact been a very different accident. The accident was that Adam was in the car and not her. Adam was never meant to die in her car. Adam was never meant to ever be *in* her car. Adam was never meant to ever *drive* her car. Everything had obviously gone wrong with the plan for sabotaging her car as it sat in the driveway in front of her house.

She tried to think about the guilt and shame that the perpetrator must be feeling, having accidently killed Adam instead of the intended victim.

When Claire returned home, she stood under a hot shower for a long time, trying to wash away the knowledge that she had not been the target of vandalism. She had been the intended victim of a deliberate act. She was the one who was meant to get into the car and drive down the hill into whatever disaster awaited; and whatever consequence resulted.

Even as this thought chilled her, she knew that she was not in danger of further harm. There would be no purpose for the perpetrator to try again. She was safe, of that she was sure.

When she sat down quietly and tried to unravel the mystery in her mind, she could only feel immense guilt. She had planned just as many ways to get what *she* had wanted; just as *this* perpetrator had. She had plotted and schemed in the most dire ways. She herself had come close to committing the same crime. Only by the grace of God had she been saved. She meant that thought literally. She remembered sitting in Saint-Patrick Basilica listening to the priest read the Ten Commandments out aloud, and how those words had impacted her when she had been at her lowest ebb.

But there had been no quiet voice to cool the temper of this crime. There had been no sane moment when they should have realized that planning a crime, and committing it, was the difference between life and death.

Sitting quietly alone in a house that would never again welcome Adam, her friend, her companion, her lover, she knew that she would never be able to voice these suspicions to anyone, especially never to the two detectives. They were never going to hear from her any suspicions of what had truly happened. She would not talk with them again.

There was only one act left for her to do to put closure to her relationship with Adam. She would have to give assurances that she would never disclose what she now knew to be the truth.

Her final thought was how tenuous the boundary between desire and will was. Not only the act performed, but the desire to fulfill it.

Finality

When you are sorrowful look again in your heart, and you shall see that in truth you are weeping for that which has been your delight.
Kahil Gibran. *The Prophet.*

Detectives Sam Mullen and Michel Giroux left the police station office, deciding that it was time to talk with the wife of the dead man. They had not been the ones who had knocked on her door and informed her that her husband had died. A female officer and her male partner had been sent to break the news and offer comfort. The two detectives had debriefed with their colleagues to find out what the wife's reaction had been. They reported that she had become hysterical, had needed support, and finally a tranquilizer to calm her down.

They had seen her at the funeral and known that she had been very distraught. They realized that she would still be very upset after the funeral, but if there was any suspicion about the accident not being an accident, the sooner they asked their questions the better.

They arrived at the Lambert house in the middle of the morning to find Luce alone. She had insisted that the children go to school that day. She had allowed them to stay home since the day of their father's death, but the sooner they got their lives back to normal, the better would be the recovery from their loss. She herself was trying to do just that, but she was finding it very difficult. She feared that she would never be able to deal with what had happened. Her sorrow, her anger, and her guilt were overwhelming.

The doorbell rang while she was sitting in the kitchen drinking tea laced with gin. She was surprised, as she was not expecting anyone to call. All their friends and acquaintances had offered condolences at the funeral, and she hoped that they would now leave her and the children alone for a few days, to mourn on their own. You could never tell how helpful some people felt they had to be at times like this, she thought. With a sigh, she got up and went to the front door. She put a smile on her face to receive what she expected would be a helpful neighbour. She froze when she saw the detectives standing on the doorstep.

"Mrs. Lambert, we are sorry to disturb you. I am Detective Inspector Sam Mullen and this is my partner, Detective Giroux." Sam produced his identification and held it in front of Luce for her to see.

"May we come in and talk with you for a few minutes? We have some questions that need to be answered about your husband's accident."

Taken aback, Luce nodded and stepped back into the house, leading them into the living room where she sat on a wingback chair and pointed the detectives to the sofa.

"Please sit down," she whispered.

"Mrs. Lambert, we are investigating the accident that your husband was involved in. We have been informed by the investigative branch that there is a strong possibility that the car was tampered with. That is why your husband could not stop the car when he got to the busy intersection. If this *is* the case, then the car had been deliberately damaged so that it would be unsafe when the next person got into it to drive. Do you know of any reason why your husband would have been in *that* car on *that* night?"

"No," said Luce briefly. She felt as cold as ice. The effect of the gin in the morning was not helping; it was making her feel light-headed. She needed to concentrate carefully with these two men in her house asking questions.

"Mrs. Lambert," continued Sam, "did you know that your husband was dining with Miss Hardick on the night of the accident?"

"No, I did not," responded Luce non-committedly.

"Mrs. Lambert, did your husband know Miss Hardick well?"

What does he know? thought Luce. What is it he is expecting me to say? I need to be very careful with my answers.

"He skied with her at Mont Tremblant," she finally answered.

"Is that all the time they spent together?"

"I do not know. They did take the children out once or twice when I was in France some months ago. The children like her."

"And how much did your husband like her?" prodded Sam.

Luce looked up at him coldly, never blinking. "My husband is not here to ask, Inspector, so I do not know."

Michel cleared his throat and looked at Sam. He thought that his partner was being a bit rough on a woman who had just lost her husband in a sudden accident, and hoped that Sam would soften the questioning.

However, Sam looked right back at Luce and asked. "Mrs. Lambert, did you suspect that your husband was having an affair with Miss Hardick?"

Luce stiffened. "I don't think that is any business of yours, Inspector. If you have no more information on how my husband died, I will ask you to leave please. I have just lost my husband, and I would like to be left alone so that I and my children can mourn the loss of a man who we all loved very much."

"I am sure that you did, Madam. But someone may have been trying to kill Miss Hardick by tampering with her car; we have to explore every possibility. Thank you for your time. If you remember anything else that we should know, please contact us."

With those words the two officers rose, gave a business card to Luce, and left the house.

Luce watched them walk down the driveway, get into the unmarked police car and drive away. She felt as cold as ice as an overwhelming fear gripped her. Walking through to the kitchen she poured another shot of gin into her now cold tea and took a large gulp.

"Merde, mon dieu, cette une catastrophe! Quel désordre! What am I going to do? I have to protect the children. With Adam gone I am all that they have now and I will have to make sure that I am always here for them," she said aloud in a quavering voice.

Walking into her studio she stood in front of the now completed portrait of her dead husband and spoke aloud in French to his image.

"Je ne vous pardonnerai jamais. I will never forgive you, Adam, for what you have done to our family. Why were we not enough for you? Why did you have to spend time with that other woman when we were all here at home waiting for you, loving you, caring for you? You have brought such sorrow on all of us. I could not cope with the triangle you created. God forgive us all, for we have ignored His commandments and followed our own disastrous way. And now we have to live with the consequences."

"Wow, Sam, what were you thinking? That was damn rough on a sorrowing woman," remarked Michel Giroux as they drove away.

"Well, stop and think about it for a moment," responded Sam. "If your husband is having an affair with a gorgeous woman, and spending too much time with her, you get scared thinking he is going to leave you and your kids. So, you hire someone to tamper with her car so that she gets killed and your worries are over. Or, maybe she just gets into a bad accident and cannot walk, or cuts her beautiful face, or whatever. Suddenly she is not as desirable as before. You see what I'm getting at?" he began to explain to his partner.

He continued, "I just wanted to watch her reaction to the possibility. She was pretty cool about the whole thing. My guess is that she knew all about the mistress and the faithless husband; but whether she was capable of any of the other stuff, I don't think so. Too soft. She's an artist I hear, and a mother. She would not risk the lives of her kids by doing something stupid like that, and then get caught. Then she would *really* lose her husband. She is just the poor woman who was played by her husband and the mistress, and now she's lost her husband for the second time – only this time it's permanent. Bloody shame all round."

"Yes, I think I agree with you," responded his partner. "There is, you know, always the possibility that this *was* just an act of vandalism. My brother-in-law came out of his house the other morning and found that all four of the tires on his car had been slashed by some crank. Boy, was he spitting mad. They will never find the punk who did it of course. Stevie is the nicest guy who would never have enemies, so we figure some punks came by. You know they tie long knives to their ankles, and walk around and kick the tires on cars and then run away with a guffaw. They know they've just caused a hell of a lot of trouble for some poor sucker. This may be what has happened here. What do you think, Sam?"

"Mmm, could be. It's worth thinking about."

With that, they returned to the station to take another look at the report from the lab, and examine the notes they had taken from their investigations.

The case lay dormant on the police books for months. The detectives canvassed the neighbourhood again, but no leads surfaced. The car was re-examined for other possible signs of vandalism, but the wreck was too damaged to draw any further conclusions.

Finally, feeling that they had reached a dead end, the two detectives wrote a report stating that they suspected that the car had been vandalized.

"I still feel damned uncomfortable about this," muttered Sam Mullen as he signed off on the report. "I know we're missing something, but I can't put my finger on it. So we just have to let it rest. But, bugger it, I can't help feeling sorry for the unfortunate guy who died."

"Well, he was the one who was two-timing, so don't lose too much sleep over it. You know there's an old saying that says, *Man proposes, God disposes.*"

Epilogue

What we call the beginning is often the end.
And to make an end is to make a beginning.
The end is where we start from.
T.S. Eliot

The tree lined street in Westmount was quiet; there was no traffic on this mid-week afternoon. A garden company truck pulled into the driveway of a large home set back from the street to work on the manicured lawn surrounding the house, as were all the lawns in this upscale neighbourhood of Montreal. The mature trees lining the streets cast cool shadows onto the pristine flowerbeds edging the lawns.

Claire drove down a street that she remembered well. She recognized the house. Pulling up to the curb, she took a deep breath and climbed out of the car.

She wondered again whether she was doing the right thing. She did not want to open any wounds, but she hoped that she would finally be putting something to rest that could be causing the bleeding ache to continue. Three months had passed since Adam had been buried, and it seemed to her that it was time to make this call, and then to walk away from the grieving family.

She could not anticipate what response she would get when she knocked at the door and had to face Luce again. At the funeral, she had seen the pain in her face, in her posture. She felt the agony the woman was suffering for her children, and their grief.

However, the questions Claire had faced over the past weeks were haunting her. She was sure that her conclusions were correct. This woman she was about to see was the only one with whom she could share her thoughts.

There was no one she could trust with what she was sure was the truth about what had really happened to Adam. She would have to tread very carefully as she broached the subject of the accident; as she mentioned the facts that she knew to be true; as she hinted at her suspicions. If she *was* mistaken, the damage to this family would be profound.

She walked up the long driveway, climbed the stairs to the front door and rang the doorbell. She thought about the last time that she had been to this same house. It had been the time when she had walked up to the door, not expecting it to be opened. It was the time she had crept in as an interloper, as a ghoul, wrought on destruction.

That had been a time when she had been happy with Adam. They had also been very selfish times. She had known then that she was an intruder and did not belong in the house, however much she had wanted to be.

The door opened and Luce stood there. She looked at Claire with a surprised look on her face; then she relaxed and opened the door.

"I thought you might come. I'm just surprised you did not come sooner after his death. Come in, we have things to talk about, things to share," Luce said as she turned and walked down the hall and into the living room.

Claire stepped into the hall, closed the door behind her, and followed Luce into the room.

"Would you like a drink? I think it may help us both," suggested Luce.

"Yes, thank you, a Scotch would be good," replied Claire.

Luce walked to the corner bar cabinet, poured two strong drinks, and handed one to Claire. She seated herself in one of the large wing back chairs, and indicated for Claire to sit.

She raised her glass and said, "To amour, to loss, and to all the grief it brings with it."

Both took a large gulp of the amber liquor and looked at each other. Neither spoke for a long time.

Claire broke the silence, "I felt that I had to come and see you. I don't quite know how to say this, but maybe I should start with an apology for the past two years. I know that what I am going to say will hurt you, but I need to say it."

Luce narrowed her eyes and drew her mouth into a firm line. She was not going to enjoy what this woman had to say, but she had to listen.

"The past years have been the happiest years of my life," continued Claire quietly. "In my euphoric state I selfishly took what I wanted. I grabbed at all the joy, the togetherness I could get, and hoped for a future. I was totally self-centered and self-absorbed. I never stopped to think much of the other side of Adam's life."

Luce suddenly sat forward, looked sharply at Claire and retorted, "No, you did not."

Feeling embarrassed, Claire hesitated for a moment, and then continued. "I know that I did not. But Adam was always so present when he was with me. We shared so much, so many inner thoughts. He shared his fears, his highs, his successes, his joys with me. He never held back, so I suppose I thought that he was all mine. That there was no other place that he wanted to be or should be."

Luce stood up abruptly, turned, and walked out of the room. Claire sat still in the chair and waited, hoping that she would return so that she could complete what she had come to say, no matter how painful it was for both of them. She sipped her drink and slowly looked around the room. This was the other life that Adam lived when he was not with her. She had never shared any of this part of him; this was totally his wife and children's domain.

Luce came back into the room and Claire noticed that her eyes were red and puffy. This conversation was causing so much grief for the woman, but it had to be borne, Claire reasoned.

And so, when Luce was seated again, she continued, "Luce, I am sorry for my selfishness. In the end, I came to realize that Adam would never leave you and the children; that he was yours, and all I really got was to share a small part of his time and his life. And for that I am grateful."

Luce looked at Claire for a long time before answering.

"All I want is my husband back again," she said in a flat robotic voice. "I feel like this grief is an illness from which I will never recover. I find myself sitting at my easel painting and feeling that I'm being disloyal to him, because I am actually doing something productive. I deal with the children and their grief. They too, are overwhelmed by the sudden loss. They feel betrayed by him, and I don't know how to comfort them. Because, you see, they *were* betrayed by him, as you know. I will never tell them that. Their memory of him is all they have, and it will always be a positive one. They do not know that he was planning to desert them – and me, and his home."

"But he wasn't at all!" interrupted Claire quickly. "He never talked about leaving you, and I know that he never would have. As much as he loved me, his loyalty to you was everything to him. The children need to know that, to the last day he was always their father and was there for them – and for you."

Luce stared back at Claire as if she was telling lies. She did not believe what this woman was saying; this woman who took her husband from them at every spare moment. She could not believe that Adam was not tempted to go to this beautiful woman permanently. That is why I was not going to let him do that, she thought.

"Luce," said Claire softly, "there is something else I have to say to you. I know how he died. The accident was not an accident. The whole thing was meant *for me*, not him. I know that the car was tampered with. The police are still investigating, but they have no leads. Their best guess is that it was vandals being destructive. They think it was some kids getting up to no good. I will never reveal that I know the truth. I was on the metro with you one Wednesday. This is our secret and it will stay that way forever."

She stared straight into Luce's eyes as she said this, and saw that her fears were true. Luce looked back at her, blinking back tears that were starting to well up in her eyes. Luce realized that Claire knew the truth about the accident.

She sat and stared at the woman who had caused her so much grief; the woman who had forced her to take enormous risks: the woman who was now saying that she would hold their secret close to themselves.

"I just want you and the children to be happy; to remember their father with love. We have all lost a wonderful man, who was not perfect, but we all loved him dearly," finished Claire.

With that, she rose and moved towards Luce. She leaned down, gave her a gentle kiss on the cheek, and walked out of the room and out of the house.

When she got to her car she sat for a long time thinking about the guilt that Luce would be living with for the rest of her life. And then she reflected on her own participation in this tragedy.

She remembered the words that she had heard in the cathedral. The words that had saved her from making a destructive choice: 'Thou shalt not covet thy neighbour's wife.'

"Or husband, for that matter," she said aloud. She had coveted someone's husband, and, like King David of old, God had wrought his vengeance upon her head and those of an innocent family.

Questions for discussion

1.   The three main characters become involved in a love triangle that ends in tragedy. Of the three, who do you feel contributed most to the tragedy?

2.   Claire becomes obsessed by her need to be with Adam. What other literary heroines/heroes fell victim to an obsession? For example, Poldark with Elizabeth; Maryanne with Willoughby.

3.   Was Luce justified in taking the action she did, or was there another way in which she could have saved her marriage?

4.   At one time during a low ebb in his life, Adam wonders if he is a 'weak male'. What do you think? Why?

5.   Claire runs away to remove herself from her addiction. Was this a weaklings way out? What else could she have done?

6.   The novel hints at the suggestion that her dead father is 'there' for her, watching over her. Can

experiences like this occur? Have you ever experienced such a feeling?

7. Claire gets close to Adam's children. Was this fair to the children and to Luce?

8. When Luce receives the poison pen letter she has a very strong reaction. Do you think that she over-reacted? How would you have handled such a situation?

9. How would the love triangle have ended if Claire had pushed Luce onto the train tracks? Imagine the follow-up.

10. Claire never actually tells Luce that she went to the garage and knows what happened. Should she have done so? How do you think Luce would have reacted if she had?

Made in the USA
Columbia, SC
11 March 2018